The Cabernet Legacy

THE DERBY DEBACLE

BOOK ONE

NICHOLAS HUNTLEY

"He who does not at some time, with definite determination consent to the terribleness of life, or even exalt in it, never takes possession of the inexpressible fullness of the power of our existence."

– Rainer M. Rilke

Act 1, Prologue

Few can recognize a sunrise as majestic as the one that comes across the Nattau Valley on a late summer morning from the highlands when the skies are clear. To see skies that are normally blue be entirely a soft yellow for that one instance is an opportunity a great many of us are sure to miss in our lifetimes. To see the many stretches of trees, hills, and fields below glow in the sunlight should remind all of us that we rely on this sun for our existence; its own existence of which relies not on us, but whose power fuels the natural world from the littlest of creations to us, the most dominant and powerful of creatures. The sun alone could vanquish all of life itself and be our doom, and all our power in us would be futile to stop it. For as powerful as we may be, we are also powerless. The power that we have is a gift to be used responsibly, and this tale is a testament to a man whose humble life should remind us of that fact.

Derby Martel Cabernet sat upon his saddled colt as he looked out across the valley from high above the grassy hills at the base of the Rocky Mountains. The top of the hill looked down upon the entirety of the region and beyond, beginning with the evergreen forests ahead to the plateau where a settlement and human civilization could be found, to the stretches of virgin lands around it and like a rift in the scenery, the Nattau River cut into the land and its waters clearly reflecting the sunlight above. A gentle breeze brushed the dry golden grass around Derby. His horse, a brown-haired mustang, and he a blonde-haired young man. His hair was medium length, parted to the right, and like his surroundings, a warm and golden color. His skin was fair, although tanned slightly from the sunlight, as much as his skin could be sun kissed. He was youthful, not a spot or wrinkle to his face. His body slim although with structure, an upright back and posture. His eyes were greyish-blue, or steel-colored. The whites of his eyes healthy and rested. He wore a felt hat over his head and his chin like his chiseled jaw and cheeks had a stubble of facial hair having not been shaven in two or three days. His hands, holding the reins, were gloved, and his feet at the stirrups wore dirtied leather boots. He wore dark beige rancher pants and a like-colored collared shirt with the sleeves rolled up. Around his hips was a belt with many pouches, and behind his back was a Lee-Enfield rifle strapped to his torso. Derby looked out to the sunrise with a hand shielding his eyes, looking down below and then kicking his horse to move forward as he made his descent downwards.

By noon, Derby brought his horse around to a creek whose waters flowed swiftly but was still shallow enough for him to cross. He took his horse around the edge for a drink of water, and then he brought each other through to the other side where they then climbed up a ledge to the top, and then came out towards a field. The field stretched out on either side for a few acres and consisted of tall grass that was dry and easily a fire hazard. Derby and his horse walked through the grass as the sun above beamed down its rays, going towards a smokestack in the distance at a clearing near some deciduous trees. Derby raised his hand again to shield his eyes as he looked ahead where there was a tent pitched and a man sat besides the fire. Near the camp there was an appaloosa horse, beautiful with its dark spots on a white coat, eating at some grass as the man poked at the fire. Derby approached with caution as he got closer, looking closely at the man with unfamiliarity and then stopping at the outskirt of the camp. The man tipped his hat up as he noticed Derby's presence, smiled, and then stood up. He was an older man, dressed in a greenish-brown plaid suit and he had a brownish beard across his face; well-groomed.

"I thought it was considered rude to linger around another man's camp," Derby expressed, speaking in an eloquent East Anglian accent.

"It would be ruder if I let a telegram be undelivered to you, young man," the man replied. "No less if it was paid to be delivered with the upmost urgency. You are Sir Derby Cabernet, aren't you?"

"It's just Mr. Derby Cabernet – I haven't been knighted," Derby expressed. "How did you find me?"

"It was not difficult," the man responded. "We don't have many visitors to these parts, and word around town is that there was an eccentric young Brit spending his summer in these parts, on his own, in the wilderness no less."

The man approached Derby as he took a paper from his suit pocket and offered it to him.

"All respect to you and your townsfolk, this region is a wonderful little haven that you have here," Derby replied. He looked at the man as he came forward and then reached over to take the paper. "I would be blessed to have my home in these parts than anywhere else." He unfolded the paper and then silently read it. Suddenly, as he read the telegram, his face grew pale and then let out an exhale. "Damn," Derby acknowledged, folding the paper and putting it into a pocket, "well, thank you for delivering this news to me."

"Is it bad news?"

"No, not exactly," Derby remarked, turning his horse to face east.

Derby looked ahead, where ahead the fields continued up to the cliffside where there was a drop to the beach. Even further ahead, there was the riverbank and waters of the Nattau River, and then on the other side, fields and many ranches scattered across that field. Derby took a moment to pause.

"The telegram was just a word of warning that my… my father is coming to visit me. He's due to arrive via train soon."

"Better news then than some have been receiving, I'm sure then," the man remarked with a chuckle. "All the best to you, young Mr. Cabernet."

The man tipped his hat and then went over to his own horse to leave. Derby looked at him as he left his camp, and once he had left, he watched him ride off northward towards a wooden bridge that connected a dirt road that ran north. Once the man could not be seen again, Derby hopped off his horse and began to put out the fire as he then looked around at his own camp and proceeded to put together some belongings.

Derby equipped his horse with his camp gear, mounted his horse, and then guided him away from the campsite and eastbound. He came around close to the cliff edge and went a similar route that the mailman had went. He went a few yards north, reached a dirt road that went further northbound and merged with the wooden bridge over the river. He rode his horse over the bridge to the other side where a dirt road continued and proceeded across a larger plain that led to a hill. Across this plain there were many farms and homesteads spread out with acres of land to themselves. An automobile drove past Derby as he proceeded along the dirt road and came towards the base of a hill that went up towards a plateau. From the plateau, there were a few more homesteads as the land gradually urbanized to a small urban centre. The dirt road persisted and at the arrival of a town square with a park in the middle, Derby turned left where there was a manor to his left and then came around to the right where he stopped in front of an inn. Derby looked around himself as he saw the townsfolk mill around the town. His eyes focused towards the opposite corner from where he was and there was train station. He could hear the whistle of a train in the distance which prompted him to dismount from his horse. Derby led his horse towards a place set for horse leads to be tied up to and then walked into the inn.

An hour later, Derby exited the inn, dressed in a different set of clothes, hair dry and neatly combed, face cleanly shaven, and without any of his bags or gear. He wore a modest suit and came around to the front of the inn where there was a café with metal tables and chairs on a patio. Derby could see at least two couples on the patio, drinking coffee and sitting together, and then one lone older male. The man wore a fine three-piece dark grey suit with a top hat that covered his medium length dark blonde hair. His vest was a silky green with a line pattern on it. Around his vest was a gold chain. Below his neck was a silky ascot tie in the same color but different eccentric pattern. He wore glasses and had a neatly trimmed beard. He was a few inches shorter than Derby in height, but was a larger, stockier build than him. As he sat, legs apart, he rested his gloved hands at the top of a cane with a metal handle with carved grooves. The pole of the cane was a polished black wood. There was nothing served at the table he was at, but he simply sat there, tapping his cane into the patio stones with rhythm. Derby approached the man, which caused the man's eyes to shoot towards him and for him to stand up as he got close.

"Father," Derby greeted, extending his hand.

"You're late, *Darby*," Mr. Cabernet spoke in a local accent. "What have I told you about being late?"

"Apologies," Derby responded with shame, "but the telegram…"

Mr. Cabernet looked him with disdain.

"It's my fault," Derby instead said.

"Sit down," Mr. Cabernet remarked, sitting down.

Derby pulled the seat out while his father signalled a waiter to come around. They ordered some coffee and then Mr. Cabernet reoriented himself in his chair to face Derby. He took off his top hat to wipe it with a handkerchief, exposing the rest of his hair which was balding along its widow's peak.

"What have you been doing all summer, *Darby*? Wasting your time in a place like this? You haven't spent your entire summer here or in the outdoors, have you?"

"Actually, I have father," Derby answered. "I like it out there – the fresh air and the breeze around the base of the mountain…"

"There's fresh air and mountains in Harlech."

"There's a lot of people too."

"There's people here," Pepin remarked, spreading out his arms and then looking at his son. "You could have spent your time doing some real work than out here, rather than…"

Pepin immediately took his handkerchief to his mouth and proceeded to give off a hefty cough. Derby looked at him as he coughed and when he finished, he cleared his throat.

"You were saying?" Derby responded.

"I was saying, you could have been familiarizing yourself with Cabernet Corporation than wasting prime time playing in the dirt. You're nearly twenty years old, my son. The time for adventure and thrills is at its end. It's time for you to begin to think about the company, the family legacy, and the legacy you intend to leave behind."

"What if I don't want anything to do with the corporation?" Derby asserted. "I have it understood that all that is to be left to Alcmene. She's more involved in the company than I am, and she likes it too. What do I have to do with a company, or a business, when I don't even like any of it? I don't want that life for me, father. I want to make my own life – I want my own legacy."

Pepin took in a deep breath, let out a brief cough, and then exhaled in a sigh.

"What legacy, my boy? Do you want to be remembered as the fool who left a successful business, a business that I've held on to through these hard times, all behind? I'm sorry, son, but there's not much more for you to achieve than to take the reins of the company… and as for Alcmene, your dear sister, she's made her decision."

Derby raised an eyebrow.

"Earlier this summer, that American businessman that your sister had met long ago proposed to her, and they're due to wed late next spring. As such, as a father and head of the household, in order to secure our legacy, I've decided to remove her from the corporation and ensure that she holds no leadership position. The last thing I would want is for Cabernet Corporation to merge or land in the hands of the Americans."

"So, you've decided that now you need your son to ensure that it stays with the Cabernct name," Derby declared, uncrossing his arms, "but what if I don't want to?"

"*Darby...*"

"I want to be an explorer and explore the empire," Derby asserted. "I'm not a leader..."

The two were interrupted as they heard the ring of a bell and a paperboy begin to shout out the headline of the morning paper, "Britain declares war on Germany! France to support Britain in the invasion of Poland!" Derby immediately shot a look towards the paperboy.

"What did he say?" Derby questioned as he bell rang again. "Oy! Over here!"

"*Darby*, sit down!" Pepin complained.

The paperboy walked over and paid for a newspaper. He then read the headline as the boy had read it aloud, 'Britain Declares War on Germany.'

"Did you know about this father? The empire is at war with the German Reich," Derby stated. "They've actually gone to war against the Huns, haven't they?"

"*Darby*, please sit down," Pepin requested once more. "No, I did not know, but there was speculation it would happen. Seems as though the Germans have made friends with the Russians and put Poland into a corner like they did with the Czechs."

Derby looked at his father briefly and then continued to read the paper. He asked, "Do you reckon the commonwealth will join?"

"Likely. I had a meeting with the board and expect to hear from Ottawa for potential military contracts, which would be very good for us."

"Good for everyone. It's about time they declared war," Derby remarked. "A war like this one is a once in a lifetime opportunity – this must have been how you felt before you went over during the last war, father. The excitement…"

"Do you mean to tell me that you intend to enlist if Canada goes to war?" Pepin questioned in a strict tone. "If you do, then I have no intention that Canada should join the war regardless of any military contracts. I will not have my son shipped off overseas to Europe."

"Father, I'm going back to school in Europe after Michaelmas anyways," Derby remarked, looking away from the newspaper with a smile on his face. He then lowered his smile as he saw the stern look on his father's face. He folded the newspaper and placed it aside. The waiter came around with their coffee and sat it down on the table. "Please reconsider, father. Yes, I've heard the stories you've given about your time in Europe, but I've also heard differently from other people. Some folks here, they fought in the Boer Wars and it was nothing like what you said war is like. They had a grand old time fighting in those bush wars, and it was a great experience for them. Perhaps this time it won't be anything like that."

"Here's what will happen after the Germans have invaded Poland, *Darby*. The German army will turn right around and attempt to invade France again, and it'll be the same stalemate that we had the last time around. There will be no change."

"What if I'm not shipped off to Europe then… alliances are made, and the war could develop elsewhere like it did last time."

"Then let me not remind you about your uncle, Lupin Cabernet, my older brother. As the eldest, he enlisted before the rest of us, and such, they sent him to the Middle East to fight the Ottoman Empire where he died in Gallipoli," Pepin stated. "Is that what you had in mind? You will not join the Canadians but instead return to England to finish your studies."

"But father, you fought in France and the experience was not at all as devastating than you said it was. You survived and even met mother in Belgium."

"My survival in that war was a fluke, and even then, the horrors of the western front were not worth the 'experience' or the 'adventure,' because the cost of those were the lives of my friends, and even the friends I made along the way. I survived, but they did not, and all that was left to chance, and you will not gamble your life like some degenerate."

Derby did not respond anymore. He looked away with a displeased look on his face. Pepin shook his head and proceeded to cough into his handkerchief.

"I was wrong..." Pepin wheezed as he finished coughing. "I was wrong to believe that you were right to take control of the company. I will have to make a deal with Alcmene about the future of the Cabernet Corporation, but in your hands, they best not be left."

The look on Derby's face as his father finished his sentence and began another coughing fit turned to further frustration and scorn.

Act 1, Scene 1

The mew and haw of seagulls could be heard from above as they passed by like airplanes, in a V formation across the clear morning skies. The common roar of waves could also be heard not too far as the lips of the sea came onto the short beachhead common in the East Anglian countryside. The beach consisted of a dark beige sand that had a dust-like composure to it, driftwood, and short cliffs that cut perfectly along the coastline as if the land suddenly came to a halt. The cliffs were less than a few feet tall, only a danger to fall over if you weren't looking where you were walking, and the grass above them was a healthy green, neatly trimmed, and with a dirt path that stretched along the entire length of the shoreline in this rural part of the region. On the other side of the dirt path there were fields according to every homestead mixed with trees and other buildings along the pathway. Unlike the rural country in Allabrese, the countryside in East Anglia was compact and had numerous buildings along the road with farmland behind them. Even a lighthouse existed in the midst of the farmland, keeping watch towards the North Sea, and from its peak an Anglican church could be seen too along the road. Further north, around the end of a small peninsula and shaded with tall trees, there was a manor with a straight gravel road that pulled in from the main path.

The Cabernet country home in England was a fair-sized house with a large rectangular gravel courtyard at the end. The lawn around the house was nearly trimmed and green, and likewise the trees around the property were large, tall, and leaves very green too that rustled with the breeze. The front yard divided between the gravel road stretched far whereas the rest of the property was surrounded by coastline and less than a few yards to stretch outwards. A stable was detached from the house and connected with the courtyard to house vehicles and horses. A few vehicles could be seen parked inside through the open barn doors and outside along the gravel lot. The house itself consisted of a light beige brick and copper green rooftop. Including the attic, the house consisted of three-stories and a basement. There were dormer windows across the rooftop with white curtains, like the rest of the windows, that blocked sightline into the home. The windows along the main and second floor were tall and rectangular with white frames. The main entrance was a single but tall door that led into the main foyer.

From inside, the Cabernet home consisted of walls split between wooden panels at the lower third and wallpaper or painted walls on the upper two-thirds. Crowns were placed along the corners with the ceiling and walls. Along the non-panelled portions of the walls there were various decorations, ranging from framed paintings, photographs, to featured artefacts and cultural items taken from across the entire world. The foyer floor consisted of a clear white marble while the walls were painted a shade of goldenrod. The wooden panels and mouldings were a dark brown wood. At the end of the foyer there was a set of steps that went up to a landing and then diverged into additional steps left and right that came up to the second-floor gallery that stretched around. A taller and wider window sat behind the middle landing between the stairs and looked out towards the patio on the other side tucked between the two wings of the home and shaded by both sides as the rays of the sun moved from east to west. At the end of the patio were balustrades and steps in the middle that came down to the rear. A small garden with a fountain in the middle stretched around the rear of the house with gravel paths, and likewise there were gravel paths that went out on both sides and connected with the main gravel parking lot. At the rear of the property, trees were neatly positioned with a few yards between them along the cliff. An individual path went from the patio, through the garden, and to a wooden staircase that came down to the beach. On both the rear face of the west and rear wing there were additional patios enclosed with balustrade railings. Each connected back indoors through French windows, where on the east wing the door led into a ballroom while on the west wing it led into a grand study. From the west patio, sitting upon a chair at a circular patio table with a leg crossed over his knee, an older Derby Cabernet sat smoking a pipe in his right hand and looking out to the sea.

Nearly thirty years had passed from then to now, an entire lifetime, and it displayed in Derby's stern face having survived the Second World War and living in the midst of the Cold War between East and West. Derby Cabernet in this time of his life had a stockier appearance, gaining mass over the years as he became a matured adult. His formerly blonde hair was shorter than he kept it in his youth, combed to the right and now faint and grey. His clean-shaven face, still clean shaven except for short moustache atop his lips. His eyes were still light blue, but at the creases of his eyes were crows' feet that stretched outwards. His jaw still square, and his cheeks round. He wore a grey suit with a tie and sweater vest underneath. His height was more or less the same to the height he had grown at nineteen. He sat at the patio porch, smoking his pipe with a cup of coffee in the early morning, newspaper beside him, but untouched. Rather than read the headline news, Derby instead sat back and looked out towards the see in silence listening to the ambience.

After twenty minutes had passed, Derby finished smoking his pipe and drinking his coffee, so he stood up and entered into his study. The household study was large and spacious with a wide desk directly in front of him. Two armchairs were on the other side, split between each other and on an angle. On the left and right was an open space with rugs on the floor and lamps hung from the ceiling. On both sides of the French window there were tall rectangular windows with tables in front of them that had all sorts of cherished artefacts on display. On both the left and right side there were two windows with tables before them that had maps, books, and other documents stretched out with chairs before them. At one of the tables there was also a typewriter with stacks of paper nearby. Directly across the desk and French window was a set of double doors that led out from the study. Besides this doorway on both sides there were tall bookshelves that covered this face consisting of a mixture of books and additional artefacts and picture frames on display, such as an effigy of a raven. Derby put his pipe away and then walked towards one of the tables on the right where he picked up some drawings, rolled them up, and placed them in a cylinder. Nearby the drawings on the edge of the table there were some that bore depictions of a six-point star in different forms, and others of drawings of a harp and maps of the Middle East. Nearest to where Derby had taken the drawing, he put away a map of Europe in the early nineteenth century.

Derby left his study and stepped out into the library with a row of bookshelves on his left and right for the first half, and then an open space for the latter. An additional enclave was on the left and right of the former portion, creating three spaces in total where on the outer spaces there were more bookshelves and display cases in the midst of them with more artefacts and items taken from around the world. On the walls shared with the study there were newspapers hung on both sides that featured headlines such as 'Derby Cabernet recovers Irish Diamond from South American' and 'Cabernet locates Sword of Islam in India'. There were also photographs that showed Derby in various locations from across the world with his wife. Derby approached the exit to the foyer where a maid was dusting some photographs kept on a table next to it.

"Mavis, have you seen my wife?" Derby questioned.

Mavis sprung to attention as she turned to him.

"Yes, Master Derby," Mavis answered. "She's in the parlor. You can't miss her once you step through the foyer."

"Thank you, Mavis."

Derby exited through into the foyer and stopped as he could hear the soft tune of a cello play from the other side of the house. He wandered into the right side where he came into a corridor. The music could be heard coming through one of the doors. Derby opened the nearest door and stepped into the dining room. He then went by and entered into the kitchen, a continental kitchen with an island in the middle, and then he came to the other side to exit through to the parlor, or ball room. Derby entered through into the ball room and stopped as he looked towards his wife with a smile.

Ophelia Cabernet played the cello gently as she sat on a low platform at the other end from a regal armchair like a throne. He walked towards the platform, put his hands behind his back, and listened and observed his wife as she played methodically with her eyes closed. Ophelia Cabernet wore a purple dress that came down to her ankles. Her medium length light brown hair was pulled back in a braided bun. She had fair skin that had taken less stress than Derby but still showed age from her own anxieties. Around her neck was a pearl necklace and at her ear lobes sapphire earrings. Her hands were in white gloves that went up her slender arms, and at her feet were flattop slippers. She played a harmonious and calm tune, which soon turned to a saddened song towards its end. When Ophelia was finished, Derby clapped his hands, and she opened her blue eyes to look to him with a smile.

"Well done, my dear," Derby remarked with a wide smile.

"Derby," Ophelia greeted in her breathy Londoner accent, "why don't you play with me. It's been a while since you picked up your clarinet."

"I wouldn't have the time, I'm afraid, my ray of sunshine," Derby expressed, looking to the armchair next to her. "I just popped in to let you know that I was going to fetch Charlemagne from his practice. Did you still want to go out to shops afterwards? We could all go out and have some lunch in town."

"A pleasant idea, Derby," Ophelia said, putting the cello wand on a table next to her and standing up. "Let me get ready first – where did you have in mind? Norwich? Ipswich?"

"Nothing too far, I'm afraid. I have to be back later this afternoon for a business meeting."

"Right," Ophelia remarked, standing in front of her husband.

Derby was a few inches taller than Ophelia. She looked at him with a kind face and placed a cold hand on his warm cheek.

"My dearest little hammer," Ophelia expressed, looking lovingly at him. "I wouldn't know what I would do in this world without you. I've come from another world into yours for you."

Derby took her hands and lowered them as he looked back at her in the same way.

"You followed me, remember?" Derby expressed with a laugh. "I made no obligation towards you."

"How could you not have? After we had met, would you not have come back if I-"

"To confront your father the same way? The odds were shifted when I knew about the life we had created together. For as much of a pain that boy has been, the greatest joy he gave was to bring us together in this lifetime."

"Forever."

Derby smiled at her and then began to lead her towards the ball room exit.

"You know, my love," Ophelia expressed, "there is another joy that we owe to our son."

"What's that?"

"Our dearest little Charlemagne, of course."

"Yes, a son that is not our own, but has been raised as though he were our youngest," Derby remarked. "I don't suppose it's worth to ask…"

"When Everest will take him? Let's not ask that question – let him stay with us."

"I agree that Charlemagne is best in our care for our sake, but not his own. The boy needs to be with his own parents; even if I have my worries that he be raised by the German and that Charlemagne could turn out of more a savage than a gentleman, it does no good to Everest to avoid his duties."

"Leave him be, Derby," Ophelia expressed. "They are both young and it will be not too soon that another child will befall them and then they won't be able to run anymore. Have a bit of patience. For now, the power of our existence is to rear Charlemagne and soon he will be old enough to decide for himself."

Derby nodded to his wife as they reached the doorway, kissed her on the forehead, and then they parted as she went to get ready. Derby remained in the ball room to look around for a moment. He glanced at the white tile floor and chandelier ceiling. The walls were similar to the rest of the house except they were pure white in panel and wallpaper. Between each window were vases that overflowed with greenery. He walked around to the center of the room and then spun around to look towards a large shield with swords inserted between to make an X mark. On the metal shield was a herald that contained the emblem of a wolf and a cross. Derby looked at the family crest and then came around to look at some photographs on a table besides the exit to the patio.

A few photographs placed in the ball room were older ones, one of which consisted of his father and mother, Pepin Waelsing Cabernet and Esme Therese Batiste. His father appeared much as he did thirty years ago in Allabrese, though in an half-button white shirt with a golden necklace protruding outwards, while his mother had wavy blonde hair and wore a white dress. Her face was very pale and eyes light. She held on to her husband's arm, both in this photo and in their life together. He placed the photo down and then picked up the next one which showed Derby and Ophelia from close to fifteen years ago with two children before them. The color photograph showed Derby with his blonde hair before it had greyed, same moustache, and his wife with shorter hair than she did now. The children in front of them consisted of a male approximately seven years old and a female approximately five years old. Everest Cabernet had medium length straight light blonde hair and a face similar to his father, while his daughter, Britannia, had golden blonde hair and wore glasses. Her face was like her father's too. Next to these two photos were close portrait photographs of Derby and Ophelia's fathers, on the left being a closer photograph of Pepin Cabernet in his finest suit and one the right being a closer photograph of Louis Mountbatten in his military dress. A crack in the glass of the photograph frame was evident, but the glass held together, nonetheless.

Once Derby had finished admiring the decorations in the ball room, he exited through the kitchen and came around to a corridor on the side that connected with the patio. He then led himself through to the dining room and back into the foyer where he waited for Ophelia, and then the two of them stepped out of the house to venture into the local town.

Act 1, Scene 2

Derby drove a 1963 green Bentley S3 around the gravel lot and up to the front step in front of the manor. He then exited out and came around to the passenger seat to open the door for Ophelia who held on to her summer hat as she took careful steps down to the gravel and then came around to sit down. Derby then came back around to the driver's seat and entered in, and then proceeded to drive around and out down the gravel road. At the end of the gravel road were two posts that attached to a fence that stretched along the front of the property. There was no gate, but Derby paused as a car passed them going northbound. He then merged onto the dirt road and proceeded to go the same direction. They slowed approached a paved road, but before they did, Derby pulled the car over and went to a mailbox to pick up some mail. He then returned to the vehicle, passed the mail to Ophelia, and they went along their way into the local village. Ophelia reviewed the mail while Derby drove. Derby passed a few villages, waving towards some people, homeowners tending to their gardens, pedestrians walking, and farmers, but for the most part they shunned Derby as they looked back. The couple entered the small village, passing the small town centre with a clock tower across a stone-built Anglican church, and passed through. Derby drove the car along a coastal road as Ophelia put the mail aside and looked out the window.

"Nothing but rubbish," Ophelia expressed. "A letter here for you, but I can't make out the name. The handwriting is awful."

"I'll take a look at it later," Derby expressed, pulling down the sun visor as the sun shined towards them.

"What are these changes I hear about in the news all the time?" Ophelia questioned. "Perhaps you know more than I do – the changes to do with the Church."

Derby's hands tensed around the steering wheel as he looked at the rear-view mirror for his periodical checks and then looked forward again.

"I have the faintest clue what is going on with the bloody magisterium," Derby expressed. "Father Keaton has not been entirely clear, nor has the bishop or the diocese."

"Those three and some years they spent in Rome discussing what needed to be changed with the church to raise attendance, and modernize the church and such… All those things that the radio talked about which they would do, and then you told me that it wouldn't happen and that it was all nonsense, but now it seems like they're taking reform, *Darb*."

"I was not wrong," Derby expressed. "Those agitators on the radio – the anti-Catholic media spoke a different lingo than what was really being discussed during the Second Vatican Council. I reviewed the final documents, and although I have my quarrels with some of the final words that were put out, in no way were the media's claims true."

"They want to do the Mass in English, like they do in the Anglican church," Ophelia stated. "The hymns sung in English, most of which will be taken from other sects. How does that not validate the claim that the Church was seeking to become more like the protestants?"

"It doesn't," Derby argued. "These changes won't be tolerated – even in this era of change, of decline. Understand, my dear, you did not leave your life behind to join me, to be ostracized by English high society and made an outcast, to not make the most important decision of your life and come into communion with Rome, the Catholic Church, from outside of which there is no salvation, for nought. The gates of Hell shall not prevail upon Her."

The car ride went on for fifteen minutes to reach the outskirts of another town on the coast. Just before they arrived into that town centre, Derby turned right into the parking lot of a secluded property. Ahead of them was their local Roman Catholic parish, St. Edmund's, which in comparison to the stone-built Anglican church nearer to the Cabernet country home was newer and consisted of tan bricks. The church had a tall bell tower at the front as part of its façade and a garden on the left with a cemetery to the right. At the left corner of the parking lot there was a separate building on the property, the rectory, which Derby pulled in towards and parked his car.

"I'll just pop in to get the lad and I'll be right out," Derby remarked, opening the door. "No need to come with. Just stay in the car."

"I'm going to go into the rectory," Ophelia stated. "Don't worry about me."

Each opened their door and got out of the car. Derby walked across the parking lot to the front of the church while Ophelia went into the rectory. The doors at the front of the church were large but had a smaller set of doors within them to allow people in and out. Derby opened the door and entered into the rear of the church where he could hear singing come from the other side of the narthex, the narthex of which was empty and quiet. Derby stepped forward towards three doors ahead of him, walked through the one on the right, and then entered through.

The interior of St. Edmund's Church consisted of a lengthy nave up to the altar with side aisles that had additional pews to create four columns in total. The sanctuary around the altar was round and there were two doors on each side that went into the sacristy. Just before the sanctuary was a transept with confessionals on the left and benches for the choir on the right. At each side of the transept there were also transept chapels with devotional shrines, one for the Blessed Virgin on the right and another for Jesus Christ on the left. The walls in the church were similar to the ones at the Cabernet home with an embedded panel on the lower one-third and a plain wall on the upper two-thirds. Likewise, around the ambulatory around the sanctuary, there was a darker grey stone brick used for the lower one-third and a clear wall with three rectangular murals separated by pillars. The depiction on the right displayed the Creation of Man with the hand of God in the corner reaching downwards towards Adam on his back and extending his hand upwards, similar to Michelangelo's painting except in a coarser and simplistic art style. The second and central depiction showed Christ as King crowned on a throne ruling with an iron rod, beneath him there are kingly figures worshiping him, and then below them noblemen and clergy, and then peasants. On the right was a depiction of the Annunciation with the Blessed Virgin on her knees in obedience before the Angel Gabriel, and a dove coming down from the sky towards Mary parallel to the hand of God in the left-most depiction. Beneath the central depiction sat a gold-colored tabernacle.

Derby dipped his hand into a cup of holy water on his right and then made the sign of the cross as he entered. He then proceeded down the aisle to come closer to the transept. He looked to his right towards the choir benches as less than a dozen young boys sang together. An older woman waved her hand and conducted them as they sang in English. Derby genuflected at the second bench and then sat down to look towards the boys as they sang. His eyes focused on a particular fellow, a young male nearly eight-years old, in a white alb. His snowy white face was soft and pure, and his lips as they moved let out an angelic sound as he sang. His cheeks were round and ruddy. His eyebrows fine. His short blonde hair neatly combed. His blue eyes like the North Sea and the whites of his eyes clean. They shot towards Derby as he took notice, but his voice continued to let out the serene sound they produced.

"For the Kingdom – and the Power – and the Glory, are yours forever," Charlemagne sang, *"and ever."*

Derby gave a nod of approval as the song finished, refraining from clapping in the church. His teacher turned the page and then noticed Charlemagne present as well as another figure nearby which notified her that practice was now over.

"Well done," the teacher remarked, closing the booklet, "that'll be all for today."

Derby turned around to notice who else was with them. The figure was none other than the parish priest, Fr. Paul Keaton. He was an average-sized man with curly dark hair and was a slim but tall figure. He wore a black cassock that showed his Roman collar around his neck. The children stepped off the choir bench and proceeded towards the altar server sacristy on the left to doff their robes. Derby stood up as the children were then dismissed and stepped away from the pew, genuflected again, and then watched as Charlemagne rushed towards him.

"Not so fast, Charlemagne," Derby remarked, embracing him and turning him around. "First, we must show our reverence to the everlasting presence of God."

Charlemagne bowed towards the tabernacle and then turned back around to embrace his grandfather.

"Where's nana?" Charlemagne questioned.

"She's with us, don't you worry," Derby expressed. "Her and I thought it'd be a good idea to drive into town, have some lunch, and perhaps we'll go down to the pier and get some ice cream. How does that sound?"

"Sounds great," Charlemagne approved, embracing his grandfather again.

Derby laughed and patted his grandson on the back and gave him a kiss on the forehead. They then turned around to face Fr. Keaton who had snuck up on them.

"Hello, Mr. Cabernet," Fr. Keaton greeted, offering his hand.

"Hello, Father," Charlemagne responded, shaking his hand.

"Your grandson has quite the voice, doesn't he?" Fr. Keaton remarked. "We are certainly blessed to have him sing in our choir."

"Yes," Derby agreed, "it is only too bad that we discovered Charlemagne's gift to sing too late that he should not have been learning the Gregorian chants in Latin to sing for us."

"Well, Latin can be a difficult subject to learn for the youngsters," Fr. Keaton reasoned. "With the upcoming changes this spring, after Lent, we expect there to be a lot more church engagement than there currently is. The purpose of the vernacular is to better engage with the lay community. You may not understand it, Mr. Cabernet, but the traditions as sacred as they are, will be kept sacred, but aren't enough to engage the people."

"The Mass isn't meant to engage people, but people are meant to engage in it. The Mass isn't an entertainment nor meant to draw people like a radio or TV show. When did the Church become interested in viewership?"

"I won't get into it with you again, Mr. Cabernet," Fr. Keaton acknowledged. "The changes are final, and they are for the best of the Church. I firmly believe that we are acting under the guidance of the Holy Spirit in this greater decision making."

"Yes, well, I pray then that these changes will not in the least be the beginning of the end for the Latin Church. I know for certain that the protestants relish in this victory that we should stoop to their levels – if people wanted a protestant service, they would have gone to an Anglican church."

"You and I both know there is so much error in the Anglican church that will not change in our church."

"I should hope so," Derby expressed, attempting to walk away with Charlemagne, but stopping himself as he walked back towards Fr. Keaton. "I suppose though that when the Holy See decides in some ill-thought revelation that contraception is acceptable as the Anglicans did, then that will be the end for us too and we'll know that the Church has fallen. The spirit of revolution is in the air, Father, if you haven't noticed. The Second World War was the death of the old world, and from its ashes comes the new world with its reforms. Let us hope that the Church is not swept up in that tide as the rest of the world is set to."

"The Church is a house built on rock, not sand, Mr. Cabernet," Fr. Keaton remarked. "The flood you so speak of, should it ever reach us, will not sweep us up. I trust that the Church and the liturgy will be kept sacred and reverent, and these changes will be for the better of the Church as a whole."

Derby shook his head in disagreement and then left down the aisle with Charlemagne. They reached the door, dipped their hands into the water, made the sign of the Cross, and then exited into the narthex.

"What was all that about, pa?" Charlemagne asked. "Is this church in danger? Is it going to be stormy?"

"In a certain sense, Charlemagne," Derby answered, taking his hand, "but don't you worry. Everything will be alright, I'm sure." Derby came down onto a knee. "God will never forsake his people again, no less when a flood comes. Don't you forget Noah's ark. God made a promise, and when the Lord makes a promise, he keeps them. As long as we are faithful to God, he will always be with you, Charlemagne, but the power to say 'yes' is within you."

Charlemagne nodded to his grandfather.

"Good lad," Derby said, smiling and embracing his grandson. "Come now, let's go meet with nana. She's just gone down to the rectory to chat with the ladies no doubt."

Act 1, Scene 3

Derby drove the family back to the English manor in the countryside at half an hour past two o'clock. The day was crisp in temperature, but the skies stayed clear, and sun was bright. Charlemagne fell asleep in the back of the car throughout the car ride home. Ophelia kept to herself to do some knitting in the front seat while Derby focused on the car ahead. He turned right onto the gravel road that came to the front of the manor, driving slowly along the path as he noticed numerous cars parked in front of the manor.

"Oh, damn," Derby cursed, "I forgot about the bloody meeting."

"Oh dear," Ophelia expressed, "well, what's the worry, love. You're the owner of the company, the sole owner, and these men work for you. What's the pain in letting them wait?"

"The pain is that I forgot I had to deal with these scoundrels in the first place and that I am now remembering that I have to put up with their nonsense now," Derby expressed as he turned the car and parked it in front of the stable. "No less, I loathe to be late and doing so gives these animals reason to criticize me."

Derby parked the car and turned off the car engine. He then turned to Ophelia who handed him the mail from earlier.

"Why don't you take Charlemagne with you upstairs and I'll see this meeting through."

"Don't rush anything for our sake," Ophelia requested. "As much as it is a bother to you, these are the men that are keeping the family company afloat. They deserve some respect for doing so."

"Hmph, how hard could it be to keep that 'legacy' from capsizing?" Derby remarked. "I'd think I've done a well enough job to establish a greater legacy than what was present."

Derby looked at Charlemagne in the rear-view mirror.

"Alas, you're right," Derby said, still looking at Charlemagne, "the family legacy deserves my full attention, and it should be my duty to ensure it can pass on from father to son."

Derby opened the door and then exited out. He came around to open the car door for Charlemagne as Ophelia stood behind him.

"Come now, Charlemagne," Derby expressed. "We're home. If you're feeling tired, why don't you have a nap in your room?"

Charlemagne didn't respond as he woke up and rubbed his eyes. He got out of the car and took his grandfather's hand. They then walked up the steps and to the front door. Derby opened the door and guided them inside, looking forward towards the group of around five men that sat and stood on the left side of the foyer.

"Gentleman," Derby greeted, looking towards Charlemagne after, "go with your nan, Charlemagne."

"Come now, Charles," Ophelia expressed, taking Charlemagne's hand and walking past the executives.

Derby closed the door behind him and then approached the executives himself. All five executives were males older than Derby, between their mid-fifties to late sixties. They all wore black suits and were of fair skin. The initial man to approach Charlemagne and seemingly the leader of the pact approached him.

"Mr. Cabernet," the man greeted. The man had dark greyish short hair that was held back with pomade. He also had a brush-like moustache.

"Herman," Derby greeted. "Gustav. Carl. Julius," he said, shaking the hands of the other males in the group. "Horace."

The last male in the group shook Charlemagne's hand with less distaste than the others, but had a firm composure. His greyish-white hair was medium length, parted in the middle, and kept together with pomade. He had light eyes and glasses. He had a short moustache and appeared to be in his early sixties.

"Good afternoon, Mr. Cabernet," Horace responded.

"Sorry I'm late," Derby expressed. "I know how much of a bother it is to come out here for our biweekly meetings."

"Yes, and yet here we come and wait," Herman replied. "Perhaps we should discuss relocating our headquarters to London from Canada to ease the strain that we should waste our time in the air."

"Oh, but I think that all that time is in itself productive and useful," Derby quipped. "Yes, gives you lots of time to think for yourself and be a bit more… analytical and insightful in your decision-making."

Horace raised a smile at Derby's somewhat sarcastic tone which did not please the others.

"The headquarters stay in Allabrese, I'm afraid," Derby stated. "Besides, this is my vacation home, and should I decide to some day return to Allabrese, what an inconvenience it would be for all of you to have to travel from Heathrow to Harlech every other week." The executives continued to remain unimpressed and instead rolled their eyes. "Gentleman, now if you'll please, to my study for the agenda items."

Derby led the men into the library and from there into his study where Derby sat down in his desk chair while Herman and another executive took a seat in the armchairs, while the other three were required to take wooden chairs from the tables around the room. They set them up so that they all faced Derby.

"Well then, let's not keep me waiting now," Derby expressed once they all sat down. "What is on the agenda for today? How is my family legacy doing?"

The men looked at each other and then Herman spoke up as he said, "Generally speaking, Mr. Cabernet, Cabernet Corporation is doing well." He picked up his briefcase at his side, placed it on his lap to open, and then took out a dossier. "Employment numbers are good. All sectors are within their target goals. We've had no major issues to discuss since our last meeting."

Herman passed the dossier to Derby who opened it and proceeded to flip through some pages. He then placed the dossier aside and looked towards the men.

"Looks like we're set to have a short meeting then," Derby expressed, "we should have rescheduled for next week. Let's not have this time together be in vain – how is the spirit of the company, our workers, our managers?"

Herman looked to the others as though annoyed with the question. He then looked back at Derby and said, "Good."

"Good," Derby repeated, "very good. Well then, it's been a pleasure meeting with you all then. We'll reconvene two weeks from now unless there's anything else you wish to discuss."

"Mr. Cabernet, we are perfectly transparent with you on a day-to-day basis. Cabernet Corporation is well off right now and we've had no major problems in the last two weeks that deserve in depth discussion, unlike other times in the past."

"No, I know, Mr. Miller," Derby agreed, scratching the side of his head. "You are all good at what you do, no doubt, and even if most of you have been in your position for only a year, we've had a better past ten years than we did earlier. At least, that is as much as Mr. Turner tells me."

Derby nodded to Horace who nodded back to him. His eyes then quickly reacted to the nudge an executive, Julius, provided to Herman. Herman cleared this throat.

"Something else, Mr. Miller?" Derby questioned.

"Uh," Herman hesitated, "just a small thing, Mr. Cabernet; something of which this board has discussed together and which we thought we should voice as a… concern and nothing more."

"Go ahead."

Herman paused for a moment as he hesitated again. He then said, "It is to do with your television interview on Thames Television a while back when you were brought on, and the remarks you made… about the Second World War."

"Go on."

Herman continued to hesitate as though unwilling to speak on. He finally said, "You were brought on to discuss your latest publication on the history of Jewish peoples and during that discussion, it was determined not by us per say, but a general consensus, that the remarks you made, in particular towards the mass murders of Jewish peoples at the hands of the Germans, as being antisemitic, sir."

"And so, what is the concern that you have for me, Mr. Miller?" Derby asked.

"The concern is the public perception," Carl stated. "It is your surname on the company name, and any attributions on your part reflect on Cabernet Corporation as a whole. Any antisemitism is irresponsible of you to do so as it negatively impacts the company. The Holocaust of Jewish people is a sensitive subject, especially when you have wars in the Middle East and increasing discourse on the mass murders and extermination camps that existed during the war."

Derby nodded and put his hand together. He thought for a moment and then brought them apart. He said, "Yes, I can see what your concern is now. Thank you, Mr. Severin."

"Even your most recent publication, although historical in nature, has been seen as somewhat antisemitic with the assertions brought forward."

"What assertions do you refer to, Mr. Miller?"

Herman scoffed as he was put on the spot and then after a moment of hesitation said, "Well, for a start, your assertion that the Jewish people are not the same people during the time of Jesus Christ, or King David, or even Exodus – that the Jewish people are not Israelites. You assert a distinction between Israelites, Judean people, and I can't remember what other term."

"You say that Jewish practices are not the same as Biblical time," Carl noted.

"You also say that Judaism did not exist until after Christianity."

"You speak in length about anti-Christian attitudes of Jewish people, of the blood libels as being true and that their hatred for Christians from the time of the crucifixion of Christ throughout history."

"Anything else?" Derby questioned.

The executives looked at each other and then did not respond.

"Well, thank you for expressing your concerns, but let me clarify my positions. I won't go into detail about the event that has now been commonly referred to as the 'Holocaust,' and the deaths of six million supposed Jewish people, because those details can be unclear, and the entire truth has unfortunately been obscured by propaganda. I do not deny that Jewish people were targeted and killed during the war, and that those murderous savages, the Germans, hunted them down, both men, women, and children; or that there were death squads and mass executions of many in the concentration camps. However, what I do challenge is this event as being one of religious significance as that would be antithetical to my Catholic beliefs. You see, the Jewish people have long believed since their diaspora that a sacrifice of six million Jewish lives would be required before they could return to the Holy Land, which is why I have problems with this contemporary term that refers to the mass murders as a 'Holocaust.' That term, from the Greek, means sacrificial offering, and in Jewish lore, their beliefs assert that when they do return to their Holy Land, which they did when they rebelled against British control in Palestine and created their occupied state of Israel, they fulfilled that prophecy which is also tied to their beliefs that once they've returned to the Holy Land, after nearly two-thousand years in diaspora, their messiah would appear. Catholic belief firmly holds that the messiah has already come to Earth once – I cannot in good conscience participate in the beliefs of the Jewish people, no less as that occupied state of Israel has become a murderous and thieving state worse than the one that got them there. Otherwise, I made no such claim as to deny that there were not mass murders and executions of Jewish people during the war, but simply asserted my right to not participate in their prophetic vision.

"As for my writings, my book is peer-reviewed and has branched upon both contemporary and traditional work on the study of Judean peoples. The Israelites consisted of twelve tribes, the Judean tribe of which was more successful due to the ascension of King David to the throne of Israel. The Judahite and Benjaminite tribes were the only ones that survived the Babylonian exile. By Roman times, the Judahite identity had become both ethnic and also civic, a resident of the Judean region, which prompted me to clarify between ethnic Judahite and civic Judean. Additionally, assimilation of other peoples and cultures had made it not guaranteed that every Judean was also a Judahite – for example, King Herod was not a Judahite, but an Edomite. The term 'Jewish' refers to the modern people who practice the modern Jewish religion which did *not* come about until after 70 AD. Ancient Israelite, or Mosaic traditions, were not perfectly practiced from the time of the Exodus onwards. It wasn't until the time of King David and onwards that some of the Mosaic law was rediscovered and adopted. Even then, these practices were cultural traditions, not a formal religion. The formal religion did not organize until after the diaspora by the remnants of the Pharisees to counter the organization of Christianity, and to counter its theologies where they developed their own mysticism and put together their most prominent writings and beliefs in a writing known as the Talmud, like a catechism for Jewish people. From the diaspora to now, Jewish belief have diverged from the tradition and Mosaic customs – it is a common misconception that Jewish customs and traditions are exactly as laid out in Deuteronomy, but that is not true. The Disputation of Paris, or Trial of the Talmud, exposed this glaring difference between practices pre-diaspora and post-diaspora as being savage and barbaric, giving reason to believe that so-called blood 'libel' was not at all libel.

"I maintain, as a practicing and devout Catholic, that the Jews of today are the descendants of those who sentenced our Lord, Jesus Christ, to the Cross, and who shouted out that the blood be on them and their descendants. I maintain that Jesus Christ is the Messiah prophesized in scripture, and that the arrival of the Messiah was already fulfilled, and that no 'sacrifice' of Jewish lives is prophesized or required, or that their return to the Holy Land will result in a doomsday event. I could believe that their return could result in an arrival of an Anti-Christ, but nothing else. I maintain that the Roman Catholic Church is the New Israel, and that the State of Israel is nothing more than an occupying force in the Holy Land who oppress both Arabs and Christians. I maintain that the Roman Catholic Church, through Jesus Christ, maintains the priestly succession from Ancient Israel, and that the sacrificial offerings, or holocausts, continue in our tradition and form through the Mass. I believe in the integrity of the Catholic Church, the succession of St. Peter through the Pope, and the apostles through the Order of Bishops, to be the One Holy Catholic Apostolic Church. In short, the Catholic faith is antithetical to the modern Jewish one. And do you know what else I say to you lot? I will not relent on anything I have just said, nor will I refrain from speaking of it to the public."

The executives looked back at Derby without another word. They promptly left as the meeting concluded with those last words.

"Pleasure to see you, until next time," Derby expressed to Herman in the foyer.

"Thank you, Derby."

Derby stepped outside as he watched executives disperse to their vehicles. Horace stayed put at his vehicle as the others got in and drove off. Once they had all left, Horace returned and walked up the steps.

"I believe you had them well spanked," Horace remarked, removing his hat again.

"Yes, well sometimes they need one to get absurd ideas out of their mind," Derby replied. "To think they'd challenge me on my beliefs – to think that they'd expect me to hold false beliefs for the sake of the company."

"They don't know you," Horace stated. "If they knew you, they wouldn't have even had thought about it, or perhaps have stuck around."

Derby chuckled. "Do you want to stay for dinner, Horace? Have a drink?"

"Certainly," Horace replied, tapping Derby on the shoulder, "how can I say no?"

Derby and Horace sat down at patio chairs and a small round table near the cliff edge overlooking the sea. Mavis served them a glass of scotch, and each took a cigar to smoke from atop of the cliff. At this time, the tide was low.

"I'll tell you what, Horace, the times have changed, but at least we can still enjoy good company and things such as these."

"Yes, that's for certain," Horace replied, lighting his cigar.

Each man took in a breath of their cigar and then let out a puff.

"How's your little one been, Derby?" Horace questioned.

"Which one? The eldest or the youngest?"

"The youngest of course."

"He's getting along well, as you can see," Derby remarked, pointing towards Charlemagne below, playing on the beach. "A remarkable young lad as it were, full of many potentials, and highly intelligent too. He's more intelligent than I could say I am at least. It's my hope that with all this wealth to which I have found little use for, he should have the means to see that potential through and become a great man – greater than I could have been. I have no expectation for little Charlemagne other than that he do something great with his life, whatever it may me, and that he decide on his own legacy for himself. He can take the reins of Cabernet Corporation, leave it all behind and make his own path ahead of himself, or any combination of ambitions – I only wish to see him live gloriously. Whatever he wishes, his grandfather in the least will approve of it. In a world that is on its way to its end, it will need a good man like him to see it through."

"Tell me, Derby," Horace said. "You say you have all this wealth and no use for it other than to see potential through, then why not use that wealth to resist the changes?"

"Resist," Derby repeated. "Resistance is futile, my friend. The winds of change cannot be resisted; history has seen that time and time again. No less can I, a single man, seek to stop the changing world. I would be like Atlas with the whole world on my shoulders, and I don't have the hubris to claim that all the world's problems are my own. I leave it all to God, my friend. No, the least that we can do in our power and might as men is to rear our children the right way. If a good number of us do so, it could be done. I only hope that Charlemagne will be able to understand as I do to be able to live in the world that is to come as though in exile, not assimilated to the barbaric, pagan culture and the lies of which it will create for itself. For those lies will all come down upon them and be their demise."

"Do you still believe that an entire international clique is responsible for this change?"

Derby looked to his friend and then out towards the sea.

"A clique? Perhaps so – you yourself, Horace, were a freemason as a young man at the end of its hold on power in a liberalized world. You and others have told me of the decline of freemasonry into the last decade. What group, if any, drives the world now…? I could not honestly say I know for certain who or what, or even if it were a coordinated change (although I suspect it to be just pure chaos). I do know that the interest of a few is at play, and that they've inherited the power that freemasons once held in their political power and influence. Their power is just now establishing in this *Pax Americana*, and financial power aside, their cultural power is inherently anti-Christian and seeks to destroy Western Civilization."

Horace did not respond as he puffed on his cigar. He let out a blow of smoke outwards, like a chimney, and then looked to Derby. The reflection of the sun shined in his glasses.

"Do you believe the Jews to be behind it – as Hitler asserted to have been the case in Germany?"

Derby looked towards Horace and puffed on his own cigar. He then let out a cloud of smoke and replied, "The only qualm I have with Jewish people are those in the Israeli government and those that have taken the tragedy of the mass murders for the purposes of propaganda." He then shook his head. "I hate no man, Horace. I wish for all of mankind the saving grace of our Lord, Jesus Christ, and love my fellow man. I cannot deny that a great deal of Jews are in places of power, especially in Hollywood. The troubles ahead of us though are a result of the liberal-democratic world and not the result of their power, but the power of many in places of power. The existence of all those people, the legacy of the freemasons, and the power of their existence is what spells our doom."

Derby looked towards Charlemagne as he played in the sand.

"I wrote that history on Judean people in reaction to the Six-Day War, my vehement opposition to that phony state of Israel. I'm not antisemitic, Horace, but I very well am damn anti-Zionist. The entire statehood is a mockery of the Catholic Church – a warring state that has not known peace since its founding; its very founding of which came from insurgency. The Catholic Church is the New Israel, the chosen people, and it is us who struggle with God as a bride, but it is they who struggle *with* God as adversaries. So long as that occupation continues to massacre innocents, it should keep its mouth shut about the German state-sponsored mass murders during the war. No less when millions more than their people died fighting in that war, the majority of whom were likewise innocent people..."

"You fought in the war, didn't you?" Horace questioned.

"Aye, I did," Derby remarked, puffing on his cigar as it went out, "and every day I question still for what did I really fight for. I certainly did not do so for the State of Israel."

Derby felt into his suit jacket for his lighter but rather than retrieve it, he felt something rigid in his pocket. He took out the item and it was the letter from the mail. He placed it on his lap, took out his lighter to relight his cigar, placed the lighter on the table and then looked at the envelope. As Ophelia had said, the writing on the letter was ineligible but the post stamps suggested the letter came from the United States. Derby felt the lip of the envelope and opened it, and then he removed some papers and began to read them.

"What's that you have there?" Horace questioned.

Derby finished to read the letter. He then looked over with a smirk.

"A letter from the U.S. government it seems," Derby stated. "They seem to be seeking to enlist my help in some matter of archeological concern. I'm due to meet an old friend of mine, Dr. Dumas. I'll have a discussion with him on it – the last thing I want to do is help the Yanks."

Act 1, Scene 4

The next day, Derby left the Cabernet home in the early morning just as the sun began to rise. He wore a dark suit, white shirt, and blue tie. He also carried a briefcase with him as he came around to the 1963 Bentley. He opened the car door, entered inside and placed the briefcase on the passenger seat, and then he ignited the engine and pulled out and forward. Derby stopped at the end of the gravel road but rather than travel south, he went northbound and away from the village. He passed a sign that stated Norwich to be little more than twenty miles away. Derby travelled further than just Norwich from the coastline, driving past Cambridge, and reaching Oxford in the late morning as it began to pour heavily. At the northeast corner of the township was the famous and old university campus.

The University of Oxford consisted of an immense city campus, of which its architecture and buildings ranged from various styles used and built in the United Kingdom between the ages, the most notorious buildings of which in the heart of the campus being of English Gothic and Baroque style, built between 1400 to 1900. These buildings were constructed of tanned bricks and grey slat rooftops with spires at the corners. The windows on various buildings were small and rectangular, some of them arched, but all of them crossed. They would very between black and white frames. Neoclassical architecture was also present in the campus, building facades consisting of several pillars with a pediment resting above. The stone bricks used to construct these were larger than the ones used in the older buildings. The windows were larger, but the doors not as large. Around High Street, where Derby entered, and around the very center of the campus there were more than just the primary faculty buildings by their notorious architecture style. Between the gaps, there were other buildings in traditional European architecture used for shops and homes that could be found anywhere else. These buildings consisted between tanned and red bricks of varying sizes. There were many of these buildings along High Street in between the traditional buildings, and then all around the periphery closer to the rest of the city centre. At the outer edges, the gaps and spaces between the buildings consisted of mowed lawns and parks that added space between each building. The roads around the campus were difficult to navigate around, so Derby parked the car on the outskirts of the university, took out his umbrella, and picked up his briefcase to venture through the promenades between buildings to reach the Faculty of History.

Derby was capable to navigate through the labyrinth of paths with ease, reaching a courtyard, and then the front door that led into the hallways of the history building. He walked down the corridor, steps echoing across by his lightly heeled shoes and the emptiness of the hallway. Finally, Derby reached a set of double doors, to which he carefully opened by his backside, and slid into a darkened lecture hall room. The room had a few windows that looked out to the dreary downpour and a field on the other side with trees on the outskirt. Thick and dark curtains covered most light from pouring through. The lecture hall was set up with benches and tables that faced a wall with numerous bookshelves. In front of the bookshelves a projector screen was pulled down, and before the projector screen, on a small table, was a projector and an open briefcase with various notes inside. There were at least thirty students present in the room, listening attentively to the speaker at the front of the room who spoke in a loud voice that obscured the creak of the door and Derby's motion. Derby was able to sit down on a chair closer to the front of the room where he placed his briefcase at his side and then listened in.

The lecturer was a young man, in his mid-twenties, and wore a tweed three-piece suit. He wore glasses and had fair skin. His hair was light brown and cut short, and he spoke enthusiastically, although in a coarse and deep voice, and French accent.

"Based on our most recent excavations last summer, it can be said with certainty that the site located is where the battle took place," Dr. Dumas expressed. "Amidst the field, after setting up our excavation sites, we analyzed the ground and were able to dig remains of weaponry that had long been abandoned in the dirt. Some may say that any sort of weaponry is not necessarily evident that this should be exactly where the legendary fight had taken place, but interestingly among the items that were discovered was weaponry uniquely Islamic."

Dr. Dumas changed the slide on the projector to show drawing examples of spearheads. Most of the spearheads appeared the same with a triangular shape, except the middle had a noticeable meridian while the bottom most had a thicker meridian.

"Here you have three examples of weapons from these times, the bottom two of which were commonly used in the Frankish and Byzantine Empires. The spearhead at the top is match for similar weapons used by the Umayyad caliphate and recovered in Spain and the Middle East."

Dr. Dumas changed the slide to display examples of swords, some of which had simple and straight designs, while the others had curves to their blade.

"You may say, one spearhead recovered in a dig site is not evidence of Islamic presence in the middle of France, but it was not just one that we had recovered, but a good dozen. However, the prize of the excavation was one of these," Dr. Dumas stated, pointing towards the Islamic curved sword. "Likewise, this blade was recovered at the dig site amongst two Frankish swords, and it was a positive identification for swords that too were used by the Umayyad caliphate. The combination of evidence suggests that the location we had surmised was indeed the site in which the Battle of Tours took place."

Dr. Dumas changed the slide to display a depiction of the battle. The depiction was Charles de Steuben's 'Battle of Poitiers'.

"The Battle of Tours determined European history as not only being Christian but secured Frankish rule in Western Europe and rise of the Kingdom of France in later years. Imagine if you would, what France would have been like if conquered like Spain? There would at that point be no power on the continent to stop total Islamic domination. The combined forces of the King of the Franks, Charles Martel, with the Duke of Aquitaine, Odo the Great, brought an end to Islamic expansion into Europe at least until the collapse of the Byzantine Empire and rise of the Seljuk Turks. Their power as rulers had alone stopped what could have been a very different change for the continent, and it could not have been done without their alliance that brought them together to defeat the Emir Abd al-Rahman Al Ghafiqi. What battle has singlehandedly been such a one that would have an impact on the rest of a continent's history, the history of the entire world, for so many centuries? Imagine if you would too, the attitude of the men to march into battle, not realizing that their actions on that date would result in our entire history as it was, both European and Christian. I am certain that in a thousand years from now, a battle from the Second World War will hold a similar legacy to cause the path of our history and stopped any alternative path. Say for example, the Normandy Beach landings or Battle of the Bulge – what if the battle had not been won and the Allies instead defeated in Western Europe? The Soviets were already on the offensive at this time, so a defeated Allies in the west would have been a delayed but gradual advance from the East that could have seen all of continental Europe under Soviet occupation. I tell you, the success of those battles dispelled not only German occupation, but freedom from both Soviet and German tyranny. A more important battle than that would be the Battle of Stalingrad; a German victory would have secured the

East and provided resources to repel the Allies in Italy and France, and a Soviet victory put an end to Axis dreams of total domination.

"There exist particular battles, particular moments in our times and our lives, in which our actions whether we know it or not, could determine the path of the entire future and stop revision or change. Not all moments are like that though; think Waterloo or Sedan, and how although these were important battles, the losers of those had already had their fate sealed. There are moments in which our actions may not have a particular effect, but those moments are more obvious to us. Never underestimate though the moments that could really have an impact, or even the power that all of us have in our own existence in this world."

A student raised his hand and asked a question, "Did you manage to recover the hammer of Charles Martel in your excavation."

Dr. Dumas gave a chortle and responded, "The hammer of Charles Martel? My boy, that magnificent man who saved all of Europe was the hammer. There exists no weapon; a hammer is an inefficient weapon, no less for a mounted soldier due to the weight of it." Dr. Dumas changed the slide and then said, "Let us move on."

Derby listened intently as he held a hand on his cheek. Dr. Dumas continued with the rest of the presentation, and when the hour was finished, the lights were turned on and presentation came to an end. Derby stood up from his chair and slowly approached Dr. Dumas as few students approached him to ask questions. Dr. Dumas proceeded to put away his slides and notes into his briefcase as these students asked him questions. Derby listened as they spoke to him enthusiastically.

"My friends, if you would please direct some of your questions to the leader, and sponsor, of our expedition, I'm sure Mr. Cabernet would be happy to answer."

The students looked and faced Derby. Derby towered over the young students by his height and stature, causing most of them to look back at him with intimidation.

"I have a question," a male asked. "What's going to happen to all of the artefacts collected? Are they going to go to a private collection?"

"The artefacts that have been collected are in a secure location, to be studied, analysed, and preserved," Derby answered. "Although I am avid to add some pieces to my personal collection, my priority always lies towards the academics and exposure of these artefacts to the public. I only take what would otherwise lie in storage, and I am always willing to return what I have, or even give and share to others."

"Very good," Dr. Dumas remarked. "Now my friends, if you would, Mr. Cabernet and I need to be off. I will be available later today at three o'clock. Thank you."

Derby nodded to the students and then exited the room with Dr. Dumas.

"Well, that was a charming presentation," Derby remarked. "I think your father would have been quite impressed."

"My father was a bitter and resentful man, Mr. Cabernet," Dumas said, waving a finger at Derby. "He could not be impressed, not one bit. I could have found the Holy Grail, and he, as a very religious man, would have not been impressed."

"You underestimate the sort of man I knew your father as," Derby stated. "Zacharie did not emote or express himself well to those around him, but he had heart."

"Yes, and that heart he killed with his excessive drinking after the war," Dumas replied. "Please spare me from your attempts to apologize for him. In the end, he was my father, and I still loved him."

Derby responded, "I seek only to remind you, Jean, because he was my best friend and I swore to him I would be there for you, and as it were, you are the most interesting of your siblings."

"You yourself are an interesting man too, Mr. Cabernet," Dumas remarked, walking up a set of stairs. "You have made my career here, and I am forever in debt to you."

"Well, I wouldn't hold to that praise – there are far better places to be than in Oxford."

"At least here they stand to reason, not like in France."

Dumas reached his office, unlocked the door, and then entered inside with Derby. He closed the door behind him and then looked around the small office, an eighth of the size of Derby's study and crowded too. On both the left and right there were bookcases stuffed with books of all sizes and nothing more. Dumas sat down at a small desk whose edges nearly touched each of the bookshelf and which there was barely enough space to skirt around it. Directly behind Dumas' desk was a small window, and in front of the desk was another wooden chair which Derby took to sit down. Atop of Dumas' desk was a typewriter and stacks of papers. Dumas reached into his briefcase to take out his notes and set them aside while Derby sat his briefcase down and then brought his leg up to rest his ankle on his knee.

"So, Mr. Cabernet, how have you been? What projects have you been up to? What mysteries of the world have you been working on?"

Derby gave a chuckle and replied, "Not a mystery of this world, but of my world. I've taken a recent fascination into genealogies in my downtime, particularly my own. It's kept me occupied since the publishing of my most recent book, and my pondering on whether I would write a second or third volume." He picked up, placed his briefcase on his lip, and then opened it. He removed a cylinder inside and took out the sheets of paper inside to pass to Dumas. "Have a look here."

Dumas received the drawings while Derby also took out some papers. He placed both it and the cylinder in front of him on the desk. Dumas examined the drawing, a family tree, carefully.

"Very extraordinary," Dumas stated. "How did you collect all this information?"

"Through a lot of searching," Derby answered. "I knew most of my family history from my grandfather, but little of where my family had come from beforehand. Now I know the truth, and I've put it together there," he said with a bored sigh. "I can't say I'm pleased to know the roots of my ancestors, but when it comes down to it, perhaps it was for the best that it should be that way; a punishment for any hint of hubris I may have had in my ancestral dynasty, to have come from barbarians that have been destroyers of civilizations."

"Now come now, Mr. Cabernet…"

"No, I mean it," Derby expressed. "The Lord has revealed onto me a truth, and I…" he took in a deep breath, "accept it. There is little significance in the origin of our ancestry when the greater purposes of the world orientate to His Will and our salvation. I accept my ancestry with humility."

Dumas continued to examine the family tree silently.

"Now that I've completed that project, I believe it is time that I begin to write my next volume on the history of Judean people, wishing to speak about recent times more than anything to address current events," Derby stated. "It's been addressed to me too that I have not been the clearest on the subject of the mass murders during the war, and it worries me that those tragedies will be used for propaganda purposes, especially in Israel. I wish to speak out of experience, on the whole tragedy that was that war, so as to the deaths of all innocent peoples in that war were not in vain."

"The war continues to haunt you, doesn't it?" Dumas questioned, lowering the drawings and placing them on his desk. "You can't let the past do such a thing – it will consume you as it consumed my father; it's the madness of us historians to have such a fate come over you. Set it aside, Mr. Cabernet, and focus on something else; the academic season is nearly over, let us set off on another expedition this spring. I have an idea for one, in South America."

"Oh really?" Derby questioned, little keen. "Perhaps you are right to some regard, my dear boy." He reached into his jacket pocket and took out a torn envelope with a letter. "I did receive this the other day. From a U.S. official in Washington who seeks to meet with me for some assistance."

Dumas took the letter, opened it, and silently read it. He then looked back over to Charlemagne. "I have never heard of a Captain Clayton."

"Neither have I, but he wishes to meet with me in Italy. No details as to what exactly the archeological expedition he intends to enlist me on is for, and I am in no mood to run favors for people willynilly."

"I'm surprised a foreign official is reaching out to you, but it does remind me of when the Americans were in touch with my father, during the occupation. He ran weapons for the resistance – nearly got all of us killed for it."

"That's the problem with these yanks, they don't care who or what they hurt when they have their missions. They're self-interested, even when they seem to care about the good of other people. They're also so arrogant. If I had to guess, the nature of this assignment would have to do with the Russians. As much as I loathe communists, I have no desire to be used by anyone, not anymore." Derby sighed and stood up. He walked over to a bookcase and pressed a fist into the frame. "I'm tired, Jean. Perhaps it's time I retire. I was supposed to have given up the adventures when I took in my grandson, Charlemagne, and taking on any of these projects, whether they be with you, or on my own, pulls me away from him."

Derby looked at the letter and then put it back into his pocket.

"I'll go and meet with this Captain Clayton, gauge him, but by no means will I help the Americans in their games against the Russians. I am nobody's pawn no more."

Act 2, Prologue

Derby Cabernet looked ahead of him with a pleased look on his face as he glanced ahead of him. He stood on the portside of a transport ship as soldiers in combat gear climbed the ramp to join the ship on its destination. The ship was a large, carrying not only people but freight as well. The ship was moored at a large port where there was various freight situated about. Aside from the troops that climbed up into the ship, there were officers inspecting the troops and other workers moving about to load cargo onto this boat and another. The Union Jack flew from a flagpole at the front of the dockyard, and also at the superstructure of the transport ship as well as the flag of the Royal Navy, the white ensign. The skies above were grey, and it was cold enough to see the vapor of another person's breath. Derby wore his brown battle dress, a wool serge button up jacket and matching trousers with numerous pockets. The torso piece had two breast pockets on either side. The trousers had a large pocket on the left side, and another key pocket in the right side. Around his waist he wore at thick belt. Around his left shoulder was a black lanyard with a whistle. On his shoulder there were regimental titles, 'Royal Norfolk' above and three black triangles on red that together created a larger triangle with a gap. Above those were his epaulettes for his rank, a single star at the lower end. The top buttons were exposed slightly, showing a collared shirt and tan-colored tie. Overall, the uniform was clean, pressed, and free of any spots or stains. Derby appeared healthy, youthful still and his face clean-shaven; hair cut very short from how it was two summers ago but neatly trimmed.

A man in a similar battle dress approached Derby from the side and stood beside him. He had the exact same epaulettes and regiment insignia as Derby. He was also around the same height as him but had a moustache at the top of his lips and dark hair.

The hair at the top of his head even had a bit more length than Derby's whose was cut very short.

"Can you smell the excitement in the air, Otto?" Derby expressed with a smile. "The adventure of a lifetime begins here, right now. What a fitting start it should be that it should start on a boat destined for sea? This is just the beginning of something much grander than any of us could even hope to comprehend. From this date, the British Empire goes on the offensive against Germany."

"I don't mean to give you a rude awakening, *Darby*," Otto expressed, "but this boat isn't destined for Europe, nor are we expected to fight Germans where we're going."

"In a certain sense, it is, my friend," Derby offered. "From North Africa, we will take our first steps towards reconquering the continent, but that begins with kicking the Italians out of Libya and securing the coastline. Who do the Italians think they are, threatening the British Empire? We may have lost the fight on the continent, but that weakness is on the French, not us. Now the fight extends outwards towards the rest of the wider world – this decade will be dedicated to the great struggle against the Axis powers as their alliance grows, as so does our strength to resist them grow. The Italians will rue the day in which they threatened the empire, and it will be their end for they will not be successful.

"I'll admit, I never envisioned such a turn of events when I listed. I thought for sure our fight would be in Europe proper, and not elsewhere. I was on the cusp of being deployed to France when it had fallen, and my waiting and waiting in England for their invasion has made me antsy to finally get out to exact vengeance. Sure, what awaits us in North Africa may be Italians, but the fight we give them affects our greater enemy, the Germans. They say that the battle ahead of us is of immense stakes and could have massive proportions. It's still nearly incomprehensible to believe, perhaps because I was not there, but France has fallen and now the British Empire, the English-speaking world, is at risk of takeover from a hostile enemy. Even now, the Italians of all peoples threaten our realm and livelihoods. Well then, I say, let's give those saucy bastards a proper kick up the arse to show them their place in this world," Derby said, taking in a deep breath. "I've dreamt of this moment for a long time, Otto. Far too long. Now it's finally happening. My adventure – a true, once in a lifetime adventure, is beginning. Ever since I was a child, I grew up with many legendary tales, mostly those of outlaws and cowboys that I held so close to my heart. In secondary school, education gave me the folk tales of legendary figures, Cadmus and Perseus, and epic heroes like Jason and Odysseus, or Achilles and Aeneas. My lifelong aspiration has always been to have my own adventure like these great men, and I often fantasized about it when I was younger. I never aspired for the glory though; if I could live their lives and even not be recognized or remembered for my deeds, then I would die happiest. I could... never stand to be revered by others, or the subject of limelight. I've always preferred to be distant, alone, and quiet."

"What's the use in it if not for the glory there, mate?"

"The thrill," Derby answered. "I've known the attention of the newspapers and media through my family's business since my earliest memory. My father kept me close to him when I was young, to model next to him as a young face, creating a sense that our company was a family company. The flashes of those cameras sickened me then and still do."

"If it's thrill you're after, then why not join the Royal Air Force?"

"I couldn't," Derby simply stated, looking up to the sky. "I couldn't face my enemy while crammed in a cockpit and flying at dizzying speeds."

"You get motion sick, *Darby*? I hope not, otherwise this'll be quite the long trip."

"No, nothing to that extent. I've ridden in trains and automobiles, but both air and sea warfare unsettles me. The uncertainty and the probability that you be left helpless... I rather have the flexibility of land, and not just that, but to see my enemy face-to-face too."

"Not much to be seen nowadays with the mechanized monstrosities that are out there doing the fighting. We may be riflemen fighting on land, but there are terrors that roll forward on the land, mounted with cannons. There are terrors in the skies, shooting at you and dropping bombs. Blimey, there's even monstrosities in the sea that fire missiles from underneath the waves and you can't even sea. War has changed, mate. The stories I've heard from others... it toughens me up inside to realize that this isn't just fun and games – the lives of those that we lead are in our hands, and our efforts bridge together with others to successfully defend and repel the enemy on the frontlines."

"The modern monsters of land, sea, and air," Derby acknowledged. "All monsters of man's creation, of his inventive power."

"We'll see if you feel that contemplative when one of those tanks are staring you down."

"Every monster has its weakness," Derby simply replied. "It's important to let the men know that, to deliver them courage."

"You seem courageous enough now, *Darby*, but let's see if it holds in combat," Otto remarked. "The men rely on us to have composure. Our leadership is entirely in our action and deportment. If we cower, they cower. If we show anger, they must show anger too. Yes, together we form a regiment, but the part we play determines so much more in the battle ahead – that power is in our hands, to lead our men to meet what is needed from us. Our existence is not just for adventure or thrill in this war, but to lead these men and see the greater story play out so that history books will learn of how the British Empire overcame the Axis powers. How the power of an entire generation stood up against tyranny and secured the English-speaking world. You've got a lot of personal romantic thoughts about what lies ahead, but they won't share in it. You've got to compartmentalize those thoughts otherwise you won't be with it and your troops."

"I'll have a hand on it," Derby acknowledged, slightly annoyed. "Don't you worry about me. I won't let any of them down."

"A small mistake won't give you the time to see them let down."

Derby didn't respond.

"You speak about chance not playing out in the field, but it does. During the bombings, a lot of people I knew were either left homeless or dead. Entire livelihoods, wiped out in an instance."

"For that reason, God bless the Royal Air Force to have repelled the Germans. The battle was won, and now we can move on out," Derby replied. "Don't you worry, my friend. The Germans will pay for every British life that was taken. If it were up to me, they should send ten times the hell they've cast onto us, for even just having threatened us no less to take British lives. The life of a British man or woman is worth just as much as that of a German."

"With this much fire, Derby, it's no wonder they let you, a Canadian, join the ranks," Otto noted. "You were lucky for them to have let you through to let a colonial lead British men."

"I'm not a colonial," Derby snarled. "I'm not even French. The Cabernet surname – a name that I most detest, is nothing – a made up moniker to advance our vineyard business when it started in the late last century. My family comes from the British Isles, and we've stayed British and loyal to the monarch through and through. Why else do you think I have the accent if not because my father and grandfather would want nothing more than to retain my native identity? I've spent more days of my life here at home than I have in the New World."

"Whatever you say then, *Darby*. Don't get yourself tied up in a knot. I didn't mean to insult you."

"A colonial…" Derby repeated. "I'm no mere subject but a citizen of His Majesty's esteemed British Empire, while I do respect the colonials and their grit. Their land is some of the most beautiful of this world that I have seen (although I do wish to see more of the world to compare). Their people are less to be desired though, and I prefer not to interact with their kind than I would to wander their lands in solace."

"Like an established member of the elite, you'll fit right in, no doubt. Balking at the colonials for the backwardness, the French for their sliminess, the Germans for their savagery, and the Italians or Spanish for their… well, I suppose their rigid religiosity – bloody Catholics."

Derby gave a short laugh as he looked at Otto and replied, "Yes… their Catholicism…" He then looked straight forward as he slowly lowered his smile. "Think of the kind of world we would live in if the savages had their run of the continent? Could you imagine it – speaking German or Italian rather than the most proper language of them all? As Englishmen, we didn't let it stand when the French thought that they could do the same to Europe, nor will we let it stand now."

"They say though that the British Empire is dying."

"The British Empire is not dying," Derby corrected as though insulted. "She is only just about to live. The world will know this century belongs to the British just as the last, to the Anglo-Saxon race, under the rule of an Anglo-Saxon king. The power is within us, by our existence, to defend our realm for both king and country. Am I wrong?"

"No, you're quite right, *Darby*."

"Let us then extend this patriotism forward to our men if we are to lead them through," Derby suggested, "for that power you recognize we need is within us in that form, to be fiery about our way of life and nation. The Anglo-Saxon race is the truest race of power, and it is us who have been the principal actors in creating the world's largest and mightiest empire, by our collective existence, and who have tamed the other savage worlds of the orient, Americas, and Africa. We, our people, have shaped history for years to come, left our stain, our watermark, on the history books. Who cannot say in the future, the world we live in is the result of the colonizing and saving efforts of the British Empire? Now, that world we have created to better the lives of all people across the globe is under threat of savagery reborn, so let us go forward into the breach, to fight for what is our own by our ancestral right and subdue our enemies to deliver them straight to the gates of hell!"

"Right!" Otto yelled. "For king and country!"

Act 2, Scene 1

Derby stepped out of a passenger airplane and looked out towards the tarmac around him at the Naples International Airport. He covered his eyes from the glare of the sun as he looked out around him. The airport building ahead was a small structure with the sight of two mountains behind it in the horizon. Behind the airport was a long field with the runway situated in its midst. Once he took in the sights around him, he took in a deep breath, and then took hold of the young child's hand as he positioned himself next to him.

"Easy there, Charlemagne," Derby said. "Watch the gap."

Ophelia walked behind them as Derby took careful steps down the stairs. He held his luggage in one hand and then reached the bottom to turn around and check on his spouse.

"Welcome to Italy, dears," Derby stated, looking around. "To think, twenty-five years ago this was all collapsed and rubble…"

"You were last here during the war?" Charlemagne asked.

"Yes, that's right," Derby responded, walking forward with them towards the airport. "I've had no need to come to Italy until now."

Derby took the family through the airport and then to the streets of Naples where they boarded a car that took them to a hotel.

"At least it's a lot sunnier here than in Britain," Ophelia remarked, looking out the window of their hotel suite. She took in a deep breath. "Reminds me a lot like Spain."

"Yes, perhaps a getaway was a good idea mid-Winter, even if for a few days to return Charlemagne to school," Derby remarked, flipping through a newspaper. Derby sat atop a chest at the foot of their bed. He was dressed in his suit. "Always good to get out off the island and visit elsewhere."

"Even better when you're not doing so for work," Ophelia stated, turning around and placing her hands behind her back.

"Honestly, darling, when are we going to get to visit some place for just a holiday?"

"This is a holiday," Derby remarked, lowering the newspaper and placing it aside. "My business later today is not related to either the Cabernet Corporation, nor my academic work. Think of this trip as more of a social call, than business."

"A social call?" Ophelia questioned. "Who exactly then are you visiting later today?"

"U.S. government officials at the naval base," Derby stated. "They'll be sending a car later to pick me up from the hotel, and I'll be away for the rest of the day most likely."

"Americans? What business do you have with Americans?"

"None," Derby replied, "but I wanted to see what business they may have with me. They're the ones that have reached out to me to meet them here. All I'm to do is to answer the call; you know how I am to say no to an invitation."

"Right, well, I suppose it's obvious for me to say it, but be safe," Ophelia remarked. "You don't need this reminder either, but the days of adventure are at their end with us, no less with Charlemagne in our care."

"I know it," Derby stated. "The Heavens know all too well that I've had enough adventure for a lifetime."

Later that day, Derby, dressed in the same suit, left the suite and went downstairs to the lobby. He passed the reception desk of the hotel, walking along the checkered tile floor and exiting onto the street where a car awaited him. The black car had men dressed in black suits waiting beside it. A Caucasian male in a grey suit, tanned fair to olive skin, white-collared shirt, glasses, and greyish dark hair stepped forward and offered his hand to Derby.

"Mr. Cabernet, pleased to meet you," the man greeted in an East Coast American accent. He had a smile on his face.

"Pleased to meet you too," Derby replied, looking at the man suspiciously. "Captain Clayton?"

"No, I'm Mr. Clayton's assistant, and it's just Mr. Clayton, at least as he prefers. He hasn't been in the navy in a long time, although the U.S. naval base here is where we're set to meet. You can call me Kory."

"Well then, a pleasure to meet you, Kory."

"As I said, Mr. Clayton hasn't been in the navy for many years, but his punctuality remains the same," Kory said. "We should leave now to make haste."

"Yes, let's do so," Derby agreed.

Kory turned around and approached the car. One of the men in a black suit opened the rear passenger seat door for Derby to enter inside. He timidly approached and looked at the tall man. He had fair skin but a stocky build. He was at least six-foot and four inches tall with a square jaw shape and short hair. He was young too, at least in his late twenties. The other bodyguard came around to the driver's seat while Kory entered into the front passenger seat.

"Thank you," Derby said, stepping into the car. The man then closed the door and came around to the other side to sit down next to him. The car engine started and then pulled out onto the streets of Naples.

"The letter I received was not very clear with what desire Mr. Clayton had to meet with me," Derby stated. "I hope whatever intention your Defense Department has in me, can do some good."

"I don't think Mr. Clayton would have sought you out if he didn't think you could do some good for us, Mr. Cabernet," Kory replied. "I have no further details to disclose so you'll have to wait until you meet with Mr. Clayton."

Derby nodded and then sat back as he looked out the window next to him. The car drove through Naples along a stone brick road. There were cars parked on the curb, various cars, most of them small in size and non-conventional in shape. They passed numerous apartments that were between three stories to four stories tall, recently constructed and their exterior colors of the light variety between a light blue, light grey, white and crème color. Each window was tall and rectangular with balconets. The windows were covered with either translucent curtains on the others side or opaque shutters from the outside. Almost none of the buildings had sloped rooftops and were instead plain. A majority of the buildings followed with contemporary architecture with shops on the lower street levels and homes above. Derby took notice of a domed copper rooftop in the distance as they passed a courtyard, but otherwise saw nothing more on their trip through the city. There were numerous people on the streets midday, dressed in usual clothing and nothing irregular about them than the common British person other than their tanned and sometimes olive fair skin. The hair of most people was dark colored, the men usually clean-shaven but some with facial hair. The younger men with longer unkempt hair than the older men. Eventually the car passed a larger square with a statue of a man on the right-hand side. Derby nodded as he read the name of the statue at its feet.

"There's the man responsible most of all for modern Italy," Derby said to those in the car. "Giuseppe Garibaldi, hailed as a hero in not just Italy, but most of the modern world. I'm sure you Yanks like to give yourselves all the credit for Italy now, but there's the man who sowed the seeds of liberalism and democracy."

"We would actually like to take no credit," Kory replied. "The modern Italy is the invention of the Italian people as they have seen fit, and you are right, Garibaldi played an active role in that process decades after his death. Such is the legacy of one man, his power, to cause change in the nation of so many, and beyond. He's called a "Hero of Two Worlds" for a reason, you know."

"Yes, an adventurist and a war hero; a hero of the liberal world," Derby stated with distaste. "What a life he held in a changing time..." he said. "Bloody freemason..." he swore under his breath.

The car continued to drive south until it reached an intersection with a wider road that had palm trees at its sides and a decent flow of traffic going either way. The car turned left and then began to speed up as it exited the city and travelled northbound. From Naples, the car travelled close to two hours, passing countryside to reach a town on the outskirts of the city named Gaeta. The drove in as it was now afternoon, and the sun beamed down hard on them. They drove through and Derby took notice that the buildings in this town were smaller, its streets cleaner, and its sidewalks quieter with less people. There was a lot less car traffic, and the occasional man, woman, or child on a bicycle. The car pulled out onto a beachside avenue divided with plants and palm trees on either side closest to the sea, and apartment buildings inwards.

After a moment, Derby could see the marina and a green hill ahead of them on the road. The road wrapped around this hill and went left at a roundabout. It continued where on the right there was a decayed ancient wall before the hill and secured structures behind tall fences and barbed wire that replaced the bayside view. The wall fell away from the road and inland to be replaced with a few more structures, a hotel, and then they made their final turn towards a gate where U.S. military officials stood on guard with rifles on slings behind them.

The driver rolled his window down, showed his ID, and then the gates opened for them to drive through into a large lot. They continued through and past two buildings to reach a dock. Ahead of them, moored on the dock, Derby saw an immense battleship. The battleship was nearly two-hundred meters in length, thirty-five meters in height at its tallest point. The hull was ten meters tall. It had four Mark 7 heavy armament turrets, and several lighter guns that were pointed inwards and away from the sea. The car drove ahead to the end of the dockyard where there was a ramp that went up and onto the ship. They stopped just before the ramp.

"Well, here we are," Kody stated, exiting the car.

"Finally, nice to stretch my legs," Derby remarked, attempting to open the door. The door was locked.

Kody opened the door for Derby, and he exited out and came around to the other side of the battleship where the bodyguards guided him towards the ramp. Derby stopped at the start of the ramp and looked upwards, towards the top where a man in white suit stood and looked down to Derby with a smile. The man had fair skin, tall nose, and an oval face. He was stocky and around the same height as Derby. He was clean-shaven though and had short grey hair that was neatly combed to the side and flat.

"Well, I'll be, if that isn't the man, myth, and legend himself," the man stated in a Midwest accent, approaching ahead. "Derby Cabernet, it is so good to meet you in person. Sorry for the travel situation, but it was the only way I could assure we'd catch each other." The pair met each other midway and shook hands. "The name is Clark, Clark McAllister Clayton, U.S. Secretary of Defense. Wow, it's so good to meet you – I've heard a lot about you, sir. Your latest publication, what a diamond – nevermind what those critics think."

"Thank you, Mr. Clayton," Derby responded. "I appreciate the feedback on my work."

Clayton looked at Derby star-struck for a moment and then turned around to the battleship. He said, "Well, come on aboard, *mi casa es tu casa*, even though this isn't my house. The United States government welcomes you for all your work and service to the free world in the course of your lifetime."

Clayton led Derby up the ramp and onto the portside of the battleship. From where they entered, they went towards the bow and to a set of reclined seats set up with a view of the bay. Derby took notice of the few sailors in white dress around, avoiding eye contact with them. Kory and the guards that came with them stood nearby, but Clayton stayed close.

"A drink, Mr. Cabernet?" Clayton questioned, pouring himself one.

"A small one, please."

Clayton poured Derby a glass and then sat down next to him.

"What a beautiful day, a perfect day to be on the seas," Clayton acknowledged. "I come from a landlock state, Mr. Cabernet, so imagine the irony that when war broke out, I chose to join the U.S. Navy."

"Yes, you were a captain?"

"Yes, I commanded a vessel much like this one. Aren't they beautiful creatures of the sea? Do you know the name of this beauty?"

"No."

"You are on USS Illinois," Clayton stated. "She was nearly cancelled but became the last of her kind of Iowa class fast battleship. Currently only her and her sister, the USS New Jersey, are active battleships in our fleet."

"And what ship did you serve on?"

"I served on many vessels, participated in many battles, mostly in the Atlantic and Med, from Operation Torch to the Invasion of Sicily, but I was the captain of the USS Baldwin in her time. They unfortunately scuttled her in 1961, but she was a fine ship. She partook in both of the invasions of northern and southern France. She then spent most of her days in the Mediterranean around here. I left the navy shortly afterwards in 1946 when the government decided to decommission her, and that's when I returned to civilian work."

"Politics?"

"Civil service," Clayton replied. "I'm not one for big speeches. No, I was reassigned to be the assistant to the White House's naval advisor. When I left the navy, it was to become the naval advisor to the President until the end of Truman's presidential term. Between 1952 to 1958, I practiced law. Before the war, I was a lawyer you know, just a simple lawyer in our little county. I never imagined I would have gone from Kansas to overseas, to the White House in such a short span, but I respected the power I had for what it was worth and did what I could with it. My father, Mr. Cabernet," he said, leaning in, "he was an evangelical pastor in our little community, and he raised me and my siblings on strong moral principles. I knew when I moved to our nation's capital, I was going to uphold those morals the way I did in the war."

"Very noble of you, Mr. Clayton."

"Anyways, I retained the connections I had in that decade. One of my clients was a senator who then became president, President John F. Kennedy. I had a dislike for President Kennedy initially, but in 1963, his vice-president, President Johnson, brought me on as an advisor, and I stayed put up until recently when I became Secretary of Defense."

"A humble upbringing to come to serve your country's leaders."

"The power we both wield is done so responsibly," Clayton stated. "I knew it from the moment I joined the navy that I was doing a service to not just the United States, but to the freedom of all peoples. To move from the combat zone to the behind the scenes was an honor, and I stuck to the mentality of what I was capable of. I never second-guessed it, and I never took it for granted. I'm sure you could understand – you served in the war, didn't you?"

"Yes, I did."

"Well, go on, tell some more."

Derby gave a light chuckle as he looked at Clayton. He then replied, "Some stories are best left untold."

"Please, Mr. Cabernet, if there's any detail about you that is not in the open, it's that you served in the war, even fought on the frontlines at Normandy, and yet you've been recluse about your involvement and experiences in the war. All that is known about the eccentric businessman is of the many adventures and fame he's earned for himself afterwards in his archeological and academic work. Please, show some of that humility I know you have for me."

Derby looked at Clayton with a plain face and then took in a deep breath. "Very well. I was an infantry officer in the Royal Norfolk Regiment, 1st Battalion, B Company. At the start of my commission in 1940, I was a Second Lieutenant, the second-in-command of a platoon within B Company, and by the end of the war I was promoted to First Lieutenant where I led my own platoon. I fought in nearly every campaign in the Western Front except the initial Invasion of France, from North Africa, Italy, the reclamation of France, and the final invasion of Germany. After the fighting had stopped, our regiment was put on guard duty in the occupation zone, but I didn't stay very long and left to get married."

"And how is your wife? Children?"

"She's well," Derby replied, causing a pause of silence. "Are you married, captain?"

"Yes, but I married before the war, and by the time I returned, all three of my children were children no more.

Derby nodded and then looked behind him. The bodyguards had disappeared, but Clayton's assistant, Kory, remained nearby although at a distance. Derby then sat straight.

"Sorry if I may seem blunt, but for what reason did you extend your invitation to me? I'm no stranger to the call of duty, nor am I to a potential business venture, so I can in the least suspect what the nature of this meeting is for."

"You don't believe it's because I wanted to meet the most mysterious businessman of the century, do you?"

"I'm hardly a businessman," Derby replied.

"Straight to the point then, I can admire that," Clayton stated. "You know, there's two facts I've caught on about you, Mr.

Cabernet, at least from the information that is on hand. The media has called you to be an anti-Semite, but I've read your early work on Germanism and find it hard to believe that a man could hold so much hate for the Nazi regime and yet also for Jewish people."

"I'm afraid you are mistaken on both ends, for as much as I loathed the German war machine and their fascist ideals, I do not hate the German people, nor the Jewish people for that matter."

"Yes, but you did hate the Germans in the past; you at least hold a particular bias against them as a race. The Jewish people though, no – there is no comparable evidence that you hold any hatred, and if anything, your most recent work was a breath of fresh air for someone like me. Did you know that despite what the media may say, your piece of work was well-received in Israel? Aside from the few political dissidents who reject it because of its damaging value to their political beliefs, your publication has been affirmed by Jewish scholars for speaking truth about Jewish legacy. Good work."

"Did you extend your invite to praise my work in person, Captain Clayton?"

"No, I did not Lieutenant Cabernet," Clayton replied, pivoting his legs around. "Here's the request – as you may know, after the war, the Allies prosecuted and tried war criminals, Axis personnel that were ideologically invested and participated in numerous atrocities committed during the course of the war. These trials took place in Nuremberg until 1949, and while a great deal of them were convicted and executed, a handful of them got away. You imagine, to the victims of these atrocities, the escape of these criminals did not go well, but the United States government was not interested in pursuing these figures and even shielded some of them for their use against the Soviets. A network was established in the early days that allowed these criminals to escape, most of them to Spain where they then fled to various corners of the Earth. For the victims of the war crimes, independent efforts took place to apprehend these perpetrators and take matters into their own hand until the Israeli government then got involved and has been involved ever since. The concern that I want to bring forward to you, is the existence of an ex-Nazi personnel who has been known to have been active in the United States and in allied lands. His name is Erich von Liudolfings, former member of the Schutzstaffel." Clayton snapped his finger to have Kory come by with a report in hand. He received it and then passed it to Derby. "Herr Liudolfings has a notorious track record of torture of prisoners, mass executions, and such, as per his own confession during interrogation. He actually escaped capture on his own, fled to Bolivia where he laid low, and then re-appeared in the last decade where he worked on classified projects with the United States government. In the last decade, he disappeared again, no doubt out of paranoia and suspicion, and we haven't seem him until we received an intelligence report that he was in Italy. Last page."

Derby turned to the last page and read the report.

"The war criminal was enlisted in an archeological program with connections to Vatican City established under Pope Pius XII. His current whereabouts are mostly unknown except that he may be travelling with this team wherever they currently are, which is where you come in."

"So, the United States government hired a war criminal to work for them, lost track of their captor a second time, and now that he's reappeared wishes to have him back for what reason?"

"Liudolfings has had access to classified information, and it is unknown to whom or what he's been up to in the course of the last ten years. Our personal interest with him is to learn what he's been up to, but there is the just component that he be delivered to trial and face the consequences of his actions during the war. Now here's the problem – we're not the only ones that wish to capture Liudolfings. Both the Israeli government and independent agents are searching for him, but they don't intend on being as nice with him as we do. We believe their intent is to capture him, dead or alive, and if alive, bring him straight to trial to face execution. I know there is not much the U.S. government could hope to offer to recruit you in the interest of our national security, but rest assured you would be in personal debt to the government and whatever you wish to have from us, you could have it."

"A Faustian bargain," Derby stated.

"What's that?"

"Don't worry about it," Derby replied. "Do you have any other leads to the location of this man?"

"Nothing more than what's in that report," Clark replied, "but my entire department is set to aid you with whatever resources or access you should need."

Derby looked at the report and the black and white photograph of a man in his SS uniform. He was a young man, clean shaven, with dark eyes. He has a round face and tall nose. He was expressionless.

"What do you say? Do you wish to claim the bounty on a war criminal? To hunt him down in a chase around the world?"

"I... I couldn't possibly," Derby expressed. "I'm not in my youth anymore, and I have the responsibility to care for my wife and grandson. I wouldn't even know where to begin to help bring this man to justice."

"I would suggest, being a Catholic man, you would start at the heart of your religion, the Vatican state, to learn more about this archeological program. From there, with your expertise and reputation, I'm sure you will find out what you're looking for. How about it, Mr. Cabernet? Do you accept the chance to bring this outlaw in like an esteemed bounty hunter?"

Derby took in a deep breath. He then looked at the lifeless photo of the man once again.

"I'll do what research I can and will be in touch," Derby answered. "My answer is neither yes nor no. I'm in no position to accept your terms on a whim, not anymore," he said, standing up. "I'll visit the Vatican, see if I can find his location, but nothing more."

Clayton stood up and took Derby's hands, "I wouldn't beg for more. Thank you, Mr. Cabernet."

"Your assistance is much appreciated," Kory agreed from behind, hands behind his back. "The United States government is in your debt."

Act 2, Scene 2

The sound of bell chimes could be heard in the distance. Derby looked out the window at the narrow streets of Rome. The buildings in the Italian capital were tall, but had a plainer surface texture, but at the same time came in more of a variety of colors. Like in Naples, the street level of these buildings consisted of shops and had no visible roofs. The roads in Rome were made of smoothened cobblestone, and the sidewalks of stone brick. There were numerous small cars parked on the sides of the roads which constricted the space around them and made travel narrow. The car reached an intersection and then a bridge, the Ponte Vittorio Emanuele II that crossed the River Tiber which was wide and green. The car then passed another intersection, continued forward and then continued straight forward. Derby caught a quick glance of St. Peter's Basilica at the end of the road they had just passed, but they drove past and reached a wall with some tunnels. The car went through and then turned left onto the parallel road and went in the direction of the basilica. Derby observed there to be lots of people on the streets in the early morning, walking around and in similar complexion to those in Naples, except in warmer clothes as the skies were grey at this time and seemed as though they may pour.

Derby sat in the rear passenger seat of a car similar to the one that picked him up in Naples, except they had a local chauffer who picked them up from their hotel and was set to drive them into the Vatican City. Next to Derby was Charlemagne dressed in a black suit, hair nearly combed, and next to him was Ophelia in a black dress and with a veil that covered her hair. She had applied makeup to her face, including eye shadow and mascara. Derby wore a different suit than the one he wore in Naples. This suit was darker, pressed, and tailored for him. He wore a black tie and had combed his hair.

Derby observed that they had moved away from the Vatican City by an approximate city block. The car turned left at an intersection and then passed a few more shops before reaching the end of that road. A sign on the right stated that there was no travel through on the one-way street. The car had reached a white gate at the end of the road where there stood two Swiss Guards in the traditional uniform. Derby looked closer at the gate and saw two white eagle statues perched atop of the post. The car stopped in front of the gate and then made a left onto the one-way street to carry onwards and go back towards the direction of St. Peter's Basilica. Derby observed at the end of the road were two tunnels, and behind those tunnels were the tall arches that marked the boundary of the city-state. The car travelled through slowly and they proceeded to travel along another one-way road at the front of the Vatican. Derby observed many civilian and tourist pedestrians around.

In anticipation of their arrival, the car was directed to stop so that policemen could restrict the flow of civilians to make space for them to travel inwards. Derby looked ahead and then out his window as the car made a turn towards the left and they entered into St. Peter's square.

"Come right here, Charlemagne," Derby expressed, sitting him onto his lap so he could see. "From behind these walls, the successors of the Apostles have sat with the power invested to them by Christ to lead billions of Christians over the years as His Church."

St. Peter's Basilica looked down upon them as the car kept left and they proceeded towards a side entrance where a Swiss Guard stood, saluted them, and let them pass through. The entrance that they passed through was known as the Arch of Bells. The car continued forwards as it drove at the side of the basilica, reaching another set of two brief tunnels, and then reaching around the basilica on its right. Derby looked at the exterior walls of the ancient church with awe and a warm smile on his face while Charlemagne appeared clueless. The car drove around the perimeter of the church and then reached a tunnel at the end of the road that passed through many small courtyards to finally reach a larger one.

The car reached the courtyard of the apostolic palace where it drove around in a circle and then parked in front of an entrance where there stood many to greet them at the end of a red carpet.

"I didn't expect we'd receive a dignitary welcome," Ophelia stated.

"Neither did I," Derby stated. "To think that we'd be welcomed this way."

"Why not? Perhaps sometimes we both simply forget who you are and the immense corporation that you own; a corporation that does so much in this world."

Once the car came to a halt, Derby opened the door to let himself and Charlemagne out, while the chauffer exited to open the door for Ophelia. A man in a black cassock stepped forward. He had an amaranth belt and zucchetto skullcap on his head. At either side of the entrance were three Swiss guards on either sides, carrying pikes in their right hands and saluting them. Behind the priest who stepped forward were three more priests who also stepped forward, but maintained their distance.

Derby looked around the courtyard and took notice of some details. The courtyard was surrounded with an arcade led through by arches and steps. From the entrance where the amaranth priest stood to greet them, there was an entranceway into the apostolic palace on the other end. There were also large round pots with hedge shrubs among the other arches. Above the arches were tall white arched windows on the second and third floor, and then above them were tall white rectangular windows. On the other side from the entranceway, there were no second levels and instead one could see the terracotta rooftops as well as the sun shining through the gap in the courtyard, and the clouds, to add some light to the occasion. Derby looked at a car, similar to the one that brought them into the Vatican, and which had been following them, pull up behind them with a man in a suit step out and provide protective presence for them. A smaller, older man opened the trunk of the car to remove a veiled item and bring it forward while Derby turned around to face the amaranth priest as he approached them.

"*Buon giorno,*" the amaranth priest greeted. "Monsignor Dario Bizzotto, pleasure to meet you, Signor Cabernet."

"A pleasure to meet you too, Monsignor," Derby replied, shaking his hand. "You are the keeper of the Holy Father's abode, I presume?"

"You would presume correctly," Monsignor Bizzotto confirmed with a smile. "We are pleased to welcome you to the apostolic palace and apartments for this visit."

The monsignor stepped aside and greeted Ophelia, and then Charlemagne.

"Say hello, Charlemagne," Derby instructed.

"Hello," Charlemagne greeted in a shy tone, sticking close to his grandfather's side.

Derby placed a hand on Charlemagne's shoulder. The family walked together as they were led to some of the servants and workers at the palace who dressed in formal clothes, suits with tailcoats. They greeted each of them. Derby took notice of a tall man in the back, near one of the Swiss guards. He had medium length grey hair and fair skin. He held his hands together and kept a professional deportment, much like the bodyguards that joined him on his voyage to meet Captain Clayton. Once Derby and Ophelia met the servants, they were then introduced to several priests who wore black cassocks and had no colored belts or skullcaps. They all had an Italian appearance and shook hands with the family before they were then led inside. Derby held Charlemagne's hands as they were led through the decorated foyer hall with Ophelia.

Msg. Bizzotto guided them through the entrance of the palace and towards a set of stairs. The Swiss guards remained outside and the only ones that followed them were the priests and the tall man in a suit. The family were led to a room where the veiled item that had been brought inside was placed on a table. It was next to another veil that hid something underneath. Derby looked at the other side of the room to see a set of wooden doors on either side.

"How has your time been in Rome?" Msg. Bizzotto questioned. "Have you been here before?"

"It's been fine. Ophelia and Charlemagne have never been here before, but I have once, close to twenty-five years ago," Derby answered. "I only got to see the basilica from afar, no time to visit because I was here for work though."

"Bravo," Msg. Bizzotto replied, "and how are you finding it so far?"

"Well, all this is quite beautiful," Derby answered, looking at his wife.

"We are honored to be guests today," Ophelia added. "We can't wait for the tour, nor to meet His Holiness."

"His Holiness will be out in just a moment," Bizzotto stated. "He has just finished a meeting with some bishops."

Derby and Ophelia stood around as they continued to absorb the atmosphere of the apostolic palace. Then suddenly, at a moment's notice, the wooden doors opened, and Derby turned to face them as two priests in black cassocks stepped out to hold the door and then three men stepped forward from the other side in a V formation. On the left was another priest with black cassock, and an amaranth belt and skullcap, while on his right was a priest wearing a black cassock with a crimson red belt and skullcap. The cardinal, Cardinal Amleto Cicognani, appeared to be slightly older than the pope with whitish-grey hair and glasses. He had fair skin and wore a gold-colored crucifix around his neck. His Holiness, Pope Paul VI dressed in a white cassock and with a white zucchetto. Derby stood up straight as he saw the presence of pope join them.

Pope Paul VI was approximately of average height, a few inches shorter than Derby but around the same height as Ophelia. He had fair, olive skin with ears that stuck out. He had a bit of grey hair at the side of his head, bald at the top, and deep grey eyebrows. His head was oval in shape, and he was clean shaven. He appeared to be in his late sixties to early seventies. He had an average figure and wore a bronze-colored crucifix on a thick chain necklace. He looked at the three of them with a timid smile on his face, and then approached them as he extended his hand towards them.

"*Buan giorno, figli miei,*" Pope Paul VI greeted, as he offered his hand. "*Che piacere incontrare la tua conoscenza.*"

"His Holiness says it is a pleasure to meet your acquaintance," the monsignor with him stated.

"Ah, it is more than a pleasure than to get to meet our dear Holy Father," Derby replied with a smile, bowing and taking the Pope's hand and kissing the papal ring. The monsignor translated into Italian what Derby had said while he backed up and stretched out an arm to his loved ones. "Your Holiness, I would like to introduce you to my wife, Ophelia Cabernet, and my dearest grandchild, Charlemagne Cabernet."

"Your Holiness, a pleasure," Ophelia greeted, bowing and doing the same to kiss the papal ring. She then backed away.

"Say hello, Charlemagne," Derby advised.

Charlemagne stood still and simply looked back at the pope with a plain expression. "Hello," he finally said in a quiet voice, still looking at him like an oddity.

"Buan giorno," the Pope greeted Charlemagne, placing a hand on his cheek as he looked at him with a warm smile. He continued to speak in Italian, and the monsignor translated his words. "His Holiness says it is most honorable to get to meet the cherished loved ones of the Cabernet name. Although your family are renowned for their world-wide industries, even I forget sometimes that people are just people, and you and I, despite what we do, are people too, more than the same as any others, and you've carried that humility well to be a people person; a father and a mother, to a such a lovely and beautiful grandson."

"Thank you, your Holiness," Derby replied with a smile, looking to Ophelia. He struck a pause and then looked towards the table with the veils. "We brought you a gift, Holy Father," he said, walking towards the table. "Apologies for the desire to meet on such short notice, and although as you say that we are a renowned family, so too do we have an abundant wealth, but in irony, little to share with you of any value. I had a difficult time in the last week to decide what I could hope to pass on to His Holiness, so I decided on something of value to the family, and that is this…"

A priest behind the table removed the veil to expose a small wooden crate that held two bottles of red wine inside, nestled amongst straw, with a small bundle of wheat between them.

"As you know, my family business comes from the wine business, so I thought it only appropriate to share two prized bottles from our collection, and then with them a bundle of dried wheat taken from our farm in the Walham Valley."

Pope Paul VI smiled as he looked at the gifts presented to him and placed a hand on the bottle of wine.

"Your family has truly been in viticulture and horticulture for some years before they shifted to industry," the monsignor translated. "This gift is a pleasure to have, both those pieces of your family's history of which I am most fond of, the humble upbringings where they harvested the fruits of the earth and work of human hands. Like those two that can become our spiritual gifts from Heaven, with gratitude for all your family does as industrialists, I hope that in time you will return to the humble earnest work of the vineyard and produce spiritual fruits that all the world can enjoy."

Derby didn't respond as he looked at the Holy Father. He took notice that when the pope was speaking to him, he maintained eye contact. The pope gestured for them to come over to the veil next to these gifts. A priest on the others side removed the veil, and underneath there were three rosaries and a leather-bound book. Pope Paul VI picked up one of the rosaries and presented it to Derby.

"From my hands to you," the monsignor translated, "I provide you with these rosaries, blessed here by me, and which I hope you will produce spiritual fruits with each."

Derby looked at the rosary. It had a polished silver chain, and the beads were a deep purplish-red that glistened in the light. The crucifix was bejeweled and so was the medallion that had a picture of a crowned Mary. Likewise, on the crucifix, Derby took note that Christ was crowned in thorns.

"Thank you, Holy Father," Derby stated, passing it to Ophelia to admire and then shaking the pope's hands again.

"Just wait," the monsignor translated after the pope spoke, "one more gift for you, Mr. Cabernet. Something of special place in my heart and which I believe you could use especially – these are an English copy of all my published works, including all seven of my encyclicals, my apostolic exhortations and letters. I hope that you will read these and meditate on them, to share with the inspirations I have received from the Lord."

Derby looked at the book as it was presented to him. He picked it up and read the spine, 'The Collected Works of Pope Paul VI – Volume 1 (1963-1968).' He then shook the Pope's hand and placed the book back on the table.

"I look forward to having a look while I am on my travels," Derby stated with a smile.

"If you'll please now, a photograph to commemorate the visitation," Monsignor Bizzotto stated, allowing photographers into the room.

Ophelia stood with Derby as he stood next to the pope. Charlemagne stood in front of them. The photographers took the photo, and then the pope picked up the bottle and spoke to Derby.

"It would be a shame not to open," Pope Paul VI spoke in English.

"That's why I brought two of them," Derby replied with a chuckle. "Please, enjoy, Your Holiness, but perhaps wait after Lent."

The monsignor translated for Pope Paul VI, and then he nodded to him. He put the bottle back, and the family and pope were guided into the pope's private study for private deliberation. The doors closed behind them, and the contents of that conversation, were left amongst them with no trace or idea of what could have been said between Derby and Ophelia Cabernet with His Holiness, Pope Paul VI.

Act 2, Scene 3

"Welcome to the Vatican Museum," Monsignor Bizzotto stated, walking them through a corridor.

"It's astonishing that everything is so close," Ophelia remarked. "One second we were in the apartments, and now here we are."

The tour continued as they walked along and met with a priest in a black cassock, and no colored designations.

"I would like to introduce you to Bishop Matteo Giano who will be your tour guide," Msg. Bizzotto introduced. "Bishop Giano is the Archivist and Librarian for the Vatican Library, and he is our chief scholar who works alongside the museum curator."

"A pleasure to meet you and be your tour guide this afternoon," Bishop Giano greeted in a deep voice. "I understand that you, Mr. Cabernet, have a particular interest in our secret archives and library, which His Holiness has granted you access to."

"Yes, but I can visit after the tour – right now I am with the family," Derby remarked. "We've still yet to visit the gardens now that the sun is shining, and I understand there is much in this museum."

"Yes," Bishop Giano answered, walking forward, "we have a select choice on display, and all of our items come from our collections and which we believe to be of most interest to the public. These include sculptures, paintings, and anything and everything of which its beauty is pleasing to the eye. A majority of our collection comes from the Renaissance and artists from those time, many of whom are Italian."

"A museum to rival the Louvre," Derby noted.

"Funny you should mention the Louvre," Bishop Giano replied. "During the Napoleonic wars, a supermajority of all our collections and items were unwillingly shipped to France during that time. The wish of the French emperor was to store all treasures of Europe in one place. When the revolutionary government was removed from power at the conclusion of those wars, items were returned, although not all. To this date, a third of all items we originally had have yet to be returned but you can find on display in museums such as the Louvre."

The tour proceeded, and Derby and Ophelia toured the museum with Charlemagne as they viewed the many sculptures, paintings, frescoes, maps, and unique architecture. The museum was set up in an organized system of several rooms each of which held a particular theme and were connected to each other from room to room. A vast majority of all items were religious in theme, with a small percentage of item to do with history of everyday life. From the museum, the tour made its way through to the Sistine Chapel where the ceiling displayed at the centre the *Creation of Man* by Michaelangelo in all its glory. Derby paid particular attention to the figure of Adam and the depiction of God the Father reaching out to him. From the Sistine Chapel, they were brought into St. Peter's Basilica to view the art and sculptures there, including the famed *Pieta*.

"With so much on display, I wonder to think what the Vatican has in storage that does not get to see the light of day," Derby remarked, hands behind his back. "The Vatican should consider more space – I would be more than a happy participant to help make that happen."

"A welcome offer, Mr. Cabernet," Bishop Giano replied. "Pope Paul VI has had a particular interest in the curation of the museum, and it is his interest to expand what is displayed with a focus on history, specifically our history."

"I'm tired," Charlemagne complained as he held his grandmother's hand. "Are we almost finished?"

"My little Charlemagne, let us not be rude," Derby remarked, walking over to him. "We can rest in due time, but for now show a little perseverance in this minor adventure."

"We still haven't seen the gardens," Ophelia said to Charlemagne, "and your Pa needs to do some work in the archives too."

Charlemagne groaned and titled his head back. He was visibly bored.

"Have we seen all there is in the museum, or is there more to trek back towards?"

"No, typically the tour concluded in the Sistine Chapel, but the basilica can be considered a bonus room worth to visit," Bishop Giano stated. "I will guide you to the gardens now, and Monsignor Bizzotto will join you for a tour of those."

"Excellent," Derby remarked, looking over to Charlemagne, "and as much as I wish to join my family in the gardens, perhaps to hasten our stay so that we can get Charlemagne some rest, if you aren't busy right now, could I visit those archives now?"

Bishop Giano turned to Charlemagne and then over to the bored child as he stepped forward towards them.

"Certainly, I am not busy at all, Mr. Cabernet," Bishop Giano answered.

The bishop led them back into the museum through the Sistine chapel, and then into the gallery where they had met the bishop and left the monsignor. They sat down to rest for a moment as they waited for the monsignor to return, in one of six rooms of an area known as the Borgia Apartment.

"Ah, Cabernet family," Monsignor Bizzotto remarked, entering into the room. "There you are – shall we visit the gardens now?"

"Yes, a savvy idea, if you could take my wife and grandson to tour the gardens, Bishop Giano and I will be going to the archives now so that I can get to my work now rather than later in the day," Derby expressed, looking at his watch, "it is midday now, so rather get in some more time before supper."

"Very well, Mr. Cabernet," Bizzotto replied. "If you'll kindly follow me," he addressed to Ophelia. "We will meet you here when you are finished."

"Thank you, Monsignor," Derby expressed, waving to them.

Once Ophelia and Charlemagne had left, Derby turned to Bishop Giano, and the two men then walked the opposite way. They walked through the Raphael Rooms where Derby once again looked at the frescoes painted on walls of many historical scenes from the Old Testament, to the New, and the later early years of the Church.

"So much culture in the Vatican, I never knew," Derby expressed, looking admirably at the frescoes. "You have a very fortunate position, Bishop Giano. I am also well pleased that the centre of our faith is a place of so much richness."

"Many express to us that we have all the power to end poverty if we were to sell what we have, and to them I say, the people would still be poor and the walls of the Vatican without anything to remind us of God," Bishop Giano stated. "The negative effects of a Vatican without any of this beauty would be more disastrous than the value of the material goods its material worth could purchase. Do not let me mistake you, it is good to feed the poor, but there are many more ways to go about doing so, and only so many ways to feed the spirit, which we aim to do."

"Returning to the subject of an expansion effort, I know that space around here is limited, being a fixed property and city-state, but perhaps a property in Rome nearby could be purchased as an off-site museum that focuses on natural history," Derby expressed. "Just as culture and art enlighten, so do archeology and artefacts."

"We must both be guided by the Holy Spirit, Mr. Cabernet, because it is just that which myself and the Holy Father intend to do."

"I had heard that the Vatican had its own archeological team, too," Derby stated. "Is that something you are involved in?"

"The archeological team?" Bishop Giano questioned. "No. Archbishop Torrez is involved in that project."

"Would it be possible to meet with him? Is his office nearby?"

"Yes, nearby, but no, I do not think he is here today to meet. I am sure he would have benefited to meet you with you."

Derby and Bishop Giano reached the Vatican Library, which was a separate wing to the east of the same building as the museum. The bishop took keys to open the doors to the library, and they entered into a room similar to the ones in the museum with frescoes and art on the walls, except it was dim inside. They then approached another set of doors that led into a long room with wooden cabinets on the walls. From here, they entered into the next room whose appearance was closer to that of a traditional library with bookcases and tables in the center. The windows in this room were sometimes covered while at other gaps they allowed light to pour through. The structure of the corridors was similar to those in the west wing, so Charlemagne and the bishop carried on through until they reached a wide open room at the end. This main atrium looked into the Library Courtyard, a small courtyard between the library and Braccio Nuovo. It had numerous bookshelves around and was a junction to many other places in the library and museum by the doors around. Ahead, Derby could see a door that led into some reading rooms. On the left, going towards the west wing, a door also led into the Vatican Secret Archives.

"Since the library became open to the public, we let at most sixty accredited scholars into this library every day," Bishop Giano stated. "All you see here has much that has yet to be reviewed by mankind. To summarize to you, this library and our archives, much like the museum, is the sum collection of nearly two-thousand years' worth of information and books, including our own published documents and files. When you have that much information, it becomes difficult to source through and organize, but it remains here for others to dig through, and the librarians do their best to keep it somewhat organized."

"It's all quite as mesmerizing as the rest of the museum," Derby simply acknowledged. "How is it organized?"

"Typically, by subject and then date," Bishop Giano stated. "Volumes will be kept together, and any other related books."

"Are these all just books? What about documents?"

"What cannot be properly organized for public viewing is kept in the secret archives," Bishop Giano stated. "Of course too, what is here in the library is all that is for public viewing. The secret archives, although not a secret in the English sense of the word, but private, are kept private and that is downstairs in the basement."

Derby took in a deep breath as he looked all around, "There's so much wealth of information here. I assume that the Holy Father's blessing to have access to this library maintains itself for a lifetime, right?"

"Of course, Mr. Cabernet," the bishop replied as Derby began to examine the room. "If I can be of some help to you, what information do you seek at this moment?"

"My research at this time has to do with organizations and departments of the Roman Curia," Derby stated, "but I see potential that I could do research on early Church history, the early martyrs and persecutions."

"Well, generally speaking, materials to do with the early Church exist, but are limited. As for church organization, we have many documents between 1300 to 1939, anything from 1939 to present that is not already public knowledge is kept private."

"Very good," Derby stated, looking back to the bishop. "Thank you."

"Well, I'll let you begin your work. If you wish to reach me, offices are on the fourth floor of the library."

"Thank you."

Bishop Giano left, and Derby returned to look at the many books around him and proceed to get work. Derby collected a few books after a while, proceeded with them to the reading room, and from there he produced reading glasses, a notebook and pencil to take notes. With glasses on, he skimmed through the first several books he collected, pausing ever so often, and if he found something noteworthy, he would scribble, if not he would set the book aside and repeat the process. Once he went through the books he had collected, he would return them from where they came, and retrieve a few more. After little more than hour in, Derby looked towards the doors to the secret archives. He stood up from the table he was at and moved towards the wooden doors, pushing at them and then attempting to pull them. The doors would not open.

"Hm," Derby thought aloud.

Derby looked at his watch and then decided to leave. He found the staircase that went up to the third level, and from there he ventured down the corridor through more and more rows of bookshelves, to reach another staircase that exclusively went to the fourth level. From there, Derby exited into a corridor that passed several offices, one of which belonged to Archbishop Diego Torrez, S.J. (Jesuit Order). Derby looked ahead and both ways before he attempted to push through the door, but it was locked. The lock itself was a skeleton key lock. Derby looked at the lock, around him, and then taking his glasses from his suit jacket pocket, he snapped the temples of his glasses off each side to give him two pieces. With both pieces, he began to attempt to pick the old luck with success. The door opened and Derby walked inside, entering into a small office on the other side.

Archbishop Torrez had a window view that looked out towards Rome. On either side from both the window and door were bookshelves with numerous books lined atop. A lectern was positioned on the right with a text and a lamp in the corner of the room. Derby proceeded to rummage through the room. He found a few letters in the archbishop's desk, but most notable of all was a letter addressed to the archbishop from another archbishop, Rene Francois Marie-Jean Chevalier, O.S.A. The letter was hostile to Archbishop Torrez and lambasted him. He accused the archbishop of hijacking the intentions of the archeological endeavors for his own purposes and vowed revenge. Derby continued to rummage around the desk and in the top drawer where there were pens and papers, there was a notepad that outlined a letter in progress. The letter was addressed to the pope and expressed condolences that the expeditionary team had parted ways from the project and were unaccountable. An attempt was made to reach these men but was unsuccessful. The archbishop explained that he had frozen all bank accounts of the defectors and requested permission to reform the project all-together. Derby put the letter down and picked up a set of keys.

Derby went downstairs again with the set of keys and was able to gain access to the secret archives. He travelled through and entered into another room that had a few more shelves, but also a staircase that went downstairs into the sublevel. He searched through the archives until he began to find documents related to Pope Pius XII, and when he did, he continued until he found a familiar name, Rene Francois Marie-Jean Chevalier, O.S.A. The letter was polite discourse between the archbishop and pope, and nothing more. Still, Derby focused and continued to filter information as he scanned through the documents. Eventually, Derby found a letter that summarized what he was hoping to find, the establishment of the archeological project. The project was given assent by Pope Pius XII in early 1958 under Archbishop Chevalier, to be led by Monsignor Teagan McKinnon, O.P. (Dominican Order). Additional documents stated the intent of the archeological group to focus on history of the church, recovery of saint relics and artefacts, and preservation of holy sites. Several letters from 1963 to 1968 between McKinnon and Pope Paul VI (or rather Archbishop Torrez on behalf of the pope) marked increasing divide in the vision of the project, where McKinnon wished to lead ambitious projects. These projects culminated with an expedition to Antarctica which Torrez expressly forbid due to danger and lack of funds. Nonetheless, McKinnon secured funds. A final letter to McKinnon asked for his resignation and that the team cease all activities – this letter was dated August 1968. In the letter, Torrez expressed that the team held ulterior motives that McKinnon was not to blame for, but which he failed to account for despite stern warnings. The last sentence stated that McKinnon had allowed radicals and revisionists within the team (O.S.A.) to hijack the project for the purposes of their own ulterior motives outside of the vision of the Holy See. Derby looked at the abbreviation again, O.S.A., which belonged to an order he was not familiar with. He lowered his glasses, which he held by his hands, and then took note in his notebook before he continued to do some research. Derby went back upstairs to search through some texts on orders in the library to learn more.

After an hour in the library, Derby accumulated some basic information about O.S.A., the Order of St. Athanasius. The Order of St. Athanasius was a religious order established in the late 1700s by Fr. Jean-Claude Desrosiers, an opponent to modern thinking developed in the Enlightenment which he viewed to threaten the Catholic Church and support Protestant movements. For that reason, the order adopted St. Athanasius as their patron saint, whose notable efforts involved conflict with heresies. Fr. Desrosier stated that Protestantism was the reincarnation of heresies defeated, and called upon St. Athanasius to give them strength in combatting them. For that reason too, the motto of the order would be, '*Athanasius Contra Munda.*' The order would operate mainly in France up to the start of the French Revolution and then expand into Europe and even go overseas to the United States. As of 1920, the order operated in the following provinces: Ireland, France, Portugal, United States, and Germany with missions expanding to the United Kingdom, Belgium, and the Netherlands (and their respective colonies). That same year, there were an estimated 900 priests in the order. The most recent piece of information about the order came from the mid-twenties in which its superior general, Fr. Ambroise Rochefort, warned against modernist interpretation of Catholic doctrine, and liturgical and theological reform. In a speech from 1926, Fr. Rochefort spoke and warned about the rise of ideologies, their influence and their agents subverting the Church away from tradition, quoting St. Athanasius in his criticism of modernists, "They claim that they represent the Church, but in reality, they are the ones who are expelling themselves from it and going astray."

Act 2, Scene 4

Derby returned from the Vatican City with Ophelia and Charlemagne later in the evening, after having dined with some Vatican officials. He retired to his hotel with the family, entering into the hotel lobby with Charlemagne in both his arms, head resting on his right shoulder somewhat asleep, and Ophelia holding onto his left arm.

"Ah, Mr. Cabernet," the hotel manager remarked from the front desk. He came around to approach them. "Mr. Cabernet, the Vatican officials came with the gifts sent to you from the Holy Father. I had them placed in your room for you."

"Thank you, Edoardo," Derby replied in a quiet voice.

Derby carried Charlemagne and led Ophelia to the elevators of the luxurious but small hotel. They then went up to the top floor where they stepped out and approached their hotel suit at the end of the corridor. Ophelia retrieved the keys from her clutch purse and opened the door, and then Derby walked inside with Charlemagne while Ophelia turned on the lights.

"Alright, Charlemagne, it's time to turn in for the night," Derby said, lowering his grandson. "Go get your pajamas on and brush your teeth."

Charlemagne rubbed his eyes and then set off to his bedroom.

"Isn't this beautiful, Derby?" Ophelia questioned, holding the rosary. "What a lovely gift. I've never been one for the rosary; an old habit, I'm afraid. My mother was always so harshly critical of Catholic devotions to the Blessed Virgin."

"Yes, it is quite beautiful, isn't it?" Derby remarked, picking one up again and looking at it. "It's always so hard to find these in England, especially a nice one."

"What's this book that the pope gave you?"

"Oh, it's just a collection of his writings," Derby replied, putting the rosary into his pocket. "Nothing special to be honest, all if not most of it being modernist rubbish too."

"Oh, did the Holy Father know you were so critical of his liturgical reform?"

Derby paused for a moment as he looked at the book and picked it up. "No, as a matter of fact, I don't believe I've spoken about it on the telly or radio. I don't tend to speak at all about Catholicism or my religious beliefs unless prompted to for some reason, and even then, I've been quite silent on those channels about the Second Vatican Council and now these liturgical reforms."

"How did he know then?" Ophelia teased, holding on to the rosary. "I'm going to go make sure Charlemagne is getting changed for bed. Perhaps I'll pray a rosary with him before he sleeps."

"That'd be wise," Derby remarked, seeing her walk off. Derby then looked closer at the book. He opened the first page and flipped to the table of contents. Sure enough, the book contained seven encyclicals that Pope Paul VI had published, as well as numerous magisterial documents and letters, including all his works that were published and a part of the Second Vatican Council. Derby flipped through the book when it stopped at a folded letter tucked in between the pages. He removed the letter and set the book down to the table. He then unfolded the letter.

"Dearest Mr. Cabernet, Apologies to have this letter stowaway in a gift to you from His Holiness Pope Paul VI, but I saw no other way in which I could see this invitation extended to you in secret during your visit to the Vatican. If it is secrets that you hope to find in Rome, then search no farther to where the seat of power manifests itself in this city. Your are cordially invited: Salla de Carbonari, Via Giovanni Giolitti, 200, Roma, Italia – 00:00hrs. At the bottom of the letter was a curious emblem consisting of three triangles, two upright, and one in the center upside down.

"Charlemagne is brushing his teeth," Ophelia remarked, returning to the living room. "What's that?"

"A letter," Derby honestly answered, "tucked between the pages of the book. An invitation to some club in Italy later tonight."

"A club?"

"Yes, related to my business, I'm afraid, so I'll have to attend."

"What time?"

"Midnight," Derby answered. "I'll only pop in for a bit – you know how I feel about social settings. I could hardly stand last night's dinner let alone a social club. I've been to these places before."

Ophelia crossed her arms as she looked at Derby. Derby noticed and looked at her.

"It's only with some priestly folk; it's to do with an order, the Order of St. Athanasius," Derby stated. "I won't be in any harm or danger."

"At any rate, it's chilly tonight, so put your coat on."

"Yes, ma'am," Derby expressed, sitting down at the table, putting the letter in his jacket pocket and taking out his notebook and glasses. He placed them on the table to review, while Ophelia went to see Charlemagne set up for bed.

•

Later in the evening, Derby silently closed the door to his bedroom to leave Ophelia sleeping. He went to the bathroom to fix his hair, ensure his suit was cleaned up a bit, and then put on a dark wool coat so that he could step out of the hotel and into the cold night. He fetched a taxi and got inside.

"Via Giovanni Giolitti, please," Derby requested.

"Via Giovanni Giolitti? In Esquilino?" the taxi driver questioned.

"Yes, that'd be right."

The taxi driver looked at Derby with a bit of worry through the rear-view mirror, but did not object. He proceeded to drive Derby from EUR, Rome's financial district, to the east. Eventually, as they arrived in the Esquilino district, Derby took notice that there was a certain lack of pleasantry in the district. He noticed the streets and buildings to be dirty, the presence of young hoodlums late at night at street corners, many industrial buildings and warehouses, and otherwise a sense of poverty in the neighborhood. The taxi passed a train yard and stopped in front of a large property in front of a bunch of train lines where there was a manor of all places.

"Here we are," the taxi driver said, shifting gears.

Derby paid the taxi driver and then stepped out of the car. He looked at the manor and sure enough the address was correct. An iron gate surrounded the building, and it had a small yard that consisted of additional pavement from the sidewalk and a small enclave up to the main entrance. Atop of the pediment above the main entrance, Derby identified the building name, *Carbonari*. He looked at the black-framed windows, most of which were barred, and none of which looked inside or showed any light. Some of the windows appeared as if they were blocked to not allow sunlight from pouring through, while some were broken and cracked. Next to the main entrance gate was an intercom. Derby approached the panel and pressed the button, causing a buzzing sound to briefly set off. He took a step back and looked up at the corners of the building to notice there to be many security cameras pointed in all sorts of directions.

Suddenly, the gate latch unlocked, and the gate began to slowly creak open. Derby caught the gate, pushed it open, and then closed it behind him. He then slowly approached the manor down the courtyard pavement and around a fountain in the center that was dirty and dry. He came up the steps of the front porch and approached the front door. The door opened as he got close and before he could knock. A man in a black suit and black collared shirt gestured him to come inside. Derby could hear the sound of energetic music from within the manor. He stepped inside and nodded to the bouncer. He entered into a small but long foyer. At the end of the corridor foyer was an archway, but he couldn't see what was on the others side as there was a long velvet scarlet curtain that blocked visual of what was on the other side. Both left and right there were wooden doors with men in black suits before them. At either side of the archway there were additional men there too. A man approached Derby to remove his coat, and he allowed him to take it to a closet to the immediate left. The bouncer then gestured Derby to move forward. Derby took a step towards the velvet curtain where the music continued on the other side. Both men at either side of the archway pulled the curtains back for him to step through.

Derby entered into a wider room on the other side that had curved staircases on the left and right that went up to a balcony that overlooked this room and the room behind. The rooms were dimmer than the foyer, but Derby could just barely see that there was some sort of atrium and then a separate ball room further ahead where the core of the party took place. Derby looked around and saw a few guests in this foyer on the ground floor and above, men in suits and women in dresses, mingling around. Above the center of the foyer was a crystalline chandelier. On the immediate left was a side room with a bar where a few more people could be seen drinking and waiters picking up drinks. On the immediate right was an archway that led to a side lounge. Derby walked around the foyer, seeing two bodyguards at the archway that led deeper into the foyer towards the atrium, and then also bodyguards at wooden doors on either side of the balcony above as well. There were only a few people in the foyer, in discussion with each other, women playful and men bashful. There was also noticeably women in lewd clothes, dancing around the guests in the atrium. Derby entered into a side room on the right where he found a lot more guests, seated down, women atop of the lap of men, lewd performers dancing close to men, men with women at both arms. He also saw a person in an animal costume, climbing atop of a sofa, drunkards and bottles of liquor scattered around and empty glasses, and a man in an armchair with three women around him. Derby entered into the side room where the party continued in another lounge with a similar environment, except a lot more people dancing atop of the furniture.

From the lounges to the atrium, Derby found a colder and dimmer environment but with a lot more space between people, men with women close to them, kissing and caressing lustfully, and some men with one, two, sometimes up to four women around them. He even saw a man with another man in his arms. The performers floated around this area, and it was difficult to see due to an artificial fog cloud in the room. Derby stepped into the ball room where a live band played from a stage at the rear of the room. There were tables in this room but few chairs and a supermajority of people on their feet, dancing to the tune. Another bar was to the left of the ballroom and additional seats to the right. The ballroom was two stories tall with a balcony that surrounded but nobody there. Derby stood in the center of the ballroom as he looked around at all the degeneracies, seeing it not just in the people, but in the choice of artwork; art that depicted torture and bloodshed, sacrificial offerings of women and children, sexual subjugation and violence, sexual abuse of men, women and children, and fornication and sodomy. At that moment, Derby instantly turned around to leave.

Derby was about to exit out through the curtains when a man grabbed him by the shoulders. "Monsieur LaPadite!" the man exclaimed.

"Let go of me!" Derby exclaimed, attempting to push the man off.

The man proceeded to ramble to him in French. Everything he said was incoherent. He proceeded to guide Derby towards the staircase. As he did so, Derby noticed some male guests climb the other staircase and then approach a doorway on the left. He proceeded to help the man up the stairs so that he could join him. Once at the top of the stairs, the man began to slouch to his side, which prompted Derby to whistle out to call the attention of the guard.

"Be a dear," Derby expressed. "He's had quite a few and needs help going on over."

Derby released his arm and then left the drunken man to the bodyguard so that he could run his hands down his own suit to retain his composure, and then calmly step forward towards the door on the left. Derby entered into a corridor and saw some of the other guests disappear behind a door at the end.

From the other side, Derby entered into another dim room; a balcony arcade that surrounded a dining hall or meeting room below. The table was large and wide with seats spread out around. Some of the profane artwork could be seen on the walls below. Derby positioned himself around the balcony to get a better view, but stayed close to the only exit he knew. There were a few men around the balcony, looking down at the table below. A door then opened behind the head of the table, and a group of twelve men in black cloaks entered into the room, followed by a male in a red cloak. The room was too dim to see the faces of any of these people. A servant positioned the head chair out for the red cloaked figure to sit down, while the others were prompted to pull their own chairs out. The doors then closed behind. A servant pushed a microphone on the table closer to the leader. He looked at the faces of the others closely and then observed to listen to their voices. The men spoke in French, which Derby did not understand. He moved around the room to get a better look at some of the other people when he caught a glimpse of an effigy above the fireplace opposite the head of the table; the effigy was similar to the watermark on the letter Derby received, but more defined – an upside down triangular skull without a jaw marked the center portion, and on either side were smaller upright triangles like the horns of a devil. Upon glancing at that effigy, Derby began to see the logo elsewhere in the building, at the crest of the ceiling, marked into the corner of the railings, and at the back of the boardroom chairs. At that moment, Derby positioned himself to leave, but as he was about to reach the exit, a hand grabbed his wrist.

"What are you doing here?" the man questioned. "You don't belong!"

Derby instantly looked at the men around him as they gazed at him, prompting Derby to quickly break loose from the grip of the man and then toss him over the railings. Another man grabbed Derby from behind, prompting him to squat down, elbow the man across the face and then take him down to the ground. His actions caused an outcry, Derby stepped into the corridor, but caught sight of the men at the end who produced firearms. He then stepped back into the meeting room and decided to vault the railing, jump down as the cult members had vacated, and use the same door to make his escape. Derby entered into the room on the other side. He closed the doors behind him and saw a display case with a metal suit of armor on either side, prompting him to push one over with a bit of strength to block his pursuers. He could hear the guard shout from the other side. He took a moment to look around the room – it was an armory with medieval weapons and items on display. In the center of the room was the crest of the cult. A set of doors on the right were already locked with a plank of wood, so Derby stepped towards another doorway at the opposite end. He opened the doors and found himself in a private study or small library. Inside was another fireplace on the left and a billiards table on the right. A desk was in the center rear of the room with a French window to a veranda. Derby looked around for a moment as he could hear the battering of the room from the armory prompting him towards the French window.

Derby exited onto a veranda with similar pavement as the exterior surroundings around the front of the manor. He looked forward to the backyard and saw that it was just more pavement and the view of the railyard and city horizon beyond. A few cars were parked on the pavement below. Derby could hear some voices come from the right, took cover and peaked around the corner to see some guards on approach from the other side of the manor. He then decided to go the opposite way but stopped as he saw that the pathway to the front of the manor was fenced off. He then decided to climb over the banister and drop down. He then snuck around the edge of the manor, past sculptures engraved into the wall. He passed a set of doors that came into the lower basement of the manor, and then went around to the other side where a ramp climbed up to another gate. He reached a breaker box next to the gate and opened it. He switched a lever to open the gate through an alleyway. He approached forward and took cover at the end of the corner, seeing guards positioned around the front of the property. Derby retreated backwards and took cover amongst the vehicles. There, he paused for a moment, took in a deep breath, and then turned around to elbow a car window. He unlocked the car, climbed inside, and then positioned himself in the driver's seat. He then proceeded to pull the cover underneath the steering wheel and pull at the wires. The car roared to life as he hotwired the car, prompting him to immediately hit clutch, shift gears, and drive off. Derby exited the manor through the alleyway, passing the guards who were stationed at the front and driving into the night.

For a few minutes, Derby cautiously drove with eyes on all his mirrors in case he were to be followed, and after a while he decided to pull into an alleyway to abandon the vehicle. From there, Derby walked to a nearby bar where he phoned for a taxi, realizing as he arrived at his hotel that he had lost his wallet and keys at the manor. Once Derby was able to sort out his taxi fare and return to his suite, he sat down in the living room and put a hand to his forehead. There, he rested for the night.

Act 3, Prologue

Derby marched along a dirt road in the countryside. The sun shined fiercely down upon him and the man behind him. On his right was a bank of tall grass that went up to an open field and some trees, while on his left was a pasture tied to a farm. The pasture was cordoned off with a white fence and had all sorts of farm animals on the other side. He and the men that followed him stayed close to the bank rather than the post. As they continued ahead, they reached an intersection where at the front entrance of the farm there was a man, woman, and child in peasant clothes who looked towards Derby and his men as they passed them. The march continued along this same route through the countryside, against the warm climate, without end.

Derby at this time had a sharp look on his face, his blue eyes focused. His brow was tense as the sun shined towards him from above. His blonde hair visibly cut short at the sides. His cheek bones visible, cheeks and jaw clean-shaven, and face otherwise carrying his youth. He wore the same battle dress as the one from his deployment; trousers, jacket, collared shirt and tie all the same. His men behind him wore the Mk 3 turtle shell steel helmets, some with foliage to add camouflage. Derby wore a khaki beret to distinguish himself from the others. He was equipped with a few pouches around his belt, some attached to straps across his chest. Around his waist on his back were two larger pouches. At his side was his canteen pouch, and at his left was his handgun pouch with a revolver, the Webley Mk 4. In both hands he carried a submachine gun, the Sten Mk 2. Behind Derby, the soldiers carried an assortment of weaponry: Lee-Enfield rifles, Sten submachine guns, and the Bren gun. The men also varied in age, from late teens to early twenties, to early to mid thirties.

As Derby and the men of the Royal Norfolk Regiment continued to march along the country road, a convoy of

Cromwell tanks rolled forward along the road to pass them. Some of the soldiers of these tanks stood up through the hatch in the tank to see forward. The passing of the tanks followed with trucks behind, both of which created minor dust clouds that caused the soldiers to hack, cough, and wave their arms. At the end of the convoy was another few Cromwell tanks, the last of which slowed down besides Derby as they continued down the road. The officer from the hatch looked down to Derby.

"Good morning, Leftenant Cabernet," the British officer greeted. "Fancy I'd see you again here"

"It's France, Myles, what'd you expect," Derby replied, continuing to march forward, eyes looking ahead of him. "We're both going the same way to deliver the final blow to the German war machine before the Russians do."

"At the pace that we've got them on the run, I reckon that we'd be in Germany in a couple of weeks. It's been nearly a whole day now with no sight of the enemy, although they've certainly left behind a mess."

"We'll see them soon enough," Derby remarked, keeping a light pant as he exerted himself. "Just you wait…"

"I hope to see you then, my dear friend," the officer responded.

The tank drove forward and Derby and the men continued to march forward.

"How much longer do we got? We've been going for hours on end," a soldier complained.

"We'll be there soon enough," Derby replied in a loud tone.

"How come we couldn't hitch a ride on that armor? They've got the space."

"Not what they're for," Derby responded.

"How about we take a break?"

"We're already behind. If I don't get a break, then neither do you."

"You aren't carrying a rucksack," a soldier muttered. Derby's ears twitched, though he did not respond and instead kept looking forward. He instead picked up his canteen and drank some water.

After a few more minutes as they trekked ahead along the road, marching along the French countryside, Derby stopped his men as his ears twitched again, but this time to the sound of gunfire.

"We've got trouble ahead," Derby remarked, getting down on one knee. "Alright, everybody stay down and stick to the shrubs on this side. We can't be too far from the action."

Derby led the men forward as they continued down the road with caution. After a few yards, Derby could see a Cromwell tank in the field, in flames, with the gunfire closer than before. He could also see the convoy of trucks at a halt further ahead.

"Crikes, everybody down! Into the field!" Derby shouted as he saw a silhouette in the horizon. The silhouette got large enough to denote a plane of some kind.

Derby and his men got into the field with the tall grass near the blown-up tank. The planes approached closer and began to descend from the air nearby. Derby kept his head down as the close air support dropped their payload, detonating one of the trucks in the convoy and earth around them. The planes then flew past and ascended; once a fair distance, the team got up from their positions and rushed forward. They came out of the field and onto a road perpendicular to the one they had marched down. They returned to the former road to approach the convoy as the gunfire settled down a bit.

"No casualties. Alright let's resume," Derby remarked. "Everybody keep down and calm."

Derby led his troops along the remainder of the road up to where another tank was blown up by the close air support. On the right side of the road the rest of the tanks were positioned, opening fire at a settlement ahead.

"Everyone fan out! Hostiles dead ahead!" Derby shouted, opening fire.

Derby could not see the enemy, but he could hear and see gunfire, and the shouts of Germans from the ruins of the town ahead of them. He turned around to his fireteam as he stayed low.

"We're going to give some covering fire and then we're going to get in closer," Derby said. "All in."

The fireteam continued to give supporting fire for the rest of the fireteams in the platoon to spread out and take position in the field. The tanks opened fire at the hostiles as they hid in the ruins of buildings, destroying said buildings further but with uncertainty as to whether it was doing anything to the hostiles. Once the fireteams were in position, Derby and his men continued forward, using a stone wall as cover on approach to the town.

Once at a building, they stood up and used that full cover to come around to a window. Derby took a grenade, cooked it, and then threw it into the window on the other side as he heard hostiles nearby.

"*Granata!*" a German soldier shouted.

Derby and his team lowered their heads as the explosion set off. He then looked inside to see the scatter of German troops into the town proper. He then paused as he could hear the sound of planes on approach.

"Not again," Derby cursed. "Everybody down!"

Derby ducked as this time, rather than bombs, bullets fell down upon them and fighter planes passed from above. Once the planes had passed, Derby came around to the corner of the building and then slowly approached forward to a doorway. The others approached from behind him. Derby kicked the door open, saw it was clear, and then proceeded inside with the team. The building overlooked a fountain and additional buildings on the other side where German soldiers took position. Derby reloaded his submachine gun as they continued to lay down fire.

Soon enough, some of the tanks rolled into the town and began to provide supporting fire.

"Let's move up!" Derby remarked. "Push 'em out!"

Derby led the team out of the building where they moved forward to take cover behind the armor and fountain ahead.

"Watch for them in that windmill!" a soldier shouted.

"There's a sniper in the bell tower!"

Derby concentrated as he reloaded his rifle and then looked out to the landscape. There were a few more buildings ahead, including a windmill on the left and a church to the right towards the far side of the town. A panzer tank sat in the middle of the road ahead in flames.

"Whoa, watch it! Hostiles with anti-tank weapons ahead!" a voice shouted.

The tanks moved forward and out of the way as rocket projectiles began to fly in. Derby kept his head down as the rockets hit the fountain and buildings behind them.

"We're pinned down!" a soldier complained.

"Nonsense," Derby rebuked. "Jones, I want your fireteam to flush out them in the windmill. Smith, you're on point for us. We're going for the church. Walton, to the left! Brown, to the right!"

The team removed themselves from the fountain and proceeded forward towards the building on the right. Derby kicked the door in, and they flushed in to clear the building. Once through, they exited into a small lane and went into the next building.

"They keep retreating…"

"Soon enough, there'll be nowhere to hide," Derby replied.

The team continued through building to building before the church where the German forces had taken position at the wreckage of their tank as well as around the graveyard on exit to the town. Eventually, Sergeant Brown took point at the buildings furthest to the right from their path, while Derby was directly across from the church. Walton secured the buildings to the left, and Jones secured the windmill. The remainder of the Germans took position in the church, while others fled further ahead.

The Junker close air support planes made their approach from the east with another payload.

"Get down!" Derby remarked as they were in a building.

The close air support plane dropped its payload into the town, creating a crater in the street and causing a building to collapse. Luckily, not the one that Derby and his fireteam were in.

"Too close," Derby remarked. "Those tanks better stay out of the way or we'll be without any armor. Lee, get over there and tell Leftenant Pollock to keep back."

"Aye, sir."

"The rest of you, let's group with the others and storm the church."

"Yes, sir."

Derby led the team towards the house further ahead along a lane behind them. A tank kept oversight in their flank. They joined the other fireteam and then provided them with covering fire for them to approach the church and reach the tank. Once there, they spread out along the stone wall in front of the church to provide covering fire for them to dash on through.

"We'll lead the way," Derby remarked as the other fireteam provided additional covering fire for them to move forward.

Derby dashed towards the entrance of the church. He reloaded his gun and then waited for the others to get in position before he was about to enter in. Suddenly, he stopped as gunfire shot towards him from within.

"Ah!" Derby cursed, clutching his upper arm. A bullet grazed him.

"You alright?" a soldier questioned.

"I'm fine," Derby barked. "Get in from the other sides, surround them!"

Derby moved his hand from his arm and looked at his own blood with anger. His own skin hung, nearly detached from his flesh in the hole it had torn in the stitching of his dress. He peaked with extra caution and then went in with those still with him. He took cover at a pillar and then peaked around again. The church was quiet. Soldiers from the right entered in and looked around the sanctuary to signal to him that the altar was abandoned. He stepped inside and looked around closer to see there to be a massive hole in the left corner of the church where the rest of the enemy soldiers had escaped from. Derby moved his hand back to his wound, gritting his teeth as he touched the exposed wound.

"You better tend to that," Sergeant Brown expressed. "We'll pursue the hostiles ahead."

Derby nodded as he retrieved some first aid from a pouch. He sat down at a pew and placed his gun down at his side. He cut the piece of skin that was dangling and held his teeth together as he did so, taking slow and deep breaths. He then proceeded to patch the wound as best, placing pressure, and then secured the patching for now. Suddenly, Derby heard a noise from behind at the base of the bell tower. Derby immediately drew his rifle and pointed it towards the noise, maintaining composure not to fire over a simple noise.

From the pew, Derby took a slow step towards the base of the bell tower, looking around and then up. The staircases had been decimated but there was a ladder that went upwards. Suddenly again, Derby turned and took a gunshot as a German soldier charged at him with his rifle, a Gewehr 43 with a scope attached. The gunshot missed and the soldiers was able to tackle Derby onto the church floor, causing his beret to fall backwards and expose his fair length blonde hair. Derby took hold of the side of the hostile's rifle, with minimum force from his wounded right arm. His revolver had fallen nearby but was too far to reach. Derby glanced at the soldier who was attacking him, noticing him to be young, around the same age as Derby with blue eyes. Eventually, Derby pulled all his strength into his left arm to cause the butt of the rifle to hit the soldier in the temple, causing his steel helmet to fall off and expose his blonde hair. Derby hurried back and gained composure as he stood up, pointing the rifle and in a panic, pulling the trigger on the rifle only to hear a click.

"Huh?" Derby questioned. He quickly looked over to his revolver.

The soldier scrambled for Derby's sidearm on the ground, but Derby kicked it away and then rushed towards it. He picked it up and then turned to face the hostile that had ambushed him, but he was gone. Derby looked around with a bit more paranoia as if he would appear from whatever direction. He stepped towards his pew, picked up his submachine gun on the bench with one hand, and then placed his revolver away. Derby continued to look around with slow movement, eventually exiting the church and meeting with other soldiers that arrived.

"Everything alright, Leftenant Cabernet?" Lieutenant Pollock questioned.

"Fine," Derby replied, lowering his weapon and releasing the tension in his knees. "Just fine."

Act 3, Scene 1

"Welcome to Tel Aviv, Mr. Cabernet," Clayton stated. "Sixty years ago, this city was nothing more than a small settlement of Jewish people. Today, it's the most populous city in all of Israel."

"You speak very enthusiastically about Israel, captain," Derby replied, looking to him from across his seat in the private plane.

"Of course, Israel is the United States' greatest ally, the only democracy in the Middle East," Clayton stated. "Well, even before the state of Israel was founded, I've always been a gosh darn solid advocate for them. My father always spoke volumes of the importance that there should be a Jewish home in the Middle East. They're God's chosen people after all."

"I thought your father was an evangelical pastor."

"He was," Clayton asserted, "and we were, and still are, a family of proud Christian Zionists," he said. "Now, I know you Brits have your own opinions about the Middle East…"

"Yes, perhaps I'm just sore about the British soldiers they killed when they led an insurgency to declare their independence."

"Just like America," Clayton said. "If anything, there was a lot less bloodshed in their case. Give it some time, you'll come around to it…"

Derby looked Clayton unconvinced as the plane began its descent towards the airport. A door opened to the cabin and Kory stepped inside.

"We're about to arrive," Kory remarked, sitting down at his seat next to Secretary Clayton. "What exactly is your plan, Mr. Cabernet?"

Derby looked at Clayton and then to Kory. He sat back and replied, "I was able to collect some information from the Vatican on this archeological group that Herr Liudolfings joined. At this current time, they've gone rogue and the only connection I have to them is a religious order. I've asked around in Rome for more information about this order, but none seem to acknowledge its existence, at least anymore. An informer told me that they still do exist, but in small numbers in the Middle East, but their largest chapter being in the Holy Land. Additionally, I wanted to check on some other intel I had gathered…"

Kory looked at Derby, and then down to the table in front of him where his notebook was open and showed the triangular symbol of the cult from Rome.

"Is that the symbol of the religious order you're pursuing?" Kory questioned.

"No," Derby denied, closing his book and putting the strap on. He then put it in his jacket. "That symbol has to do with some research I'm doing on a side project."

"Ah," Kory replied, "I thought so – that symbol, it's not Christian that's for sure."

Clayton looked at him with intrigue. Kory's eyes shot to the secretary, and he let out a half-embarrassed chortle. He then looked at Derby.

"I did my undergraduate in Near East studies, and that symbol is an ancient Canaanite symbol known as the sigil of Moloch. If you're looking for more information on it, I suggest you look at Phoenician and Canaanite pagan practices. Stars as a symbol in Near East anthropology typically represent a pagan god of some sort – Moloch of whom was one of those ancient deities."

"Moloch? Hm, thank you," Derby replied. "I will."

"The one in your book though, it's missing a triangle," Kory remarked. "If I may…"

Kory picked up the pencil on the table and then took a sheet of paper. He drew the symbol, but added a fourth elongated upright isosceles triangle, creating a star.

"You see?"

"Very peculiar," Derby remarked with a half-hearted laugh. "Like the horns of a goat... What do you suppose the symbol without this additional triangle means?"

"Oh, I have no idea," Kory denied. "I only thought you may have had the wrong symbol."

The cabin became silent as Derby looked at the picture for another moment.

"At any rate," Clayton expressed, looking at Derby, "what do you intend to do in Tel Aviv and what do you need from us? You have a blank cheque for whatever you should need."

"I will need a truck, some supplies in case I should need to go into the desert, and if it is alright with you, weaponry to defend myself."

Clayton laughed at Derby's request. "Mr. Cabernet, say no more when it comes to weapons. Ask and you shall receive. I'm sure we can acquire you some firearms from the embassy once we're there. Where are you going to go?"

"Ashkelon," Derby remarked. "This order has strong ties to this archeological group, so any information I should hope to find will be in their stronghold."

"Very good, and if you need anything from myself or Kory, you let us know. The U.S. Embassy here in Tel Aviv is where we will be this next week."

Derby nodded and then looked out to the cityscape. Tel Aviv was a coastal city with beaches that had golden fine sand. Its beaches also had a particular shape and pattern to them, conclave curves side by side with each other. A vast majority of buildings in Tel Aviv were white and there was a distinct Mediterranean appearance in these many white homes, some of whom added a light blue hue, and some of them which had golden domed ceilings. At the heart of Tel Aviv, a rectangular skyscraper could be seen tall in the distance. There were of course lots of palm trees all around. Derby exited the plane after it landed at the airport, and from the top of the stairs, he covered his eyes at the intense glare of the sun and then looked around.

Tel Aviv airport, known as Lod Airport in these days, was located on the outskirts of the town. From the tarmac, Derby could see the desert spread about as well as fields of dry grass. He walked down the steps and stopped to look at some flag poles in the distances; the flag of the Israel State waved in the wind, its colors matching those of the buildings seen from above, but its national symbol known as the Star of David, being of particular note to Derby for its six-points made out of triangles.

A limo picked up the trio and then proceeded to drive them along the freeway into the city. Derby sat across from Clayton and Kory.

"If Liudolfings was in Israel, we would have known it," Kory stated. "There's no way he would risk endangerment in coming so close to people who want to kill him."

"Perhaps he feels more secure than we believe," Derby rationalized. "Only so many know his face and want him captured or killed. My thinking is that he may not be in Israel but could be somewhere in hiding and that this religious order is supporting the archeological group. The most I can narrow down his location is to somewhere in which Christian archeology would have some importance, and that leaves Europe and the Middle East (unless he's gone searching for relics of saints elsewhere, which I doubt)."

"If Erich Liudolfings is in Israel or near Israel, then the urgency to capture him doubles. We need to know what information he has passed on to our enemies."

"Find him, Mr. Cabernet. There's no time to waste."

"I wasn't keen to waste anybody's time," Derby remarked. "Although, while my supplies are put together for my journey to Ashkelon, I will need to take some time to compile some note at the local university library."

"Whatever you need to do, do it," Clayton answered. "We trust in you, and your kit should be ready ASAP."

"Appreciated."

The limo arrived at the U.S. embassy building in downtown Tel Aviv. The structure was greyish on the outside, made of concrete with tinted windows, and at least seven stories tall. The building was located on the seafront with a view from the upper levels out to the beach across the other side of a road. From there, Derby could see the gold-colored fine sand and tall palm trees that looked outward to the Mediterranean Sea. The security in the building was light and involved going through metal detectors and security in the main lobby. Derby collected papers and identification for use in Tel Aviv, as well as currency and in the meantime, a Colt M1911 semiautomatic pistol with a holster he could conceal in his jacket. He also changed out from his dark suit to a beige suit with a white shirt. When Derby was ready, he stepped out onto the city with his notebook in hand, handgun concealed. He waited outside the embassy doors for a limo that would escort him to Tel Aviv University, and as he waited, he looked around the Jewish city from the pedestrians to the traffic. Eventually, a limousine drove up past the bollards in front of the embassy and stopped in front of Derby.

The chauffer exited the vehicle and turned around to look over to Derby. "Mr. Cabernet?"

"Present," Derby greeted, stepping towards the tinted window of the limo.

"Allow me," the chauffer remarked, walking around to open the door. He opened the door and Derby folded over to enter inside, but as he did so, he noticed a man in the limousine.

Derby squinted at the man. He wore a cyan grey suit with a white shirt. He was middle-aged, in his fifties or so, and he had fair to olive skin. He was not clean shaven and he wore thick glasses. He also had fair-length grey hair. He sat in the limo nearly directly in front of the car seat door with his left arm stretched out across the top of the seat and his right hand reaching into his jacket.

"Who the hell are you?" Derby questioned.

"Why don't you take a seat, Mr. Cabernet, and I'll explain everything." He spoke English in a New York accent.

"I don't fancy taking a seat with a stranger in this strange world."

"I recommend you do," the man remarked. The chauffer drew a handgun from his jacket in his right hand. He pointed the handgun at Derby who looked at it and then frowned.

Derby got into the limousine and the chauffer closed the door behind him. He sat in the seat across from this mysterious stranger, next to the exit. Derby noticed it was just the two of them. Once the chauffer returned to their seat, he got into the limo and proceeded to drive.

"I hope I'm still being taken to the university, I have research to complete."

"I'm sure you do, Mr. Cabernet, but first we need to talk."

"Do we?" Derby sarcastically responded.

"Did you really think there would not be any consequences after what happened in Rome? After you so politely crashed our party and ran?" The man stretched out both arms across the top of his seat.

"I understand that I was invited. An invitation was slipped in from one of your pawns during my time at the Vatican."

"You were invited, but you weren't supposed to see what you saw just yet – whatever it is that you think you may have seen."

"Who are you? What do you want with me?"

"Who I am is not important."

"So, you're nobody then. Just another pawn sent out to have a word with me about whatever sick cult you're a part of."

"Not nobody, Mr. Cabernet, in fact, I'm someone a lot more powerful than you," the man stated with a strict face. "Do you think that you could hijack a government vehicle to have this conversation in? Totally unnoticed to the U.S. government and their allies? You don't know who I am, many don't, but I am the most powerful being in this world. Whatever I want, I could have it. Whatever I want to happen, happens. All the countries of the world are under my rule…"

"I don't believe you. I also won't be intimidated by a charlatan. I'm not naïve. I know that such power in this world is an impossibility. You've been sent to scare me into submission, but don't worry. I'm not interested in what I saw."

"My concern isn't that you believe in our existence," the man said, face easing to a calm smile. "If you choose not to believe we exist, it does not change our power or control. We thought to recruit you, to share in what we have to offer for you."

"And what is that?"

"Whatever you want or hope to achieve, Mr. Cabernet."

"I have all that I need."

"Why are you in Israel?"

"I'm on the hunt for a war criminal."

"Why pursue a criminal from a war that happened twenty-five years ago?"

"He killed hundreds of innocent people."

"Yes, Jewish people, and you think yourself different than him?"

"I'm not a murderer."

"You are no different than him when you spew antisemitic rhetoric, denying the massacres that occurred, and creating your own narratives about Jewish people in your publication," the man said. "Look out your window – this city and all this land, in all you have said about Jewish people, you fan the same flames that Nazi Germany had ignited, in hatred of the Jewish people, our right to exist on this land and have a place we call home. You empower the enemies of Israel and Jewish people. The Jewish people have suffered for nearly two-thousand years in exile, in persecution, and you add to that – you are no different than the monsters you had fought in the war who aimed to exterminate us."

"I hate no man or woman," Derby stated. "Neither the Jewish people, nor the Germans. I wish no harm or malice upon any person. You lot cry anti-semitism as you see fit nowadays and believe anything that opposes you to be antisemitic. Just as after the Pharisees and Sadducees called for the death of our Lord to Pontius Pilate, and after they persecuted Christians, did they cry anti-semitism as they were persecuted in a Christianized western world. It is the same cry of anti-semitism as when after the Zealots killed and rebelled against the Romans, Hadrian led his legions to slaughter the insurgents and salt the land. It is the cry of anti-semitism as when their ancestors were arrested and executed in Medieval times for practicing ritual sacrifice and preying upon innocent women and children. It is the same cry of antisemitism as others ostracized them after they acclimated wealth from usury and the slave trade. It is the very same cry of anti-semitism as reactionary forces arose to oppose their vengeful, anti-Christian avant-garde of revolutionary thought through the industrial revolution and modern times, which more than ever seek to deconstruct our Christianized civilization. It was not Jewish people that caused their own infamy and persecution, but a small, select group of rootless, treacherous, and immoral few whose hubris thought themselves as gods among men – and who timelessly branded themselves victims whilst holding the knife. Likewise, it is the Zionists now who massacre Arabs that cry out antisemitism, and it is the Jewish people who have to pay, as they have had time and time again, for true anti-semitism because of the crimes of this ruthless bunch. I hold no hatred to that people, nor to that rootless few. Unlike the German people, who have asked for forgiveness in the acts that they encouraged through the Nazi leadership, although I understand, I have not fallen bait to hate an entire people because of the actions of a few evil men that are less than

Jewish, but anti-Christian at heart. My woe though is to the common Jewish person who has to pay for the actions their elite."

The man looked back at Derby as he finished. He held a frown on his face.

"I had no idea you were such a fanatic – a devout believer of Christ."

"A fanatic? If a fanatic is one who holds an extreme devotional love for the Lord, then that is who I am. I am a Roman Catholic, and we are the children of God."

The man looked uncomfortable with what Derby had to say. He remarked, "The Jewish people maintained themselves as children of God for some time as well, for well over a thousand years when the world went their way. Let's see if the Roman Catholic Church and its people can persevere through the same..."

"Seems as though we'll find out."

"For nearly two-thousand years it's been that the Jewish people have not been in this land, the Promised Land, but they persevered to return home through their collective willpower and determination that they should exist. Do you believe the same God of the Jewish people is your God? A God who some may say abandoned these people?"

"I cannot say for certain who the Jewish people worship because I am not Jewish, anymore than I could claim for a Muslim," Derby stated, "but I can deny that the return of the Jewish people to the Holy Land was nothing more than the permissive will of God to let man act rather than an act from God. What I am certain of is that even in the treacherous act that led to the diaspora, through the centuries of exile, God had not left or abandoned the Jewish people, even if they rejected him through Jesus Christ."

The look on the man's face turned to a scowl. The car came to a halt.

"I was wrong about you, Mr. Cabernet. Seems as though our organization is not for you," the man stated. "Let's hope your pursuit of knowledge does not have us meet again, the consequences would be dire if they did – go and find your war criminal andlive out whatever fantasy you wish to live out in delivering him to justice."

Derby stood up as the car door opened for him to exit. He proceeded to exit.

"And Mr. Cabernet," the man said, "be sure you do capture that criminal. The hundreds of innocent people that he killed depend upon you to avenge them."

Act 3, Scene 2

The next day, Derby was taken to his kit kept at the back of the U.S. embassy. Included in that kit was a pickup truck with all the requested equipment in crates at the rear of the truck. Derby was dressed in a tan canvas collared shirt, canvas trousers, and brown boots. He checked the equipment crates in the rear of the truck to ensure that all the requested equipment was accounted for. Included in that equipment was an FN FAL assault rifle, plenty of ammunition, and other supplies. Derby put on a belt around his waist that held pouches. He also took a pair of binoculars and put his notebook in one pouch and a canteen with water in the other. Once all was set, Derby got into the driver's seat of the pickup truck, ignited the engine, and then drove off from the rear of the embassy onto the main road to travel south.

The drive from Tel Aviv to Ashkelon took less than an hour. He arrived in the city as it was still morning time. The terrain around the city consisted of a mixture of green patches of vegetation to coarse desert sands. The buildings from the horizon were similarly white stucco, with a majority of them being rectangular apartment buildings with plain rooftops and a few houses with terracotta rooftops. He passed through the city and exited out the south, into the countryside where he passed vast farmlands and open fields. Eventually, Derby drove onto a road that approached a large complex in the midst of a small few acres of land. He stopped at the front gate and saw a signpost on the front that listed three lines of text, each in different languages: Latin, Greek, and Neo-Aramaic. A separate signpost in front of this sign had words in Hebrew and Arabic with a stop sign in the middle. Derby exited the vehicle to approach the gate, examine it, and then walk around to an intercom at a post.

A deep voice spoke in a Semitic language to him that he could not understand.

"Hello? Hello?" Derby questioned. "Do you speak English? This is Derby Cabernet, looking to speak with someone from the monastery."

A faint voice spoke back from the intercom. There was then a muffled sound. Derby waited a few minutes as he could still hear the speaker turned on and dead air float through.

"Hello," a voice spoke in the speaker. "Is someone there?"

"Yes, I'm still here," Derby remarked. "I'm looking to enter the monastery – my name is Derby Cabernet."

"This is a sheltered community – we don't allow strangers…"

"I'm not looking for a place to stay, just need some help…"

Derby could hear some voices speaking a vague Semitic language from the other end. The speaker then cut out. Derby looked at the intercom and then through the fence. He caught a glance at the wider space of the monastery. The structure was not large, although there was a bit of land. Similar to the buildings in Tel Aviv and Ashkelon, the structure consisted of white stucco. The road continued forward and passed the main structure that consisted of two-stories and had a terracotta rooftop. Between this structure was the apparent church grounds with a rectangular bell tower and lookout. Attached on the other side of the main building was another structure similar to the one closest to the gate. On the right, besides the main structure, were some greenhouses. On the immediate left, past a row of cypress trees, was an open field with no horticulture whatsoever and instead goal posts on either side. The road passed the main structure and went further ahead past a few small houses up to an open clearing where there were taller structures with pens and an orchard nearby. Behind the main structure and along that entire side of the perimeter was some farmland. Derby could see some telephone and electrical wires connect in with the monastery from outside.

After a few minutes, Derby noticed two men in black habits approach the gate. They stood at the other side and looked towards him, eyeing him and his truck.

"What business do you have here?" the monk questioned. "We are not open to foreigners."

"I understand that, but I'm just looking for some assistance," Derby requested. "Surely you cannot deny that request – I won't be around very long, and I can pay the community to compensate for my time here. I have money…"

The monk looked at his brother monk, and then back towards Derby.

"If you have money, then why come here? We do not recognize shekels in these lands."

"Not shekels, but British pounds," Derby remarked. "I'll be honest with you, my dear brothers in Christ, I am not a Jew. I am a Catholic who wishes to meet with your superior and ask questions about a group of fellow Catholics who may have passed through. I'm looking for them and need to know if they've been through."

"Like I said, we are not open to travellers…"

"I am not a traveller, and neither are they. Let me talk to your superior – is this not a monastery of the Order of St. Athanasius?"

"Yes, and as much as we'd like to help you," the other monk said, "it's not possible. Any foreigners, whether Catholic or Jew, are forbidden from this land without consent from a superior."

"Let me talk to your superior then. I assure you; I am not an enemy. I just have some questions… it's of the up-most urgency."

The monks looked at each other. The eldest let out a huff and then looked back at Derby.

"You will wait here while we consult our superior," the eldest monk said before he turned around. The younger monk followed him, and so Derby retreated to his vehicle hide from the heat and wait. Derby looked at the perimeter of the monastery from his truck as he waited.

Half an our later, Derby spotted three men in habits, one of whom appeared older among them and wore a kalimavkion hat, a rectangular black headpiece. He had a thick grey beard and deep tanned skin. He also held a staff and approached ahead of the other men.

"I am the abbot of this monastery, what can I do for you, traveller?"

"This monastery belongs to the Order of St. Athanasius, doesn't it?" Derby asked

"You are correct – how did you know?"

"I've heard that the order had been disavowed and wished to inquire deeper. My name is Derby Cabernet, of the Cabernet fame. You may have heard of that name, but I'm an explorer and a researcher, and I'm looking for information about the order in search for a group of travellers of my esteem."

"I do not know anyone of Cabernet fame, or what fame exactly you refer to. My name is Abbot Amos and you are correct, this abbey, the Abbey of St. Antioch, belongs to provincial chapter of Syria Palaestina of the Order of St. Athanasius. Few know or recognize our existence, so how do you know of us?"

"From archives held in the Vatican City," Derby answered. "The archives end in the last half of the century, but I know it has continued to exist – I wish to enquire further because the travellers I am looking for are associated with the order and must have been travelling between monasteries."

The abbot looked at Derby in the eyes and then nudged his shoulder to the others. They proceeded to open the gate. The gate rolled open, and Derby stood across from the abbot.

"What do you intend to do with this information about our communities?"

"Nothing more than locate these travellers, I assure you. I'm an ally to your cause."

"The Order of St. Athanasius has no allies in this world, not anymore, and what cause we have, I am not so sure. There was a time in which we had influence, but it was short-lived. We are now very few, no more than a handful in each province. Allow me to explain..."

Derby followed the abbot into the monastery. He was taken through the doors into the church where he caught a glimpse of the inside of the worship space. The walls of the church maintained a light beige color in accordance with the stucco façade. The floor consisted of a slightly darker tan tile. The timber pews looked towards the altar at the end with a gold-colored tabernacle atop of it. Along the walls were some Byzantine-style caricatures of angels and saints surrounding a triumphant Jesus Christ who loomed over the sanctuary. From the central building, Derby was taken to the left and brought around to a room at the end of the corridor on the second floor.

The abbot office took up the entire depth of the building and was a share of the length. It had windows on both end, one of which looked out to the farm and another to the rest of the monastery and open field. In between those two windows were two bookcases, and then in the middle of those was a mural painted on the wall. The mural depicted Samson bound to pillars on the brink of collapse. The abbot sat down at his desk and then offered Derby a seat.

"Where do I begin..." the abbot expressed. "What do you know about our past?"

Derby began to explain to him what he collected from the Vatican archives on the founder of the Order of St. Athanasius (Derosiers), his intent to combat modern thinking (secularism, liberalism, and later socialism), and the interest of the order to protect the traditions of the church.

"Yes, that's mostly true," Abbot Amos stated, "except allow me to add a bit of detail. The Order of St. Athanasius was initially an effort to recruit impoverished and marginalized young men to the priesthood – the collective aim and adoption of St. Athanasius came a few decades later at the conclusion of the French Revolution, to preserve and safeguard the Church from the dangerous thought of the last three centuries. The rest of your information is about correct – the order grew, and then Fr. Ambroise Rochefort was our superior general... he was a passionate leader, I can remember, and then the Great Depression came.

"Since the papacy of Pope St. Pius X, the order has been in decline and Fr. Ambroise fought against the hostile change before us. He was for the most part successful, but then the Great Depression came, and we held through... and then the war came... Not even during the Great War was there so much division, ideological division, than during the last war... it was the war that forever changed the order and guaranteed our end."

"What happened during the war?"

"The ideological spirits took fold in the Church, not just the order, but reactionary ideals came through to us and it was then that the order began to drift from its mandate. This spirit that passed through lingered even after the end of the war, and as the revelation came of atrocities at the hands of the losers of the war, the priests and brothers that participated in that collaboration beat down on us. For a moment in the last decade, the 1950s, we had some tranquility in the politics of the order, but then the Second Vatican Council was announced. Suddenly, the entire core beliefs were put to the test, and there was internal strife... some monasteries left the order to embrace the change, some left because of the internal change within the order, seeing us as having become too political and to have ironically departed from tradition, while others saw us as too rigid and to be holding too tightly to tradition. Yes, the Order of St. Athanasius survives at this time, but with no organization, no leadership, and the entire order in disarray."

"What about Archbishop Rene Chevalier?" Derby questioned. "Isn't he the superior general?"

"Archbishop Chevalier? Archbishop Chevalier died last year, in a plane crash. No, the Order of St. Athanasius is no more, my brother. What remains are cells, throughout the provinces left in the world – the Province of *Columbia* (United States), *Britannia* (Britain), *Hibernia* (Ireland), *Graecia* (Greece), *Syria Palaestina* (Palestine and Syria), *Mesopotamia* (Iraq), and *Aegyptus* (Egypt). Ten years ago, we also had chapters in Canada, France, Spain, Italy, and Germany, but these have since disappeared."

"What happened to those chapters?"

"They were either silently dismantled or assimilated into other orders."

Derby nodded and then asked, "What's so radical though about the Order of St. Athanasius? I understand that there has been some dissent in the current direction of the Church, but has it really been so serious?"

"The Order of St. Athanasius held to the traditions of the Church with vigor. Some unfortunately though took the mandate of the order to extremes. *Provincia Germania* for example, our largest province, was dismantled at the end of the war due to their collusion with the Nazis. You can dismantle the chapter, but not the people – its members fled to adjacent chapters. *Provincia Gallia*, dismantled in the last century due to radical beliefs and experimentations from those same people. *Provincia Italia*, *Lusitania* and *Hispania*, forcibly dismantled by the Vatican due to their hostile opposition to the Second Vatican Council, its monasteries assimilated into other orders and most of their members fled from public life. *Provincia Borealis* in Canada dismantled too. I haven't heard any news about the chapters in South America except *Argentia* (Argentina). I only hear from chapters closest to us, as far as our mail can be sent. Seems as though every order has their own ideas, projects, and visions these days, and without a leader, they fall further from the ideas of Fr. Desrosiers."

"What does this abbey envision?"

Abbot Amos took in a deep breath and answered, "To survive in this occupied land and maintain the faith in the Holy Land. We have no other aspirations except to mind our own business. I've seen what vehement traditionalism does to a community of people, where in their despair in face of the world around them, they take what is beautiful and construct it into an idol. Here we hold to traditions, teach new priests in the seminary, but never will traditions and orthodoxy be placed above obedience to the magisterium."

"Very humble of you to lead your flock in such a way," Derby admitted. "On the subject of radicals and reactionaries though, there comes some bad news I may have for you. I believe I can trust you to be honest, so I will be forthcoming – I'm searching for an archeological party that may have passed through your abbey. I am not sure who they are led by, but one of their party members is a man named Erich Liudolfings. He was member of the Nazi Party guards, the Schutzstaffel, and is a war criminal who I am looking for to bring to justice."

"You are a Nazi hunter."

"My understanding is that Nazi hunters seek to kill. I seek to return him to the proper authorities, the Americans, so he can be brought to the Hague and face justice for his war crimes," Derby remarked. "I need you to answer my questions. Did a German man of this approximate facial feature pass though here with other archeologists, and if so, where did they go?"

Derby took a drawing from his pouch and placed it on the table. The abbot brought a hand to his cheek.

"Dear Lord," the abbot expressed as though in distress. "It cannot be…"

"I need you to focus…" Derby requested. "Did a man who looks like this spend time here?"

The abbot froze as he became endowed in a panic. Derby knocked on the desk to get his attention.

"It's important that you help me, Father. Herr Liudolfings is a bad man. He tortured and killed a lot of people, a lot of Jewish people, so I'm told – women and children of a variety. Where did he go?"

The abbot put a hand over his eyes. He began to calm down. Derby looked at him intently. The abbot lowered his hand.

"The party you speak of… it's led by a priest, a young priest – they are not a large party either. They're being led by a Father Tristan Williamson… a member of the order from *Provincia Britannia*. A few more are with them… one more priest, two scholars, and the German… he goes by the name Engstfeld – Rudolf Engstfeld."

"And this Engstfeld looks like the man in this picture?"

"Yes… yes… just like him."

"And where did they go?"

"The West Bank," Abbot Amos answered. "They stayed the night and left the next morning for an excavation in the West Bank. They're working on a project… something to do with biblical archeology of some sort, something to do with giants from the Bible."

"Where in the West Bank are they?"

"I have no idea… somewhere in the desert… I did not ask many questions about their work. Really, all I know is that it has something to do with giants. We talked lots about this land before Exodus, before the migration to Egypt, during the times of Genesis."

"Okay…" Derby remarked, jotting these notes down. "When did they leave?"

"Not too long ago, just yesterday… I understand that these expeditions take days, you won't miss them if you leave now…"

"Oh, I don't intend to," Derby said, standing up. "Thank you for your time, sir. I must be on my way." He quickly stood up and turned to leave, prompting the abbot to stand up quickly as well.

"Wait!" the abbot called out.

Derby paused for a moment.

"Mr. Cabernet, please, show forgiveness," Abbot Amos remarked. "We are all sinners, are we not? Despite this man's past, have mercy on him, please. Do not get carried away."

Derby ignored him and left the room.

Act 3, Scene 3

Derby travelled north from the Abbey of St. Antioch, but rather than return to Tel Aviv to update Secretary Clark, he drove to Jerusalem where he stopped to assess the border situation with Palestine. The accumulative drive from the abbey to Jerusalem was two hours by which time it was nearly noon. The east-west border in Jerusalem at this time consisted of barbed wire and checkpoints along roads into the West Bank that were manned with armed Israeli Defense Force soldiers. Derby observed the border checkpoint from a distance before he attempted to cross through, seeing that the IDF soldiers were more interested in harassing Arabs and other suspicious characters travelling into Israel than those leaving Israel. Since 1967, in the conclusion of the Six-Day War, Israel expanded its occupation in Palestine to include the West Bank and Gaza Strip, in addition to the Sinai Peninsula seized from Egypt and the Golan Heights from Syria. The checkpoint was not a customs checkpoint, but an occupation checkpoint to ensure internal security to screen potential insurgents. Derby travelled with caution through the checkpoint, witnessing IDF soldiers harassing and beating a woman in front of her child from the other side of the crossing as she crouched in a corner. Some of the soldiers held back their Rottweilers from a group of Arab teenagers that were held up against a wall. Once Derby was in the formal occupation zone, he travelled with caution.

East Jerusalem in the West Bank (referred to as the West Bank as it lies west of Jordan), was impoverished. The streets were littered, walls tagged by vandals, and its buildings were old and decaying. The citizens were less clean than the ones in West Jerusalem and the rest of Israel. They wore old clothes, appeared less nourished and lankier, especially the young people, and it was not as though one had stepped less into the slum of the same city, but from a developed country into an under-developed country, the first world into the third world. The Israeli Defense Force was heavily present in East Jerusalem, especially teams that had Rottweilers on leashes. The Palestinian flag was not visible on any flagpole which instead bore the Israeli blue star. The citizens walked with their heads kept down, avoiding eye contact with the soldiers lest they be the target of their foul mood and prejudice towards these people. However, even in this representation in the people and the city in the West Bank, Derby observed that the structures were old, and especially older in the district known as the old city, but for the first time since his arrival in Jerusalem (aside from at the abbey), he noticed the presence of churches. He noticed women with veils, Eastern Rite priests in black cassocks wearing large crosses openly in crowds of Muslims who did not care. Derby drove past the old city district where from a distance he could see the Dome of the Rock atop of the foundations of where the second temple had been. Rather than stop to view the sites worthy of pilgrimage and homage, Derby continued to drive through to the outskirts and then the Judean desert outwards.

Derby drove along the main highway eastbound, passing signs in English and Arabic, remnant from British rule. The land around him was rugged, as indicated in the topographic map at his side. He passed through the top of a plateau in the desert with hills and mounds around him. The highway he travelled on almost cut through the land to make its pass with neatly cut cliffs at his side. Eventually, the road came out from this sort of canyon and he could see ahead of him from above to stretches of the land below the plateaus. The freeway made a descent to the lowlands and the terrain seemed more traversable for him if he chose to go off-road. Derby drove up to a gas station around a small pitstop near a junction to assess his progress.

"Why did I pull myself into this land without at least a guide?" Derby muttered, looking at his notes and maps "I don't speak a lick of Arabic or Hebrew. How am I supposed to track these people down?"

Derby looked at the terrain map and could see that around where he had entered was an entire lowland from the northern coast of the Dead Sea, to the River Jordan further east, and then upwards to Jericho, and then slowly less and less space up to cliff walls until the northern exit from the West Bank. He circled this space in particular. The southern dredges were dominated with hills and appeared difficult to traverse. The southern freeway to the southern exit from the West Bank was dominated with extraordinary high cliffs. There were also no other roads in the land between the coastal freeway and civilization around Hebron. The north was a different story with roads travelling through the various hills and mountains in that region, going from Jericho to Shiloh, to all sorts of paths that sprouted out from around that city in the center of the desert region. In comparison to the rest of Palestine, this area of the West Bank was dominated with rugged surfaces, mountains and hills. The only traversable land in these parts was around the River Jordan. Derby looked at the map and then began to pause for a moment.

"Giants... when did we hear about the giants in the Bible?" Derby muttered as he continued to sit in the truck. He flipped through his Bible beside him and began to skim through the Book of Genesis. He stopped at Genesis 6:4, and it said:

When men had begun to be plentiful on the earth, and the daughters had been born to them, / the sons of God, looking at the daughters of men, saw they were pleasing, so they married as many as they chose. / Yahweh said, 'My spirit must not for ever be disgraced in man, for he is but flesh; his life shall last no more than a hundred and twenty years.' / The giants were on the earth at that time (and even afterwards) when the sons of God resorted to the daughters of man and had children by them. These are the heroes of days gone by, the famous men.

Derby continued to investigate as he skimmed the Book of Genesis. Eventually, that book did not suffice for his research, so he went through the Pentateuch and came to Numbers 13:33.

"*Yes, and we saw giants there (the sons of Anak, descendants of the Giants). We felt like grasshoppers, and so we seemed to them,*" Derby read aloud. "Anak..." He wrote that detail down and then continued to Deuteronomy 2-12, which said:

And Yahweh said to me, 'Make no attack on Moab and do not provoke him to fight, for I will give you none of this land. I have given Ar into the possession of the sons of Lot.' / (At one time the Emim lived there, a great and numerous people, tall as the Anakim; and like the Anakim, they were accounted Rephaim, though the Moabites call them Emim. / The Horites, too, loved in Seir at one time; these, however, were dispossessed and exterminated by the sons of Esau who settled there in place of them, just as Israel did in their own land, the heritage they received from Yahweh.

Derby then continued to Joshua 11:21-23, which read:

Then Joshua came and wiped out the Anakim from the highlands, from Hebron, from Debir, from Anab, from all the highlands of Judah and all the highlands of Israel; he delivered them and their towns over to the ban. / No more Anakim were left in Israelite territory except at Gaza, Gath, and Ashdod. / Joshua mastered the whole country, just as Yahweh told Moses, and he gave it to Israel as an inheritance according to their division by tribes. And the country had rest from war.

Derby retrieved another book and began to flip through it. He found a map of Canaan at the times of the end of the forty-years wandering in the desert and was able to compare locations on the map, i.e. Moab, Ammon, and Amorites with their location in present day Jordan. Across the Jordan was a disputed territory among Canaanites, Jebusites, Edomites, and other tribes.

Without another word, Derby ignited his engine and proceeded to drive closer towards the border crossing at the River Jordan. At a junction in the freeway, Derby drove south and proceeded south towards the cliffs of the Dead Sea until he reached a junction in the road that came to a side road. He stopped at the side of the highway with his binoculars and began to scout the land. Most of this land consisted of farmland and there was no sight of any archeological expedition. He returned to his truck and went north up until he reached a makeshift trail that traversed towards the hilltop. He took the truck off-road and began to climb the ascent to reach an open plain ahead. First, he scouted the land below from the top of the hill and then he proceeded inland. The skies at this time were greyish and there was minimal visibility from afar. Nonetheless, Derby scouted this land and saw a bright-colored banner stuck into the rock to the west. He drove closer towards as close as the truck could traverse, and then he got out and followed on foot. He reached the banner and saw that it was stuck into the rock at a man-made cavern, but this area appeared abandoned with not a sign of human life, so Derby too abandoned it to return to his vehicle. He searched this area for another few hours, reaching a monastery in a canyon where he asked questions to monks at the gates who could not speak English. He then exited out to find himself not too far from Bethlehem where he retired in the wilderness for the night, setting up camp, and then the next day he continued.

Derby searched the southern region for the entire day, passing Hebron and checking in with anyone that would speak to him and which would talk to him. Few that did talk to him could speak a morsel of English, so the conversations were fruitless to the hunt. The hunt around this region took him three days, and when he had exhausted his options, he turned northbound and went back up the way he came to return to the northern coast of the Dead Sea. Derby travelled to Jericho with hope that it would be the next possible location, but when the immediate area around him showed little promise, he continued to drive northwards to avoid venturing into hillsides and canyons, keeping an eye out towards the desert around him until he reached the end of the line at the northern crossing from the West Bank. Derby searched the area around him one more time before he travelled through an alternative route southbound and spent the rest of the day in the wilderness, searching for any sign of an expedition. On the evening of the sixth day, encamped out in the desert close to Shiloh, Derby re-assessed his notes and the next day he journeyed around the land between Shiloh and Jericho.

From these lands, Derby travelled off-road and began to take notice of some ruins in this area in the midst of the desert. He travelled closer to get a better look as he noticed white tarps and tents set up around the area. Derby parked the pickup truck nearby and then proceeded closer on foot, arming himself with his rifle and backpack, and going ahead along the desert to reach the site. A mild wind blew, and the skies were clearer than they had been earlier in the week. Derby approached the site from the side and could not see anyone around. The ruins consisted of sandstone and were not particularly tall, at most six feet at some sections, but the size of the settlement was large even if it was just collapsed walls buried beneath sand and surrounded by cliff walls. An approximately ten-yard gap between the city and the cliff walls was where there were the tents and tarps set up. Once Derby was close enough to insert, he dashed forward and entered into the ruins and walked carefully through, but it was quiet, and he could only hear the whistle of the wind blowing into the tarps and canvas tents.

Eventually, Derby reached the tents and looked towards the tarps to notice there to be tables with some equipment laid out, but not very much. There were also some crates with empty jars and bottles. A book was laid out atop of a table, and there were some smaller tarps that held stone and bones, with brushes laid out. Derby looked around and then saw many pits nearby with demarcations surrounding a general area where excavations had been done. Eventually, Derby realized that the area was abandoned, so he lowered his stance and began to look around the area closer. He looked beneath the large pits that were dug out to see that they were like graves but empty. He looked through each of them and saw that ladders were still stuck in some of them. He then came around to the tables to look at what laid out before him – bones and shards of stone. He looked at some of the items that were left out beneath in crates, fluttering the flies as they flew around the leftover food items. A few remains of scraps could be found, slightly fresh. He picked up the book on the table to see it was a copy of the Book of Enoch. Derby looked at the light book and then pocketed it. He continued to search around the dig site until he found some more items around the tents. He picked up a journal inside one of them that had been left behind and began to read through it.

The journal did not have many pages of written contents but started two weeks ago and detailed arrival in Israel through Egypt, travel through the Sinai Peninsula, and then arrival to Ashkelon. From Ashkelon, it detailed an expedition nearby to recover bones from a Philistine graveyard, some of which were above average in length. The journal then detailed the departure from Ashkelon to the West Bank through the south and arrival to this dig site, a ruined town known as Ai. Derby cross-referenced this location with his notes taken from the Bible. He then continued to read through the journal to see that it mentioned that when they finished here, they would travel east to search dig sites in former Babylon. No other details were written down.

Derby thought for a moment and the put the journal into another pocket. He stood up and exited the tent. He then proceeded to climb upwards to the tallest point of the excavation ruins to look at all the low walls around. He couldn't see a single person around him, nor anywhere worth to search, but before Derby could decide to leave, he noticed some movement along the desert road. He picked up his binoculars and looked outwards. The convoy of jeeps travelled towards him, a car pulling over at Derby's pickup truck and the rest going towards the excavation site. Derby concentrated before him as he saw the men armed with assault rifles. He attempted to identify them, but they had no patches or insignias, and their uniforms were not like the ones worn by IDF soldiers that Derby had seen so far.

As the convoy travelled closer, Derby got down from the top of the hill and began to move into position in a secluded area with his rifle ready. He took a vantage point above a cliff and went into the prone position. As he waited for the soldiers to come closer as they parked their jeeps and travelled on foot a few yards away, Derby noticed some jets fly past from above. He then returned his focus ahead as the soldiers entered into the ruin and split up into teams. Derby attempted to remain hidden as he looked down upon them, but as he shifted his body, some rocks collapsed down the side of the cliff which prompted nearly all the soldiers to shoot their gaze towards him and point their rifles.

Derby sat up and waved a hand towards the soldiers as they refrained from opening fire. He could hear them speak some sort of semitic language, but still unsure of their loyalties, he said, "I'm not an enemy – I come…"

Before Derby could speak another word, the hostiles opened fire towards him, causing him to roll over the side and get out of harm's way.

"Bastards!" Derby shouted, readying his rifle. He quickly got up and rushed down to take cover beneath the slope as the soldiers spread out into cover. He came out of cover as they scrambled and opened fire towards them. From within the ruins, Derby could hear them speaking in their semitic language, but one word he was sure not to mistake as familiar was 'Cabernet', spoken numerous times through their shouts.

Derby withdrew from his position and went up the slope, and then he doubled back and took cover from further above down towards the hostiles as they had him nearly cornered. He took some shots towards them as he was close to a few yards above them. The gunshots that came towards him chipped at the stone he hid behind. He reloaded his rifle and paused for a moment. The soldiers moved in on him, but Derby could not fire back without compromising himself. He lurched forward and slid down the side of the cliff to the bottom, unseen, where he came around and took cover around some walls. Derby reappeared into the battle as he opened fire at some soldiers at their flank, causing the small platoon to turn around and face him. He then stayed low and began to crawl forward as they shot their guns towards him. Derby approached a taller wall and then stood up to double back around.

Derby reappeared again from around a corner at a tall wall and opened fire at the flank of the enemy, catching them by surprise, but then they quicky responded to attempt to pincer him from both ends. Derby ducked back around, encountering a hostile as he was about to turn the corner. He whipped the butt of his rifle in their face and then kicked them over. He shot them and then proceeded forward to the other end, dashing towards the jeeps and taking cover behind them as they shot towards the jeep and blew its tire. He then ducked backwards to another jeep, unwilling to hop aboard lest he be shot at once. Derby decided to blow the tires with them, going from jeep to jeep until he reached the end and opened fire at the now stranded crowd. Next, Derby moved away from the jeeps and towards the cliff side and away from the excavation site as he attempted to flee from the few that remained.

From the side of the cliff, he reached a gulley and slid down it. He then went forward, coming out at the top of a slope and looking ahead as the soldiers spread out to look for him. Derby decided to sprint towards his truck as he fled from the hostiles, but as he did so, he could hear the passing of the jet from behind. Not willing to turn around, Derby continued to run towards his vehicle as others behind began to open fire towards him. With less than a few yards to go, Derby suddenly ducked down as the pickup truck detonated and flew into the air. He then quickly made the decision to rush away from the pickup truck, fleeing into the desert, not looking behind him, going towards the desert road and then going towards the untraversable hills where on foot he could hide into the mountains.

Act 3, Scene 4

From the excavation site, into the mountains, Derby stopped to catch his breath as he slid down a slope and reached the bottom. He saw a small mountain ahead and began to climb it. He stayed put for a moment and took position from a ledge. He took out his binoculars and searched his surroundings for any trace of the combatants, and then he stayed put for a few more minutes before he continued into the mountains and hiked into the mountain range. Suddenly, as Derby made his way around a mountain, he ducked behind a boulder as a jet made its pass nearby. He then stopped to listen to his surroundings before he ventured forward. He came around the mountain and stopped to look out towards the desert and see some jeeps on the road ahead. He stayed put until they passed and then returned into the mountains to go deeper inside. He trekked a kilometer to the others side to see a road between some hills where a jeep made its pass. From where Derby was located, he waited and then made his descent downwards to cross the road and climb up to the others side. Derby then travelled into the mountain range and went north.

From the late morning to the evening just before the sunset, Derby trekked close to fifteen kilometers where he stopped to have a rest at a stone wall. He kept his rifle at his side and titled his head back. He picked up his canteen to drink some water, feeling the last drops drip onto his tongue and nothing more. He put the canteen away and then looked around him. He had descended from the mountains to reach a plateau where there was a ranch in the midst of the wilderness. He tilted his head back again as he continued to rest, and what became a moment's rest in the shade of an olive tree soon became a nap. Derby quickly jerked his neck forward as he jumped in his sleep. He grabbed his rifle and bent a knee forward to take aim with his rifle, but there was nothing around him. He slowly stood up as he lowered his rifle. He looked up to the orange sky and then began to walk around the wall to pass the ranch he was at. He picked up his canteen again as he was about to journey into the mountain range again, but as he did so, he saw that it was empty. At the same time, his stomach grumbled. He looked into the pen of the ranch to see three flocks of sheep within, and further ahead, a well in furthest reaches of the property sat atop a hill. Derby's eyes looked around for a single person in the ranch, but it was empty, and he saw warm lights turned on in the main home at the furthest end.

Derby climbed over the wall and began to proceed past the flock of sheep to reach the well where he rested his rifle at the stones of the well. He picked up the bucket at the side of the well, lowered it on its rope to scoop out some water, and then pulled it back up. As he had both hands on the pale, Derby's ears twitched as he heard the cock of a rifle behind him followed with the bark of a dog behind. In an instance he froze, removed both hands from the pale and then slowly raised them and turned around. Ahead of him, beneath the top of the mound that the well sat on, he saw an older man in a suit. He had deep tanned skin, but very white hair and a neatly trimmed white beard. He wore a dark tan plaid suit with a bowtie. He aimed a Lee-Enfield rifle towards Derby, his right eye closed and left eye towards him. A shepherd dog barked behind him, stuck behind a fence near the house. The two men stared at each other until the man that pointed the rifle spoke some words in a semitic language.

"I can't understand you," Derby replied in a coarse voice. "I don't speak Hebrew, or Arabic, whichever of the two you speak. The most I know is Latin, French and Spanish."

"You are not from here," the man spoke in his coarse and deep voice. "What're you doing on my land?"

"I just wanted a drink of water from your well," Derby argued, exhausted. "I mean no harm... just passing through. It's quite a nice ranch you have here..."

The man examined Derby and then lowered his rifle and opened his other eye. Derby picked up his rifle by the barrel and then offered it to the man.

"I'm not a robber, I swear to you," Derby expressed. "Take my rifle if you want. It's quite an improvement to what you have there. I had one of those when I joined the army, they're quite good, but this is better. I think this'd be a fair trade for some water…"

The man looked at Derby and he then slowly approached. He took hold of Derby's rifle and then stepped back. Derby turned around and began to pour the water into the canteen. His hands and legs trembled as he did so, from exhaustion. Once Derby finished to put the water into his canteen, he took the bucket and poured the rest of the water into his mouth, spilling around the side of his face. He then took what remained and poured it atop of him and then lowered the bucket down. Derby turned around and looked at the man with a tired expression. The man continued to point his rifle towards Derby from his waist with one hand. He looked and then looked back at the man.

"Now if you won't mind, I'll be off…"

Derby took a sidestep and then turned around to walk back towards the wall.

"Wait," the man spoke, "why don't you come inside for something to eat before you set off? A fair trade is a fair trade…"

Derby turned around and looked at the man. The man turned to his side and gestured with his neck for Derby to come follow him. Derby followed him out of the pasture and through the gate of the fence. The dog continued to bark towards him, but the man hushed him and then led Derby towards the front of the house. He looked around the front of the property to see a truck parked beneath a shelter and a barn on the other side. The man stopped in front of the door as he set the automatic rifle down to open the door. Derby turned around and then stepped through to enter inside.

The foyer of the house was well-decorated and had a chandelier above the center. To the left were some arches that led into a living room. On the immediate left was a wooden door. Ahead of him was a staircase that went upstairs. On the right was an archway and on the right of the stairs was another archway that led to a vestibule.

"You can wash yourself in here," the man said, nudging over to the door on the immediate left. "Kitchen is this way…" The man then walked into the archway on the right.

Derby stepped towards the door on the immediate left, opened it, and then stepped into a small but lavish washroom. He turned on the taps at the sink and water fell out. He took the bar of soap and washed his hands. He then washed his face from the dirt. The skin on his face was warm. Derby stepped out of the washroom and then came around to the archway on the right that led into a small dining room. Another archway on the left showed the kitchen on the other side. In the center of the kitchen was a large pot over an open fire in the center. The man poured some strew into a bowl with a ladle, and then came around to set the food down at the head of the table. The man nudged for Derby to sit down. Derby stepped forward, pulled the chair out and then looked at the stew and smelled the herbs with the meaty soup.

As Derby sat down, he looked to his right and saw a menorah on a table between family photographs. Above that was a painting of a desert landscape. The man stayed in the kitchen for a few minutes as Derby settled in and picked up a wooden spoon to eat the stew.

The man entered into the dining room and sat his portion down at the other side of the table. He then sat down and ate his meal in silence. Derby finished his stew quickly and then looked around the room again. He saw some books on a bookshelf that had a mixture of text, Hebrew and English. The dog stayed close to his owner and sat down in a bed in the corner of the room.

"You have a lovely home, very... quaint," Derby expressed. "Do you like it here?"

The man didn't answer as he ate. Derby cleared his throat and then picked up his bowl to set it forward. He then backed up from his seat.

"Thank you for your hospitality, I truly appreciate it, but I must return outside..."

"It's not safe to go..." the man simply said.

Derby seemed uneasy at the man's words. He cleared his throat again and replied, "I insist that I'm not safe here. It appears as though I'm a wanted man. I need to get to Jerusalem at least... I need to..." he let out a sigh. "Sorry, it's none of your business. I shouldn't be here though..."

"They've already been here," the man expressed. "They wont' return."

"Who was here?"

"The soldiers, looking for a man like you."

"Did they say why?"

The man shook his head and then replied, "They call you an enemy of the Jews."

Derby huffed and then replied, "Seems about right, but I assure you, I hate no man. My strife is not with you or your people. I don't even know who these men are who are looking for me, but they don't appear to be Israeli defensemen. I fear they may be working for the government though..."

The man didn't answer. Derby looked at him with suspicion.

"Why take me in if I am a wanted man and you know it? Why risk yourselves for me?"

"Not the actions you'd expect from a Jew, is it?" the man questioned.

Derby raised his eyebrow and replied, "No, not at all like that – it's just... not decorum to assist a man when he could be a criminal – a bad man."

"Are you?"

"I certainly am an inconvenience to these men to label me an enemy of their kin, your kin. I swear though that I have not broken any law in your country."

"The laws of this country are not the laws that they concern themselves with," the man expressed, setting his bowl aside. He then put both elbows on the table and put his hands together, raised up. "It's not difficult to be labeled an enemy of the Jews, especially when you oppose their wars..."

"You opposed their wars?" Derby questioned.

The man shook his head and replied, "I've minded my own business. The same way I did when I came to this land when it was ruled by the Turks, British, and now Jews."

"Where did you come from before then?"

"I was an exile from the Russian Empire, fleeing from the revolution because although I was a Jew, I was young and naïve, like many such faces in the Bolshevik party."

"What brought you here to Israel if you were a Bolshevik?"

The man sighed and replied, "I was not welcomed – even when the revolution came, I was not welcomed." He paused and then said, "I was a mistaken man, but not mistaken to have left Europe in that time when hatred of Jewish people was unjustifiably high, because of young fools like us. We are a feckless and rootless people who can't help ourselves to exist in controversy and contrary to the majority ways. I opposed the majority of thinkers in the Bolshevik party, and as such I was exiled in West Armenia and then came here. I bought this land to be on my own, and here I have been, unable now to even escape what I escaped from – other Jewish people, or Zionists as they call themselves now."

"I'm sorry," Derby expressed, "for what they do, and for what all my own people and ancestors do and have done because of what they do."

"It's a terrible thing... but for all of our history have we known it... this isn't anything... For hundreds of years did

Jewish people turn from what was good and what was right, and we were punished for it. For that reason did we lose favor *Hashem*. Is it worth the punishment because of a few who seek to defame us all? It may well be if we do not cry out against them, but who among even us can stand defiant an increasing power that is Zionism?"

"I hear you – many blame the Jewish people as a whole for the death of Christ because of what it states in the Bible that those in the crowd before Pontius Pilate sought to take his blood onto themselves and their ancestors, but just because they say it does not make it true for us Christians. The Church has rejected such position, and I see that to an extent it is only true from within Jewish people to believe that such 'blood curse' as it were truly exists," Derby stated. "Christians and Jews have existed in this long-time conflict for two-thousand years, which has resulted in the sufferings of each of our very own innocent people. Jewish leaders persecuted Christians in the early days of the Church, and Christian leaders persecuted Jews in the early medieval years. Jews unjustifiably grew anti-Christian attitudes because of the way Christians treated Jews, and Christians unjustifiably grew anti-Semitic attitudes because of the ways Jews treated Christians. To tie it all together, it was not Jews that killed our Lord on the Cross, but humans, because it is our human inclination to evil that has resulted in this escalating behavior between the two parties as it was the inclination of evil to see to it that a man who never hurt anyone, or did anything wrong, should be nailed onto wood and made a public spectacle.

"I can only imagine the generational trauma present in certain Jewish groups, more now than ever since the events of the war, which will carry forward a desire for vengeance and destruction against Christian people. Only if we heed on Christ's words to turn the other cheek, and to pray and forgive our enemies, could this cycle end, but how can you expect divine mercy from human people? Our Catholic Church needs to lead by example, to acknowledge the blood libels as true, while also acknowledging the harm also made in the Spanish Inquisition for example, and un-Christian treatment of Jews in those times. An effort needs to be made for us to come together and end this violence between us, but it will never happen – either side would be too proud to admit the truth, and what more, this Zionist occupation continues to grow a hostile force that will be even more difficult to deal with and result in the persecution of even more innocent Jewish people around the world. Oh, how I pray for peace in the Middle East, for your people as well as my Christian brothers and sisters who live in these lands, and so do I wish for this peace and reconciliation between Christians and Jewish people, to put to an end hostile feelings between both groups."

The man chortled and said, "For as much as you do pray it, they truly will not let it pass. People like me did not ask for this regime to come, but do they insist that they have the best interest of us in mind while rockets come down upon us and they hide in their bunkers. These leaders are a people far from *Hashem* and who have taken money and power as their idols. They are beyond any sort of good, they cannot even be called Jewish in belief as much as they are like the Canaanites."

"Perhaps it's just the Christian heart within me, but even your own elites are not beyond salvation, my friend."

"You would be very foolish to believe that demons like those could be saved."

"I am a holy fool in that case," Derby acknowledged. "A man whose religious beliefs have gotten the most of him… I was not always such a man… I was baptized Catholic, raised Christian, but never did I have a sincere sense of belief until I felt salvation. I was a despondent young man, a war veteran who had integrated back into civilization, but not warmly received nor prepared for life after war. I had… regrets about the course of the war, what I thought I had entered in to fight for, a sense of adventure and patriotism to the British Empire, to a firm realization and questioning of my actions in that war… the lives that I had taken, the death that had surmounted in both innocent and combatants, of all that bloodshed… why did it have to happen and for what reason? I grew into despair, thinking about the past, when I should have been present in the home with my children. My children certainly suffered because of my actions, and it's affected them. Since my conversion nearly ten years ago, I've thought to relieve my guilt in my son by raising his own son at his request to give him a sense of liberty and freedom to live his life, but even then, I question whether what I am doing to atone for those sins is for the best. I returned to family life when I should have been set to retire and explore the world instead, to instead raise my grandson… and I raise him with a clear mind, a healthy mind, and as I would have raised my own son, my eldest son, Everest." He paused and then laughed, "Named for the highest peak on the world because my wife wanted him to be raised up high… I lambasted him when he made the same mistakes as me, to conceive out of wedlock, and I am so critical of him that I should not have been his parent. I was… not fit to be his father, but he will never know of the forgiveness I wished for from him."

The man looked across from him. Derby was looking to his side and then slowly shifted his gaze back towards his host. He then looked down.

"I'm sorry," Derby expressed, "I shouldn't have said what I had about my personal life. It was not my place to impose…"

"The words have been spoken, and they were better said then kept to yourself," the man stated. "What do you intend to do when you leave this shelter?"

"I need to get to Jerusalem, or any path that can get me out from this country. I need to travel to Iraq."

"Why?"

"I'm on the hunt," Derby expressed, "for a wanted man – a true criminal. A Nazi war criminal who I intend to capture and return to the authorities for trial."

"For what reason?"

"So that he may face justice…"

"I thought Christians believed that true justice was in the judgement."

"A Christian also believes that the powers of Heaven have empowered the states to exercise justice and laws…"

"Not unless those states have usurped power," the man expressed. "Nearly all the countries of this world have in some way rebelled against the divine right of majesties in their time. What gives you cause to believe they hold legitimate power and not the power of man?" Rather than wait for a response, the man then also said, "Let him go – rest your heart… return to your grandson."

"I… I can't," Derby expressed, "I still have guilt within me that needs to rest first. Can you help me reach Iraq?"

"What do you have in mind?"

"All I would need is a horse, nothing more reliable than that. I have money to buy supplies once I reach a town, and I'll be able to make contact with my people too. I can pay you well…"

The man looked at Derby and nodded, "I'll take you into town tomorrow, you can make contact with your people. I have no horse to offer you, but I've enjoyed our time here together tonight and it is now dark… I hope I can offer you water, food, and shelter for the night."

"I am in your debt."

"Not necessary," the man responded, standing up. "The bedroom upstairs on the left is open to guests. You will find a bath in the next room – tomorrow morning, I will take you into Jerusalem."

"Thank you, my friend."

Act 4, Prologue

Derby stood in front of a table in a trench bunker as it vibrated with artillery fire from a distance. He looked upon a map ahead of him with tokens laid out, his own icy breath before him. He was dressed in his battle dress but overtop he wore a white smock and white trousers. He also wore gloves. Next to him was his helmet in white camouflage on his right and a lantern on his left. The structure vibrated again, and Derby was joined by three others who entered into the bunker, two of whom were similarly dressed as Derby and the third of whom wore a different uniform. The third person wore a green winter jacket and helmet. Around his neck he had a dark green scarf and around his waist he had a combat belt with pouches. He also had a belt that crossed his chest and tactical vest with additional pouches. He wore baggy green trousers tucked into light brown boots. One of the two men that was with Derby was a familiar sight to him by his dark brown moustache but noticeably tired and baggy eyes – Otto Murdoch, now First Lieutenant. An older male in the same uniform but without a helmet was with them and took lead to approach the map with the other two at his side. Two more older men in white uniform entered the bunker to join the other officer. Derby stood in salute as the senior officers entered the room.

"At ease, Cabernet," one of the senior officers remarked.

"After a moment of discussion with our American colleague, we've agreed to disagree" the other senior officer said. "This salient is getting out of hand. We're to stop its advance any further and push them back tonight. Captain Davis and his armor will lead the charge. We've got good reason to believe that they've pushed as far as they can for now, so we're going to hit them hard and hit them fast. We move forward with the battle plan as discussed, so unless there any more questions…?"

"No, sir."

"As I thought, then you are dismissed, sirs."

Derby left with Otto, while the American officer remained with the senior officers in the bunker. Later that same day, Derby caught sight of his companion as he grouped around his men in the snowy trenches. A thick snow covered the ground around them, even at their feet in the six-foot-deep trench they were in now. Their breath was visible before them, and all their fair skinned faces as pale as the snow around them, and cheeks red.

"What if they've not lost wind?" a soldier asked Otto.

"The chances are slim, mate, but a little resistance can be expected. We're not on our own though – American tanks will be leading the charge while we follow through from behind. The Germans have had us on the run for days now, but they've surely ran out of steam."

"And if they haven't?"

"Then we fight as we've been doing so since the start of this war, and we won't stop fighting. I can't guarantee you that everything will be alright, but we stick together then we will get through this just fine. We're not alone in this either."

"I've heard stories… about what the Germans do to you if they capture you. They massacred an entire company not too far from here."

"Don't you worry about that, lad. You just keep your mouth shut and your chin high, and remember, you let me or the captain do any talking."

"I'm scared, leftenant."

"So am I son, always have been. It's a normal response right before a brilliant fight. I recall being that way all the way to North Africa when I was first deployed. It wasn't until I was in trenches like these that it became so real, an impending doom, but I tell you what, you stick behind your mates here, then it'll all be alright. That's what got me through it all, nobody rubbing salt in anybody's wounds. We're all in this together, and we'll get through it together."

A whistle sounded off from the distance.

"Alright, that's cue," Otto expressed. "Everyone into position – as soon as that armor rolls forward, we're on the move."

The soldiers dispersed amongst the trenches. Artillery fire proceeded to volley positions ahead of them, prompting a response from the opposing forces. Derby and Otto took positions nearby each other.

"You've certainly have a way with words to motivate your men," Derby acknowledged, "my men too."

"They're my boys," Otto remarked. "I wouldn't want them to feel anything other than reassured that we're going to get through this to the end of the war, together for victory."

U.S. Sherman tanks rolled forward from where they hid in their own trenches, while others in repair remained in place and opened fire across the battlefield. Derby and Otto stood up and moved forward into positions behind spruce trees in the forest. Any sort of visibility ahead was diminished by fog and even above it was difficult to see through the grey clouds. Across the frontline, through the fog of war, Derby could see some German panzers spread out close to a few hundred meters ahead and at least a total kilometer wide. Rapid gunfire tore through the land from beyond the mist and artillery fire continued hit random locations around the battlefield. The Shermans advanced the line forward and engaged the armor ahead, while at the same time the rest of the Norwich regiment pushed up and took positions that came into contact with infantry.

"Move up!" Derby shouted.

Derby advanced further and began to lay down some fire with his carbine rifle. He stuck to the right of the battlefield close to Otto who was on the left of the battlefield, close to his men whereas Derby's men were to the right.

The tanks shot their cannons into the mist while panzers appeared from unpredictable points in the battlefield. These panzer tanks were not just any tanks, they were King Tiger heavy tanks with increased armor and size.

Derby ducked down as a Sherman tank nearby detonated into a ball of fire as a King Tiger shot it from afar.

"Let's get those anti-tank missiles out!" Otto shouted. "Show it to 'em!"

Some of the soldiers equipped and aimed anti-tank weapons to combat the tanks. At most at this time there were four King Tiger tanks in the vicinity, two panzer tanks destroyed for three Sherman tanks. Additional enemy soldiers advanced through the fog to take position in trenches further ahead. They opened fire and returning fire came from the British-American line. Derby observed that as some of the soldiers equipped the bazookas, they became primary targets.

The battle resumed in this position as the Sherman tanks dueled the King Tiger tanks and were able to square up the ones deployed ahead of them. At the same time, German soldiers equipped panzerfausts and attempted to repel the advancing American tanks. Eventually though, the Germans retreated.

"Move forward!" Otto shouted. "We've got them on the run!"

Derby saw Otto move forward as another King Tiger tank nearby rolled forward. Its machine gun fire targeted Otto, prompting Derby to quickly rush towards an anti-tank rocket launcher on the ground and pick it up. He aimed the rocket towards the tank and fired it; the rocket hit the ground in front of the tank causing dirt to erupt up but causing a distraction and new target in Derby.

"*Darby!*"

The tank rolled forward slightly to readjust its aim. The cannon shot towards him and Derby slid into a trench and kept down. Suddenly, a Sherman tank rolled forward and neutralized the King Tiger.

Derby looked over the trench to see the heavy tank was destroyed and then ran forward to join Otto halfway.

"You crazy bastard, you nearly got yourself killed," Otto remarked. "Keep your head together, *Darby*, this isn't the time for heroics."

"We've got to watch out for each other, don't we?"

"Not in a way that'll get yourself killed, mate. Let's go."

Derby and Otto moved forward as the tanks rolled in. Through the fog, Derby could see entrenched troops in pillboxes and additional King Tiger tanks also entrenched. The artillery fire from the enemy side began to ramp up again too. They took position in a fox hole or crater created from artillery fire.

"Not even Normandy was this fickle," Derby expressed. "This is madness, Otto."

"Keep it together," Otto encouraged. "Don't let it intimidate you…"

"I'm not…"

Derby and Otto continued to return fire from their position as the tanks continued to duel. Suddenly, through the fog, another four King Tiger Tanks, totalling seven, appeared. They both ducked down as an artillery shell nearly fell upon them.

"Did you see that?!" Derby questioned. "They've got seven of those beasts! How're we supposed to crack that?"

"I reckon it's time to get creative, Mr. Cabernet. If we don't in the least hold this line, then they'll overrun us and we'll be finished."

Derby reloaded his rifle and then peaked out the foxhole again as he continued to lay down some returning fire. Otto stood up from the foxhole and moved forward, taking cover in another foxhole. He noticed that Otto's men took lead and also pushed forward, some of them being immediately wounded in the process and others sniped and killed. Derby stayed put and continued lay down fire, looking towards his men as they stayed in place. He reloaded his rifle and then took in a deep breath before he made a dash forward.

"Otto, this isn't looking good. Half of our tanks are shredded, and who knows how many more of these monstrosities the krauts have on the other side of the fog. I reckon we retreat and get out of dodge with whatever tanks and men we have left."

"Now's not the time for cowardice, *Darby*," Otto rebuked. "Come on man, for King and..."

Derby immediately raised his forearm to cover his face as an artillery shell landed beside Otto. The explosion pushed Derby over but left him unscathed even by shrapnel. Lieutenant Murdoch on the other hand was nowhere to be seen in what remained, an extension of the crater that Derby lay in. He lay back in the hole for a moment, gun resting at his side as he looked at his hands and then around him. He breathed sharply and quickly, chest raising as though his heart would escape him with every beat. He felt around his side for his rifle, took hold of it, and with trembling hands looked ahead as machine gun fire, artillery fire, and tank fire continued through.

Derby observed barbed wire lined along parts of the frontline on the German side, overtop the pillboxes. The only opening that he could see was through a crater that breached through. He stayed put as the Shermans continued to fight the entrenched King Tiger Tanks. The other four tanks were nowhere to be seen. Derby concentrated fire towards the pillboxes as he aimed his rifle towards them.

Suddenly, an artillery shell hit in front of Derby's location, creating a cloud of smoke that gave him a chance to hide behind a tree and then slip into the trenches that the enemy had formally used. There, Derby took hold of a panzerfaust but rather than aim it towards the King Tiger Tank, he aimed towards the pillboxes to cause them to collapse and become unusable. He then focused on a King Tiger tank closest to him with his last rocket and caused the turret to explode.

The company pushed forward and took position in the trenches. Derby positioned himself with some of the men.

"We've got five tanks ahead of us, and little support our way," Derby remarked. "What do we have?"

"We can fetch some more anti-tank munitions," a soldier suggested.

"Alright, you and you go salvage what you can. I want you two to salvage what you can from these trenches."

Meanwhile, the remainder of the Shermans continued to win the uphill battle against the entrenched Tiger Tanks, one on each side. Derby picked up another panzerfaust in the trenches while the rest of the men held the line and the artillery fire began to cease. He found some rocket ammunition, loaded the panzerfaust with a rocket and took another with him to find a position that he could target the King Tiger Tank on the right. First, Derby took out the pillbox to the left, and then next he proceeded to a better position where he could aim and fire towards the turret. The King Tiger Tank exploded, and Derby retreated back as he equipped some more rockets.

Some non-entrenched King Tiger Tanks moved in from ahead as the German defenses loosened up and began to open fire towards the line. They engaged the Sherman tanks as they moved in too. Derby took a rocket, aimed it at the nearest King Tiger Tank, and was able to hit its side. The turret then moved towards them and blew a shot towards the trenches. The damage of the shell caused the trench to become exposed at that section. He then paused as he heard the turret adjust its aim, almost as though it was positioning its aim closer to Derby's location. In a heartbeat, Derby came out of the way and fired the rocket towards turret of the tank, causing it to detonate before it could kill him.

Before Derby could retreat, he noticed that there was another series of machine guns even behind this line. He took note and then retreated as enemies called him out. He reloaded his rocket launcher with the last pair of rockets he had. He moved back towards the right where a King Tiger Tank dueled with a

Sherman tank. The Sherman tank detonated into a ball of fire as Derby positioned himself to launch a rocket towards the heavy tank. The rocket blew the side of the tank and created a rupture of smoke, but as the smoke dissipated, Derby saw the turret aim towards him. He raised his rocket launcher up once more and fired the last round. Derby was then blown back by the shot of the cannon directly in front of him.

Derby recovered from the blast and looked around for his panzerfaust, but it was destroyed. He left it behind and then returned to the center of the trenches where he saw the remaining two mobile heavy tanks take position on the left and right behind the trenches., while the entrenched tank of the left continued to assert control.

"We're back," soldiers reported. "We brought ammo."

"What about the anti-tank rocket launchers?" Derby questioned. "These won't do in a German one."

"We'll go back for one."

"Never mind, give those here," Derby expressed, taking two of them in hand. He put one in each pouch and then took his rifle from nearby.

"What're you going to do?"

"Stay put and form a line here," Derby expressed. "I want this line held, corporal! Support what armor we have left, if it goes, you go too!"

"Yes, sir."

Derby put the last rocket into a pouch behind him. He then took his rifle and went forward towards the edge of the trench and began to assess the line. Very little returning fire came from the trench directly ahead as most of the enemy soldiers had treated to the machine gunners, so when the time was right, he removed himself from the trench and went forward towards the crater in the frontline. Derby slipped into the trenches and began to open fire at hostiles on his left and then his right. He took them by surprise and then fought his way forward towards the entrenched tank.

Once at the entrenched tank, Derby took one of the rockets and began to dig a small hole behind the tank. He placed the rocket and then took a grenade. He charged the grenade and then disappeared from the blast zone. The resulting blast tore the engine of the tank and caused it to detonate into a ball of fire. Not too far from where he was, another of the tanks was in position above the edge of the trench. He created another hole in the snow, placed a rocket and grenade, and then moved out of dodge as he went towards the right.

Derby aimed his rifle forward as German soldiers confronted him through the trenches. Some even hopped down from above to reinforce their comrades. Derby opened fire towards them as he placed some pressure on them. Meanwhile, the few American tanks that remained moved in and opened fire at the machine gun pits on the other side. At that point, the artillery fire from the German side resumed its barrage. Derby continued to aim his rifle down the trench as the German soldiers began to retreat.

Suddenly, an artillery shell from whichever side hit ahead of him and collapsed the trench. Derby diverted into the trench cavern and resumed to fight Germans inside. They soon fled and opened up space for him to pass through and come out from the other side. From where Derby now was, they increased their resistance to stop him from getting to the last tank.

Derby stayed put from where he was. He could feel the vibration of the tank as its cannon fired towards the British-American line. The trenches shook again as another artillery shell hit close by. He took the chance to exit the cavern and take cover behind some crates. The tank was not too far from him. He took the rocket from his pouch, weighed it in his hand, and then decided to throw it towards the tank. The rocket hit the side of the tank and did not go off, but the toss of that rocket was met with the toss of a grenade. Derby stayed put as the grenade set off the rocket, and he stayed where he was as the German soldiers continued to fire towards him until it was time to retreat.

The British soldiers hopped into the trenches and a sergeant took Derby's hand and helped him up. "Are you alright, Leftenant?"

Derby looked at him and replied, "Just fine…"

"Where's Leftenant Murdoch?"

"Dead, sergeant."

"I'm sorry, sir."

"Don't be sorry for me," Derby expressed, seeing his disappointment. "We've done a hell of a job here – Otto, Leftenant Murdoch, would have been proud. Good job, all of you."

Later that day, Derby was approached by the senior officers as he assessed the wreckages. He looked towards them as they approached. He stood before them, eyes and chin slightly down.

"Leftenant Cabernet," the senior officer remarked, "I've heard of your hand in this work. Good job, son."

"Thank you, sir."

"It's a shame of what happened to Leftenant Murdoch," another senior officer remarked. "His company also took the most casualties."

"We're consolidating his company into your command, Leftenant Cabernet."

"Thank you, sir."

"I'm also nominating you for a V.C., leftenant. Your work here will not be forgotten, I assure you."

"Thank you, sir…"

Act 4, Scene 1

Derby mounted a saddle upon his horse, a black Arabian horse with a precious, clean coat. The saddle contained pouches, a blanket, mat, and other equipment. He lifted himself up onto the saddle and placed his feet into the stirrups of the horse. He then took the reins into his gloved hands and looked down to his side at the man who had sheltered him in the desert. The man approached Derby with his semiautomatic rifle behind him, and Derby's automatic rifle in his hand.

"Thank you for your assistance, *Dariy*," Derby remarked. "It's been a pleasure to meet your acquaintance, and I hope that weapon is of better use for you than it was to me."

"I have no need for such weapon, my friend," Deriy replied, attempting to hand it to him. "You are in better need of it, to defend yourself."

Derby took the automatic rifle into his hand. He looked at it, seeing that it was cleaned. He then took the strap and brought it around his neck and shoulder. Deriy then handed him two magazines that Derby had left behind. Derby took these and placed them into his pouch.

"Are you ready to head off then?" Deriy asked.

"I have enough food for three to four days, plenty of water, and assurance that my people should meet me in Baghdad," Derby remarked. "I need to hurry to my next destination, and I have no other way to exit from Israel with the authorities after me."

"May *Hashem* be with you on your journey then."

"And also with you, in your home," Derby replied, nodding to Deriy. He then kicked his horse and departed from the side of the highway they were parked on. Rather than continue on the road, Derby rode into the desert where he carefully navigated his way through some rocks to reach up the slope of a plateau. Once at the top, Derby looked out to the desert beyond and took the bandana around his neck to raise it up to cover his face. He then looked behind to see Deriy depart in his pickup truck, and then he kicked his horse off to ride forward into the Jordan desert.

The Jordan desert was a vast desert east of the Jordan River. The desert was several times as large as the Judean desert in the West Bank, but rather than consist of rugged hills and mountains, consisted of smooth sandy plains. Derby rode east and crossed into Jordan through the Jordan River, and he soon found a road that had Arabic letters. Rather than follow the road and where it would take him, Derby stuck to his compass and continued to travel east for the rest of the day.

Within the day, Derby travelled approximately one-hundred kilometers, and then each day afterwards, he travelled another one-hundred kilometers on average so that on the seventh day he travelled about 700 kilometers in total and was now in Iraq on the outskirts of its capital city. He stayed in the wilderness that entire length of time, hunting the wildlife and allowing his horse to occasionally graze on the grass near farmland, feed on adjacent vegetation and shrubs, and drink from the irrigation trenches and oases on his way through. Derby would eat the minimum he would have to in this time, doing what he could to prioritize feeding his horse so that she could make the journey. The Arabian horse was an Oriental breed, capable and used to travel through desert, and a fast horse at that too. An average horse could travel between sixty to eighty kilometers in the day, whereas an Arabian horse traveled one-hundred kilometers on average and up to one-hundred twenty on better days.

For the seven days that Derby travelled through the desert, the nights reached degrees as low as five degrees Celsius (forty-one Fahrenheit), and during the day, the warmest it became was twenty-five Celsius (seventy-seven Fahrenheit). Most of the days were cloudy, or partly cloudy, and only during the midweek did the sunshine through to dominate the land. On this day, Derby travelled less distance to account for the exhaustion of his horse. The journey towards Baghdad took Derby along the flood plains of the Euphrates River where he kept to the road and was able to travel quicker through the countryside and finally reach the city limits.

Baghdad was a large city, much larger than Tel Aviv or Jerusalem, and its city buildings were plentiful and rectangular, but rather than pure white like snow as it was in Israel, they were tanned structures that blended into the landscape of the desert. Similar to Tel Aviv and Jerusalem, the city was modern for this time period, with vehicles and pedestrians in modern clothes. Eventually, Derby reached where he needed to be in the city centre, stopping at British Embassy. His horse entered into the courtyard of the embassy gardens where guards immediately pointed their weapons towards Derby who raised his hands up.

"Put your guns down, boys," Derby expressed in his English accent.

"Identify yourself!"

"Derby Martel de la Cabernet, gents," Derby loudly stated. "I'm here to meet with my board of executives."

The guards murmured between themselves, while additional guards appeared and pointed their weapons from all points around the courtyard, including the second-floor veranda. Eventually, some diplomats exited the building and looked down below. Derby looked at the men in suits. Suddenly, a man in a suit who Derby recognized stepped out, Herman Miller, and he looked at Derby for a moment until Horace Turner stepped out as well. Horace immediately noticed Derby.

"Dear Lord," Horace expressed, "put your guns down, it's Mr. Cabernet."

At that moment, Herman spoke to the man next to him, who then spoke to the man next to him. Eventually, one of the gentlemen in the group addressed a senior guard who signalled his men to put their weapons down. At that point, Derby lowered his arms and a single guard approach Derby's horse as he hopped down. He took a lead around his horse's neck and gave it to the guard, and then Derby stumbled towards the main entrance of the embassy where he was welcomed inside.

Derby met with Horace and the rest of the executives soon afterwards in the main lobby where he greeted all of them.

"I'm glad to see you gentlemen have made it," Derby expressed. "Have you done as I told?"

Herman looked at the others while Horace stared Derby head on. Herman then stepped forward and said, "Mr. Cabernet, even though you told us, it was the agreement of this advisory council that have a discussion beforehand to think this decision through…"

"There is nothing to discuss, Mr. Miller," Derby expressed, stepping forward with a limp. "All assets are to be liquidated and sold to the Iraqi government as I instructed."

"It was not us, but them who advised we wait to meet with you here first…" Herman expressed, nudging towards the British diplomats behind them.

Derby looked towards them and then towards Horace. "Very well," he expressed, looking past Horace and then focusing on him. "Mr. Turner, please reach out to Iraqi authorities on this matter to arrange for a meeting. I will deal with these drones."

"Very good, Mr. Cabernet," Horace responded, leaving.

"Mr. Cabernet," a diplomat greeted, stepping forward and shaking his hand.

"Hello," Derby greeted, shaking his hand and then two others in the group of six.

"Hugh Packer," the last greeted, "British Ambassador to Iraq. Your friends here tell me that you have a business venture with the Iraqi government, but your appearance tells me that perhaps it was some sort of other adventure… You look like Lawrence of Arabia in that garb."

"I've travelled across the desert for the past seven days, and least of all the countries I did travel in was in the Arabic peninsula," Derby answered. "You wish to dissuade me in my business venture, but least of all organizations I am likely to listen to, the British government cannot deter me."

"All due respect, Mr. Cabernet, it is your own organization, and even if it is not a British one, it is in British interest to express the possible ramifications of doing business with the Ba'athist government."

"The ramifications are that if I do not sell these assets now, it could be a days away from being seized as they already were elsewhere in the country in 1961," Derby answered. "The only advice I see the British government give me is to withhold assets for their gain, so that I may lose in the future."

"The Ba'athist government has made it clear to the British government that it has no interest in doing so. We are familiar with the number of leases Cabernet Corporation owns in oil fields in these lands, and the transfer of sale of this land to the Iraqi government would provide a member of OPEC, the Organization of Petroleum Exporting Nations, with control of oil fields that used to sell outside of this cartel. Currently, Iraq has the third largest oil reserves in the world behind Saudi Arabia and the United States. The fourth and fifth countries being OPEC members in addition to Saudi Arabia. Iraq is one of the few markets in which colonial investments have been held on to, and now you wish to sell them back to the Iraqi government? Are you mad?"

"Not mad, Mr. Commissioner," Derby answered, taking a drink of water from his canteen, "and don't believe this is a brash decision on my part… I've spent enough time to think it over…"

"Well, what you haven't had the time to think about is our proposal," the ambassador said, snapping his fingers. An assistant brought a dossier and passed it to him. "The current worth of your assets in this country are as such. Iraq Petroleum is offering the market value plus 150%. What is the price that you have set, or plan to set to the Iraqi government?"

"I haven't got a price, sir," Derby answered.

"What?"

"I said I haven't got a price, at least not one in U.S. dollars or British pounds."

"Mr. Cabernet…" Herman interrupted.

"Silence," Derby directed.

"Is this some sort of joke?" a man next to the ambassador questioned. Derby looked at him. "Your time in the sun must have done a number on your head, son."

"No, my decision was final before I went into the desert," Derby answered, looking at him suspiciously. "I don't take it by your tone that you're a part of the diplomatic corps, I take it you are Iraq Petroleum Company?"

"Very observant of you. Yes, I'm with I.P.C.," the executive answered. "What do you intend to receive in exchange for these assets of yours, if not money?"

Derby shrugged as he held both hands to his canteen and said, "It wouldn't be appropriate of me to talk with another interest group what I intend to offer to their rivals."

"It is *something* though?" the executive questioned.

"Of course."

"What then, is more valuable to you then money?"

"Nothing of which a I.P.C. exec, or a diplomatic team could understand," Derby answered, "and to your next question, it is nothing of which the I.P.C. or the entire British government could hope to offer me in this land. On the topic however, and I'm not much of a businessman, never have been… that's why I have these gentlemen with me and advising on the business of the company, but what I have been sure of is that the nationalization of oil in this country is not over. The Iraqi government does intend to seize your remaining assets, and it will happen soon. However, as gentle as they may be, when it does happen, it may very well provoke a response from the antiquated imperium, like it did in Suez. Her Majesty's government will then send her loyal boys in green to the frontlines to fight, so maybe then, when the dust has settled and the greed of the empire is satiated, maybe then will you see what was once mine now yours. Until then, you can back right off."

"You truly are mad, Cabernet," the executive responded. "Just as everyone says you are – you've lost it, mate. From a noble explorer of Her Majesty's realms to a bitter and resentful old man who has lost his ways. Your ramblings on the radio and telly are just that, aren't they? The deluded ramblings of an old man... You ought to be institutionalized."

"Wouldn't that be convenient for you," Derby remarked, putting his canteen away in the pouch next to his pistol. He looked to his executives with him as they looked at his pistol and appeared uncomfortable. "Why don't we leave now, gentleman, somewhere far from this unholy place, to a hotel where Mr. Turner can return the Iraqi delegation to us and we can negotiate our terms with them."

"Y-yes, Mr. Cabernet."

"Good evening, gentlemen," Derby remarked before he parted.

•

Little more than an hour later, Derby appeared in a suit that was provided for him. The suit was brown with a fine very light blue dress shirt. He was showered, shaved, and sat down at the head of a table with his executives on his left and right of him. A few minutes later, Derby and his delegation stood up as the Iraqi party arrived. Derby turned to his side as the leader of the Iraqi party, a man with very tanned skin and a thick dark moustache over his lips in a dark suit approached Derby.

"Mr. Cabernet, a pleasure to meet you," the man spoke. "I am Bashar Al-Malik, Minister of Oil here in Iraq."

"A pleasure to meet you, minister," Derby responded.

Each men sat down at their side of the table afterwards.

"Mr. Cabernet, I understand that you wish to concede ownership of your share of British concessions in Iraq for a small price," the minister stated. "Unfortunately, the government has a policy in place by which no foreign company shall receive no concessions for their oil leases at this time. Why do you intend to sell these assets to us?"

"I have no interest in these assets," Derby answered. "Cabernet Corporation has oil field projects in Canada that it wishes to use these funds to aid, and otherwise, the cost of foreign management has become too great, in my opinion."

"You must understand that we cannot pay full-price."

"Oh, I am very aware," Derby replied, looking towards Horace, "and we are prepared to put a generous price of less than fifty percent."

"Less than fifty percent is still too much to pay…" the minister said, receiving the papers as they made their way around. "We would be unable to provide that…" The minister read the paper. "Mr. Cabernet… this is less than fifty percent…"

"Yes, like I said…"

The minister looked thoroughly at what was before him. He then looked to his colleagues as he passed it to a person beside him.

"I am not interested in money," Derby remarked. "Since the end of the war, this world has become obsessed with capital as if money is all that makes the world turn on its axis. If it were up to me, and if I had no children, I would want nothing more than to see Cabernet Corporation liquidated and this tremendous power and responsibility taken off my shoulders, but alas, since my father died… unfortunately, before I could return from the war… it has been a weight that I've been asked to carry, although not alone. Cabernet Corporation is prepared to release all our assets to the Iraqi government, in exchange for assistance in the location of a fugitive believed to be in this country at this very moment. This fugitive travelled from Israel, through Jordan, to Iraq, and he has company with him. He has ties to a secret society as well, and so whatever intelligence the Iraqi government has, and whatever assistance they should provide us, I am prepared to provide half of our assets now, and the latter half later if they assist me to provide passage and protection through this quest."

"What do you have in mind, Mr. Cabernet?"

"I would need two platoons in the least of soldiers, transport, and guidance through this country as I search for this vandal."

"Your request is very strange and peculiar, Mr. Cabernet..." the minister said, looking to his colleagues. "I will need to consult with the president, but I believe that some sort of arrangement to those liking could be made."

"A successful negotiation then, minister," Derby thanked. "Very much appreciated... should I receive what I need, those oil fields are the Iraqi people's government's."

Act 4, Scene 2

"Hello, Mr. Cabernet, my name is Hussein Anwat, Mulazim of the Intelligence Company," a man greeted Derby, shaking his hand. The man appeared to be around the same age as him with dark hair and a thick moustache like the minister. He also had dark tanned skin. "I've been assigned to be your guide in Iraq, and take you wherever you need to be."

"Very much glad to meet you, Hussein," Derby replied. "With me is an executive from my company, Horace Turner, here to see me off before he returns to Canada."

"Nice to meet you, sir," Anwat greeted.

"Same here."

"I take it then you've been briefed on our situation," Derby expressed.

"Yes, Mr. Cabernet, I received a briefing on your situation... at least, the details that were provided to us. You are in Iraq to search for a war criminal, a German military officer who killed lots of people during the war?"

"That's correct."

"Where do you suppose he is?"

"Well, here's what I'll fill you in on... His last sightings were in Israel, near Ashkelon and then near Jericho. He's on the hunt, you see – our target is with an archeological team who are associated with a secret society, a former religious order, and they are most like travelling to cells to receive shelter in-between their excavation missions. Otherwise, their most likely location would be at excavation sites; archeological digs."

"What kind of archeology are they interested in? Iraq has many ruins and locations of interest to archeological teams..." Anwat said. "As you may know, Iraq is the land where ancient civilization was born – not too far from here is the ancient city of Babylon and its walls."

"Yes, I am familiar," Derby expressed. "The nature of their investigation is biblical, to do with ancient times from the Bible. I won't go too much into the details as it is nuanced, but my initial question to you and your intelligence team is whether or not there has been any irregular traffic through the country."

Anwat thought for a moment and then answered, "Such a vague question is difficult to answer, but to your specifications, nothing like that. If there was an archeological team though, they should have travelled under discretion of our Ministry of Culture."

"I do not believe this band seek to travel within the constraints of the law," Derby answered. "I've been advised that they are rogue, but not particularly dangerous."

"You say they take cover under a secret society?"

"Something of that sort, a religious order really."

"During the revolution in 1958, the Iraq government outlawed secret societies. Their properties were abandoned, seized, but not regulated. There should be no secret society in Iraq that provides them with sanctuary, but the buildings… there were two such buildings that come to mind, one of which was in Basrah and that was destroyed in a fire. The other is the city, in Baghdad, we could travel there if you'd like to."

Derby looked at Anwat and then over to Horace. He then looked over to Anwat again.

"Very well," Derby stated. "Let's travel to this abode."

"Sounds like you've got a plan ahead of you," Horace remarked. "I'm going to go – let me know when you're done in Iraq. I'll be in the city at the hotel waiting for you."

"Thank you, Horace," Derby replied, shaking his hand and then turning to Anwat. "Let's visit this stronghold."

•

Derby sat in the front passenger seat of a military truck that drove through the streets of Baghdad from the nearby military base. His horse was left behind at this time, but he travelled as the second vehicle in a convoy of four that went south from Baghdad into the countryside.

The secret society stronghold in question was situated in the midst of an overgrown field on a property. Around the perimeter of the property were hedges that were unkempt too. The grass on the front lawn of the property was dried and tall. At the front of the property were statues of lions that led inside. A road came around to a plaza with a dried fountain in the center. A set of steps at the front of the building came up to the tall front doors that went inside. A pediment was positioned above columns at the front of the door. The building, like many buildings in Iraq, consisted of smooth sandstone and the windows on the ground level were tall rectangular windows that were tinted. Above these tall windows were smaller rectangular windows, and then above those were arched windows. All windows had black frames and were inside nooks in the sandstone to create ledges on the exterior side. The building consisted of three partitions, the left and right of which were stuck out slightly and smaller than the central portion. The trucks parked around the front plaza and the soldiers exited the rear of the truck, while Derby exited his side and looked around further. He noticed palm trees at the side of the causeway up to the plaza and around the edges of the property. He then turned around and took a closer look at the building. The exterior walls, consisting of at least two ground-level floors, was tall, and there was no sloped roof but a plain roof.

Derby joined Anwat from his truck as they went to the front doors of the stronghold. As they approached, Derby looked above the front doors to see an emblem. The shape of the emblem was in a hexagon. At the bottom centre of that shape was a mythological creature, half man on the top and half seemingly lion on the bottom half with four legs, clawed paws, and a feline-like tail. The man on the upper half was muscular and had some sort of exotic headdress and beard. In Latin alphabet letters, beneath the beast was written out in capital letters, 'Babylonia'. Above this creature was a sun caricature with wavy sunrays. Derby looked at the emblem and then to the door as Iraqi soldiers cut the chain and then forced the doors open.

The team entered into the foyer of the strange building. The floor consisted of half black marble and half white marble tiled checkered floor. A chandelier hung from the center of the ceiling. On the left and right were smooth sandstone staircases that went up to the second-floor balcony that looked down. The balcony railings consisted of rectangular sandstone balusters. The architecture was rigid and rectangular. Light poured in from overhang windows on the left and right, as well as those from the façade. On the left and right were tall wooden doors that went into the respective wings/partitions those directions. Behind the staircases were three wooden doors that went deeper into this partition.

Derby carried on through and pushed open the door to enter into a central atrium. The walls consisted of both beige and dark tan bricks. This room was square and had a motif of a sun in the center of the sandstone tile floor colored in turquoise, gold and indigo and black colors. Likewise, the motif was bordered with a square frame in those same colors. A chandelier hung from the centre of the ceiling, and overhang windows around the very top. The room had rectangular columns against the walls ahead and behind with cross beams along the second floor. A tall wooden door was directly in front with smaller doors to the sides at a wall that had a slight angle. A small emblem above the tall wooden door resembled the star from the stronghold of the cult from Rome, tall triangular horns and a lower tall triangular jaw, and just those triangles with no other additional components

166

except for a pair of small dots like eyes beneath the center of the horns. Additional small sets of doors were on the side of this room as well.

Derby pushed through the large set ahead of him and entered into an even larger room on the other side. Unlike the manor in Rome, this room was not a ballroom but resembled both a church and a parliament. Immediately ahead of him were three seats that faced an open rectangular space in the center of the room with checkered floor. Behind these seats were banner stands with navy blue velvet banners facing away from Derby. On the left and right were seats, some in the corner, and then the majority on the side like the seats in a movie theater. There were two stories of seats on either side, a middle aisle between them. At the end of the aisle on the left was a golden chair with royal navy-blue cushions and a podium in front of it. Behind the seats on the left and right, on both sides and floors, were tinted windows with curtains. The balcony railing on the gallery on the second floor consisted of sandstone and had a checkered pattern to them. Directly ahead, at the other side of the room, was a slightly raised platform with three golden chairs, the one in the center of which was larger than any other chair, like a throne. The gold seats next to it were smaller than even the one with a podium to the left. Beside these seats were a few chairs pointed inward. Behind the throne and these seats were dozen more seats in a slight arc that looked inward too. Behind these seats was an organ. On the left and right of the organ were overhang windows at the very top of the wall, and rectangular columns between them. In the midst of these columns and below the windows were depictions of tall figures in ancient Near East dress with long hair and beards. They appeared almost like ancient Egyptian figures in their drawing, and they faced inward towards the organ. Above the organ was a depiction of the star of Moloch in full, with the additional triangles. As Derby entered into the room, he looked at the banner and saw the star symbol once more. At the corners of the room were aisles on an angle that led to archways with velvet curtains and secluded rooms at every corner of this large room, the ones beside the throne being large, on the side like the rooms of a sacristy in a church. Finally, Derby came around to the center of the room where there were three objects, the object in front and facing towards the throne was a gold-colored chest. Behind that chest in the very center of the room was a square display case that was empty, and behind that and facing the three seats and banner was an empty lectern. Around these items were candelabras, as was around much of the room. Finally, the ceiling in the room, above the overhang windows was arched inward to display a mosaic – the depictions of the mosaic were almost fitting to be Babylonian with depictions of temples, mythical half-lion, half-boar, and even half-man, half-bull beasts, the cultic star, and silhouettes of people in dark blue. Across the upper frame of the mosaic were words written in some sort of semitic script.

"Is this what you were looking for?" Anwat questioned.

"In a certain way, it is," Derby expressed, looking around the assembly in astonishment. "What did you say this place was, or belonged to?"

"I believe it was a freemason lodge, built in 1920 during the time of British rule," Anwat answered, "and as I said, freemasonry along with other secret societies were outlawed in 1958."

"No, this isn't a freemason lodge," Derby answered, looking at the symbol on the banner. "Perhaps at a time, I can believe so. The end days of the British empire were infested with freemasonry at every corner, once the life force of liberalism across the West, but with changing times so to did freemasonry either die, or was replaced... This place is so much larger than the one I had come across in Rome. What a chance to be in one when it is abandoned – what secrets may have been left behind."

"From the reports that I referenced, this space was already searched and its inhabitants took all that they could before they fled."

"When did they flee? With whom?"

"It does not say in the report."

"And this script above us, is it Aramaic?"

Anwat looked and squinted and then looked back at Derby.

"Does not appear to be, but I can't read Aramaic, sir."

"I would imagine, given the Babylonian pagan theme in here," Derby expressed. "I'm going to have a look around and see what I can find…"

Derby walked towards the aisle going to the room behind curtains on the left when he noticed that beneath the large figures depicted at the back of the room, there were small figures on the ground level depicted in the stone, also facing inwards. On both sides, there were at least six figures in total. Derby took mental note and then walked through the curtains to enter into a medium-sized room with a staircase that went up to the gallery above. The rest of the room consisted of bookshelves, cupboards, and wardrobes. As Anwat had said, the area was abandoned and items taken away. Derby walked towards the aisle that went towards the room on the right – this room was smaller because it had a set of doors that went into a sub-room.

Derby tugged at the doors to notice they were locked. He attempted to forcibly open them with his hands, but they were well locked with no keyhole. He looked around and then stepped back. He raised his boot and kicked at the middle of the door, below the door knobs several times until the doors finally gave in. He then entered through and came into an office. The chair at the other side of a large and wide desk was gold-colored like the ones in the assembly, specifically the ones beside the throne. In front of this desk were two navy blue cushioned chairs like the ones the audience sat from. Behind the desk were bookshelves and overhang windows where light poured in from outside.

Above the center of the room was a chandelier. There were also candelabras around the room with used white candles. Additional bookshelves were on the left and right next to the desk, which itself was above a raised platform with two steps that came down to the lower half of the room. On the left and right of this half were rectangular display cases that were smashed and its contents taken. Above these display cases, on the walls, were imprints of artwork of some kind that was taken down. He came around to the side with the desk and began to open drawers, which were also empty. Derby tugged at a middle drawer to notice it was locked, but with a bit of force, he was able to pull it out to see nothing on the other side.

"Oh, these penny pinchers have really taken all they can," Derby expressed with a sigh, stepping around to notice the floorboard creaked at his feet. Derby looked at his feet and then above towards a mosaic over the door. The mosaic displayed three figures like the ones outside, except these loomed over people in front who were smaller.

"Hm…" Derby expressed, "how peculiar…"

Derby crouched down and began to tug at the boards in the floor, which were not secured. He was able to remove them bit by bit to expose a crawlspace beneath the office. He climbed down and took a flashlight from his pouch to shine around. The crawlspace when further into the assembly around the organ area and towards the other side. Derby crouched down even more to proceed to walk through, but as he did, he kicked something that was on the floor.

The object rolled forward. Derby shined his light towards where it went and then slowly made his way over. He reached over and picked it up, seeing it to be some sort of scroll. He unrolled the scroll and took notice at the font, it was the same semitic font as used in the mosaic in the assembly, and therefore Derby was unable to read it. He put the scroll back together and then carried it in his other hand as he continued to look around the crawlspace. He came around to the center and saw that the crawlspace narrowed out at the very center into a trench. Derby climbed down and shined high light down the trench, going away from the building to see dark tunnels that curved out to the right.

Derby slowly walked into these tunnels and began to walk through, going for minutes until he finally reached a junction, a fork in the road. He looked both ways and decided to stay to the left. He carried on through and finally began to see some light around the other side. The tunnel began to narrow slightly, but there was enough room for him to duck his head and come out to a ledge. He looked out around him and saw that he was inside a cavern. The light that lit the room poured in through a crack in the ceiling and due to the fact that it was noon, and the sun was out, provided ample lightning to see inside. From where he stood, he could see some seats below around a pit, and behind those were tall statues around eight feet that depicted humans in ancient near-east garments with long hair and beards. These giants carried braziers from chains that were unlit. Derby slowly walked around the edge to come down and see the room.

The cavern room that Derby had entered was large with chiseled stone walls along the sides with archways that formed arcades. In the center of the room was a bonfire pit with charcoal and ashes inside. Derby finished coming down the slope to face a statue directly in front of the tunnel exit. The statue was tall and cast in bronze, depicting a strange anthropoid creature sat on a throne. The feet of the creature was flat, it had greaves around its lower legs and its legs were both spread apart. Its torso was flat with rendition of six-point star in full, plus a sun behind it and an eye in the middle of the star. The statue had grooves around its collar bone. Its arms were spread out at a ninety-degree angle with arm rings around its upper arm and gauntlets around its forearms. Its palms faced outward and had circular markings pointed out. The statue had semicircular wings spread out from its back. Its face was eccentric, face unlike a human or animal, mouth wide open and bulging eyes above an ox-like snout. It had a third eye between both pairs of eyes, except this one had an imprint similar to the ones on the palms of its hands. At either side of the creature's face were drooping ears, and behind those from its head were bull-like horns. The statue faced the chamber pit and a tunnel that went into the cavern and was dark. From within were some more seats, but also the entrance which was caved in. The statue was immense, at least ten feet tall, and all the statues in the room looked towards it with reverence, while Derby looked before it with disgust.

Act 4, Scene 3

Later the same day, Derby left the former freemason lodge and regrouped with Anwat to learn that religious freedoms were respected in the Republic of Iraq, and that Christians were allowed to practice the faith despite being a minority. They made a trip to a local church, and from there to another church, where eventually they were given the approximate location of a monastery that belonged to the Order of St. Athanasius. The information that was provided to them was that the monastery was located to the north of the country in the mountains. The convoy therefore travelled north from Baghdad to Mosul, and the drive took them the rest of the day. They camped in the wilderness on the outskirts of the city, near the ruins of what once was the ancient city of Nineveh, the Assyrian capital. The next day, the trip continued northbound towards the mountains, following the Tigris and going into the mountains. As the roads forced the trucks to travel slower, Derby got out from his passenger seat where he studied the scroll he recovered from the lodge to ride his horse with the team.

As the team ascended the mountain and began to travel through, the weather became more frigid but also the desert sands were replaced with more greenery and trees than they had seen before. After a few more hours into the morning of traversal through dirt and gravel roads, the trucks passed around a mountain to finally reach the secluded monastery in the woodlands of this mountain. The monastery was not a large complex, but it was located directly on the slope that looked downwards to a trench and gulley with a stream approximately two hundred to four-hundred meters below. The slope and monastery had layers with paths and stairs that connected downwards as far as the stream. The monastery was long, but the buildings were slightly narrow and built out tannish-grey stone bricks. The building has no particular architecture, although some of its roofs were domed while others plain. The windows were arched and consisted of glass. From their approach from the west, the sun shined down towards the stone bricks to give them a bright tanned appearance that blended with the tannish-stone cliff walls and sand at the side of the road. A mixture of the desert and greenery was spread throughout the grounds.

Derby rode forward to approach the gate, which he noticed to be open with the left gate collapsed into the road as though someone had broken through. A sign on the right gate read the name of the monastery, Abbey of the Two Twins, in English, Latin, and Greek. A sign on the left gate stated visiting dates and times. Derby entered through and came into the courtyard where he saw a set of doors ahead were wide open. The building in the courtyard was L-shaped with the lower half ahead of him where the main entrance was. Besides the main entrance was a dirt road that climbed upwards further along the slope of the mountain, and on his left was the cliffside wall. Derby rode around and came out to face the trucks. Anwat stepped out of his vehicle with an AK-47 in his hands. Derby rode up to him and took his own provided AK-47 into his own hands, which replaced his FAL due to low ammunition (the ammunition the Iraqi Army had was incompatible with his FAL).

"Be careful, seems as though they may have had some uninvited guests. I suggest your men take position and scout the grounds in case they were not far off. I'll be going inside... do not enter behind me."

"Yes, Mr. Cabernet."

Derby rode back into the courtyard and hopped off his horse. He took the lead and secured it, and then he proceeded towards the doors into the monastery with his weapon raised. He entered through into the small foyer of the monastery with its low ceiling and mosaic at the end of the hall that showed two twin bothers, one with blonde hair and the other with brown hair, each facing each other. They each had halos around their heads and wore long robes. Derby passed the foyer and entered into a corridor adjacent and parallel. He noticed cartridges on the floor, which caused him to take extra caution as he proceeded around the corners and hallways. He then backed up as he heard whispers and the creaks of floorboard up ahead. He came around to a door frame and stayed put, and when the two persons came around the corner, he identified them not as monks, but locals in peasant robes and scarf headdresses, known as keffiyehs. The two adult men one of whom carried a FAL and the other a Sten Mk. 2, and as soon as Derby realized these were Kurdish insurgents, he took his finger to the trigger.

"Stop right there!" Derby shouted, causing them to panic and raise their weapons. Derby opened fire before they could fire back at him, eliminating them and alerting others nearby.

Gunfire erupted from the other side of the monastery as Ba'athist forces engaged with the Kurdish rebels. Derby made his approach around to the corner of the monastery and looked around to find a set of stairs that went down. Before he proceeded downward, Derby turned around the corner to look down the corridor he came around to wait and see, but no rebels came forward. Derby then turned around to the stairs to wait and see, but no rebels came upwards. Finally, Derby moved to the other side of the building to a staircase that went upstairs, and there he waited and then slowly made his approach upwards.

Rebels in the corridor above took notice of Derby and opened fire down the corridor. Derby stayed down as they shot towards him. He then raised his rifle up over his head and returned gunfire. They did the same. He could hear the rebels shout in their own language to each other. After the second round of gunfire from the rebels, Derby did not return gunfire and instead reloaded his rifle and then stayed put. He waited with patience to see what they would do, listening to their whispers. He went down the stairs and took position around the corner where he could either hear them approach from all angles. The rebels still did not approach from the main floor or the basement level, but with a bit more patience, he began to hear them exchange gunfire with the forces below in the courtyard.

Some Ba'athist forces who entered into the main building eventually joined Derby, and he directed them to go ahead towards the basement, while a fireteam stayed put to watch his back. Derby then proceeded up the stairs again, with cautious and quiet steps, peeking around the top of the staircase to see the exposed hostiles. Derby's eyes focused on a rebel left to guard the stairs, and he opened fire first on them with an aimed shot, and then towards the other two in the corridor. A fourth hostile at the end of the hallway opened fire towards Derby, and Derby reacted immediately to exchange fire with them. Once Derby had eliminated these hostiles, he waited a moment before he stood up and proceeded down, looking into the rooms, cells, at the side and then reaching a room at the very end that had a door that led outside. Additional rebels entered through this door, and Derby opened fire at them, causing one to fall over and the other to retreat. Derby pushed forward and then took position from atop of the stairs, opening fire at the hostile who ran on the rooftop below and also seeing additional rebels below at a plaza in front of the church. Across the rooftop was another building attached to the rear of the main building, and there were stairs that went down to a building on the second layer below which was also attached to the main building and accessible from the basement of the main building via a trail. The Ba'athist forces engaged hostiles from this lower building across the courtyard between that building and the church.

Meanwhile, Derby supported from above, firing down at hostiles as they began to choose to retreat from their positions. The monastery continued with a few buildings around the side and even above the dirt road from the main courtyard where the building behind the main building connected with the trail, and another building was at the top of a turn in the road. The hostiles were retreating up a stairway behind the rear building and coming up towards this trail. Derby continued to support the Ba'athist forces from his position as he caught rebels on the run.

However, just as the first group showed up, the ground at Derby's feet began to tremble, and his face sunk and ears twitched. Not too far from where he was, Derby began to hear the creak of iron gears turning and metal screeching. This sound, all too familiar to Derby, was met with the occasional pause and sound of readjustment, an awe-inspiring sound of terror different from the gears, slow but terrifying. Around the corner of the dirt road, a cloud of dust pushed forward and out of that cloud was a modern tank, larger than the Shermans and Crusader medium-sized tanks but more nimble than the Pershing and Churchill heavy tanks. The tank design was unfamiliar to Derby, but roughly resembled that of a Pershing to him, but there was no star at the side of the tank to identify it as American. The tank came around the corner and stayed put as the machine gunner began to open fire towards where Derby was located. Derby immediately ducked down and stayed put as the spray of bullets shattered windows and chipped at the brick walls.

Derby held on to his AK-47 for a moment until he heard that awe-inspiring sound again, prompting him to move out of the way and return into the corridor as the turret readjusted and a shell was fired towards where he hid. The room he was in collapsed entirely. Derby ran down the hall and took cover behind the window as he saw Anwat below.

"Be careful, lads, they've got an American-made tank up that hill!" Derby shouted. "Do we have any sort of anti-tank weaponry?!"

"I did not think that we would come up against a tank," Anwat confessed. "Kurdish rebels are everywhere in these lands, but so are reinforcements. I will have to call for some help!"

Derby ran down the corridor, moving slower for a moment before he paused. He went downstairs and passed a short corridor to reach the door that exited out to a trail besides the slope. He went down the trail and towards a domed structure. He entered inside and saw the Ba'athist forces stayed put. He looked around for a moment, and then double-backed to the trucks parked outside the monastery where he met with Anwat.

"The closest unit is an hour away from our position," Anwat reported.

"What about air support? Surely a jet could support as faster than it would be for some anti-tank support."

"The area around us is too close to risk that danger."

Derby grunted and replied, "Then we'll need to siphon some fuel and find some bottles. There's more than one way to destroy a tank."

Derby returned to the monastery and began to search the rooms. He found seldom that could be useful until he found the kitchen and scavenged some bottles laid aside. He then went to the monk cells and began to collect fabric. With both fabric and these bottles, he tore the fabric and paired the bottles with petroleum from the reserves at the trucks. In total, he produced four petroleum bombs for himself, and left the rest of his ingredients to the Iraqi forces to produce more for themselves. He fitted the Molotov bombs into his pouches, and then approached Anwat.

"The rebels have taken a defensive position in front of the church," Derby expressed, "and from the top of the hill. In North Africa, these were highly effective against Panzer tanks in those days, but less so in the later years of the war when the armor of these tanks grew thicker. They were still cumbersome though and are our only hope in this fight before they push downhill."

"How do you intend to approach the tank, or get close enough to attack it?"

Derby looked towards the rooftop of the monastery main building and then to his side at the cliff wall.

"I'll need a vantage point, somewhere that isn't too dangerous. Just have your men hold the line, and I'll see what I can do."

"Best of luck then to you."

Derby nodded and then walked towards the cliff wall. He put his AK-47 rifle behind him by its sling and then began to climb upwards to lift himself onto a ledge in the cliff. He then began to climb further up to reach another ledge, which led to a slope and then a natural trail that came around to the trees above. From this point, Derby climbed around the side of the cliff and saw the tank ahead at the top of the road. The cannon fired downwards towards the courtyard, causing dirt to shoot upward as it decimated the stone floor. Derby shook his head and then grabbed hold of rock in the cliff to climb even further and then reached the top of the cliff.

From the edge of the cliff, Derby took position by some trees to see that the hostiles were on the approach to ambush them. He stayed put and then took position in the prone position, by a shrub where he counted four, and then eight. Derby took a magazine and placed it beside him, and then with abated breath, he opened fire at the hostiles. Confused, the hostiles dispersed, two went down at that moment, two fled, while four remained behind the trees and were unable to see what had hit them. Derby hit another, and then picked off one more as they attempted to reposition. The rebels shouted out and Derby took the moment to reload his AK-47 as they realized his location. Derby took position behind a thick tree and stayed put as they shot towards him.

Derby returned fire and moved up as they took a moment to reload and reposition. He saw the two hostiles within the woods ahead of him by a few meters. Derby shot at a rebel as he attempted to hide behind a closer tree, grazing him. The other opened fire at Derby, and he stayed put and reloaded his rifle again. He focused on this other rebel as the wounded one stayed put. The rebel shot towards him, and when he was spent, Derby moved forward as he shot towards the rebel. The returning fire grazed the tree that Derby stood behind. Derby put his rifle around his shoulder though as the rebel assumed to move in. Derby took his pistol into his hand and came out from behind to shoot the rebel as he charged him, killing him. The rebel on the ground returned fire at Derby, grazing him too.

From behind the tree, Derby assesses his wound at his thigh. He stayed put and attempted to move out, but the rebel shot towards him. He could hear shouts from the rebels behind. He waited for a moment and then attempted to step out, but as he did, he realized that the rebel that shot towards him was dead – Derby had grazed this rebel's neck and he bled out. Once the area was secured, Derby moved towards the top of the cliff where the tank was. There, Derby assessed the scene and there was only a fireteam between the tank and the building beside them.

Derby took one of the petrol bombs into his hand, placing another beside him, and with a flint lighter, lit the rag and then threw it towards the top of the tank. The bottle splashed fire, some of which poured out besides the fireteam. Quickly, Derby took a step back with the other petrol bomb, hiding behind a tree, he lit the rag and then quickly he threw it towards the tank, hitting the top of it again. Derby took hold of his rifle at this moment and could hear the sound of the turret readjusting.

The rebels opened fire towards him from where they were. Derby looked around the corner for a quick moment, seeing the blackness of the cannon barrel face him, he immediately rushed forward as the cannon fired and hit the slope, causing dirt to crumble down as well as a tree that fell towards the rebels. Derby escaped the cannon fire, although slightly deafened, he turned around to see that the tree obscured the rebels. Derby looked and prepared another petrol bomb, throwing it towards them and then escaping around to slide down the slope of the road. The rebels continued to open fire towards where they thought Derby was, but he approached them from their flank and opened fire at them.

At least one rebel fled back towards the church courtyard, while Derby could hear the shouts of the rebels from within the tank as they panicked. The hatch opened and fire spilled down from the tree inside. A rebel attempted to exit with a rifle, and Derby shot at him and caused him to fall over. The others exited from the tank with raised arms and Derby kept careful watch of them. They then ran down the hill towards the Ba'athist forces while Derby took the last petrol bomb and threw it into the hatch, leaving the tank behind to catch on fire. From the top of the stairs, Derby saw the rest of the Ba'athist forces clean up hostiles as they began to surrender, prompting him to come down and join them as the fighting stopped.

The doors into the church slowly opened, and the monks that hid inside came out and met with the Ba'athist forces led by Anwat. They shook his hand and before long, Derby recognized the leader of the pack, the abbot, as he spoke to Anwat in Arabic. Anwat began to introduce Derby to him, and Derby looked at the abbot. He was an older male with a beard and headdress like the one that the abbot and monks wore in Ashkelon. He was slightly younger than that abbot though, but wore black spectacles and had darker tanned skin.

"A pleasure to meet you," Derby greeted, shaking his hand. "The name is Derby Cabernet."

"What a blessing it is to have had you come when these men came to ransack our monastery," the abbot expressed.

"Trouble with the Kurds? Not a problem to us and glad to make your assistance," Derby expressed. "I'm sure this must not have been the first time…"

"Yes, it is," the abbot explained. "Never in the last decade have they come to us. What reason would they have? We are a small, cloistered community of sheep and goat farmers. Look at the damage they've done on our abbey."

"So what reason did they have to come?" Derby questioned, suspicious, especially as he looked around and could see a figure uphill disappear. "Are they looking for something, or someone?"

The abbot didn't answer.

"Did you have a German pass through here?" Derby asked. "A group that included himself and few others, Catholic priests?"

The abbot stuttered to answer.

"I believe these armed men were most likely sent here to search for them," Derby expressed. "Listen to me, abbot," he said, stepping closer, "where did those men go…?"

"We did not tell the rebels, so why would they go and find them?"

"Just because they did not siphon information from you, doesn't mean they aren't on the hunt," Derby expressed. "Where are they?"

The abbot looked at Derby and then towards Anwat.

"Not too far from here…" the abbot expressed, "they've gone on an expedition on a plateau near here…

"Can you provide an exact location?" Derby questioned.

"Yes…"

"How far is it?"

"Not too far… at least an hour drive…"

"I'll need to get to them at once…"

Act 4, Scene 4

Derby mounted his horse from where it was still tied to its lead in the front courtyard. He then rode off and followed the road that he had travelled with the convoy, stopping at a junction and retrieving a map with the indicated location that the archeological group had gone too. He took an alternative path that rather than exit the mountains, continued through. Derby rode horseback for two hours through the mountains, travelling along narrow roads until he finally exited and came out to a desert plain. From atop of the slope above, Derby looked down and took his binoculars to get a better sight, but there was a strong breeze that blew a mild sandstorm and made it difficult to see through the landscape. He could not see across the desert any sign of an excavation team, causing him to worry. Derby mounted his horse again and proceeded down the slope of the mountain to reach the desert sands.

From within the desert storm, Derby travelled at a slower pace and kept his head down. His horse began to struggle with him, but as they slowly journeyed through the sands, Derby soon became lost and wandered for nearly an hour. Eventually, Derby found himself an exit through the cloud of dust and found himself in the middle of the desert with dunes around him. He took his compass from his pouch and referenced the map and the position of the sun to make a decision to move northeast. Derby travelled up the dune and once at the top, looked below to see another cloud of dust approaching from the northeast, but below between this dune and the next far ahead were some tents positioned around some ruins.

Derby looked down from the top of the dune as he saw some movement around the ruins. Around the perimeter of the ruins were some armed guards in khaki clothes, at least three in total. Around the outskirts of the ruins were two pickup trucks and some horses. He identified at least four to six unarmed persons within the ruins, all of whom wore tan clothes. From afar, the dig site appeared large and consisted of many collapsed walls and trenches. Derby looked down upon the site with sharp eyes, like those of a raven, after which point he saw the sands encroach faster and decided to move.

Rather than face the site head-on, Derby moved around the side to search for an insertion point. He rode his horse around behind a rock, tied its lead behind, and then moved forward to encroach on foot. He moved towards the trucks to identify wooden crates and chests in the rear. He came around to the front of the front-most truck, and then identified a wall in which he could rest upon. From there, Derby took a petrol bomb from his pouch, lit it, and then threw it towards the trucks. The splash of the gasoline doused the rear truck in flames and alerted the guards. He quickly took another one as the closest guard came around to respond. He threw the bottle at the truck, causing it to douse the front of the front-most truck in fire and then turned the corner and aimed his rifle at the guard. The guard, taken by surprise, was immediately struck with the butt of Derby's rifle and fell over. Derby moved forward and took cover as the rest of the team members reacted to the trucks on fire.

"What's going on out there?!" a voice questioned in an English accent. "Get those horses under control!"

Derby looked at the unconscious guard and saw that he carried an Sturmgewehr 44 rifle, a German automatic rifle similar to the AK-47. He went down the side of the wall to come around to the other side where he saw another guard approach. At that moment, between all the shouts, Derby heard the deep voice of shouts in Germans that caused him to pause. He breathed sharply as he lost his focus.

Suddenly, German shouts were met next to him as the guard discovered Derby. He immediately lurched forward to tackle the guard, tipping the Sturmgewehr upwards and causing it to shoot upwards and warn the others in that way too. Derby was able to force the man down as he overpowered him, using his own rifle to knock him out unconscious. Gunfire came towards Derby from ahead, causing him to retreat behind the wall and pick up his rifle from the sand nearby. The gunshots chipped at the bricks at his side. He felt the person come up towards him and decided to retreat further and go back the way he came. As Derby was travelling down the wall, keeping low and running, the pickup trucks blew up and sent a ball of fire upwards.

"Everyone get into cover!" a German-accented voice shouted out.

Derby looked out from around the corner at the wreckage of the automobiles and saw that the desert cloud was fast on its approach towards them. He quickly ran towards the wreckage and went down the wall beside them to see the horses freaking out.

"Who's attacking us?" the English accented voice questioned.

"I'm not sure," the German-accented one replied. "I thought we lost them..."

"Get those horses under control!" the English accented voice shouted out again.

"It's not safe here... you need to go."

Derby saw from around the corner as a man in a greyish-tan jacket came out from behind a wall, taking a man by the arm and assisting him onto one of the horses. The white horse moved out of the way and Derby looked towards the man. He was an older man, around the same age as Derby, with grey hair that was flat upon his head and pulled back. His face was weary, skin fair and cold, but not pale rather pink. He was armed with a Sturmgewehr 44 like the other guards, which he held in both arms. The man was tall, around six feet and two inches tall. He wore matching pants to his jacket, a scarf around his neck, and brown boots. Meanwhile, Derby looked over to the man atop of the horse. He was a young man, around twenty-years old, and he wore a brown cloak atop of his clothes, but poking through the neck was site of a Roman collar. The man had fair skin, like Derby's, but with light brown hair and blue eyes that looked back at him with anger and hatred. Derby saw him stop before him and point him out.

"He's right here, Erich!" the priest shouted. "Get him!"

Derby's eyes looked over to Liudolfings as he raised his rifle towards him. Derby raised his rifle upwards to face Liudolfings.

"Get out of here, Father!" Liudolfings shouted out. "I will take care of this pest!"

The horse that carried the priest galloped forward towards Derby. He jumped out of the way before the horse could trample him. He hid behind the wall and stayed put as Liudolfings fired at him. The priest on the horse turned around and looked at Derby.

"I've got eyes on him, Erich! He's right here…!"

"Bothersome brat!" Derby remarked, pointing his rifle towards him. He took shots above the priest, startling the horse and causing it to rear.

"Get out, before he kills you! Run, Father!" Liudolfings shouted. "Men, keep Father Williamson safe!"

Father Williamson got control of his horse and then stamped off. Derby stayed put as he could feel Liudolfings approach him.

"So, we finally meet Herr Liudolfings," Derby remarked in a loud voice. "I suppose you didn't expect me…"

"For twenty years I've run with Death following behind me. The death that I did not experience in the war has always followed me, but I am stubborn old man who has resisted and will not give in without a fight."

"I assure you, I am no messenger or harbinger of death, you silly old kraut," Derby expressed, reloading his rifle. "I am but the purveyor of justice here to return you to face the crimes you committed years ago; I am here to ensure that actions of past are not accounted for on this world."

At that moment, Liudolfings stopped shooting towards Derby. He shouted out in German, and the shooting continued for a moment. Derby's ears twitched as he could hear someone mounting a horse behind. He peaked out around the corner as the gunfire stopped to see Liudolfings mount a horse with a reddish-brown coat. He took his rifle into his hands as the horse moved forward, prompting Derby to reveal himself from his cover and open fire at Liudolfings as he was about to trample forward. Derby's shots missed, but the proximity and volume startled the horse and caused it to rear. Liudolfings fell off the horse and fell backwards into the sand. Derby did not fire at him and instead watched for the guard on the other side as the horse ran off into the desert without a rider. Once the horse was out of the way, and Liudolfings still on the ground, the guard on the other side and Derby exchanged fire with each other, causing each of them to take cover.

"You silly Englishperson," Liudolfings expressed. "What crimes have I committed, when the thousands upon thousands of innocent the likes of your comrades took from us in my homeland…"

Derby attempted to keep an eye on Liudolfings as he scrambled to reach for his rifle while keeping down from the gunfire. The guard on the other side intensified his fire as he encroached forward and took cover behind a crate. Liudolfings crawled forward and then stood up on one knee, keeping low as he disappeared into the ruins. Derby attempted to fire at him, but the guard shot back towards him with his last magazine.

At the sound of the clicking of the guard's assault rifle, Derby stood up and opened fire at the guard, causing them to withdraw. Derby was able to graze their leg as they attempted to escape, causing them to fall over. However, before Derby could pursue further, shots came from within the ruins, from Liudolfings, and he was forced to stay back.

"If it's a fight you want, Englishman, then it's a fight you shall receive. It seems to me as though we both have unsettled scores to settle..."

Derby shook his head and directed himself the other way. He ran down to the end of the wall, reaching a gap and climbing into the ruins. At this point, the sandstorm began to envelop the area and hinder nearby vision. At most, Derby could see three or four feet ahead of him, prompting him to bring his rifle around on its sling and for him to take out a dagger and pistol. Derby kept his head down as sand tore at his face.

After a few minutes into the ruins, Derby paused and came down onto his knee. He listened to his surroundings and the whistling of the sandstorm. From somewhere within the ruins, Derby could hear the patter of boots into the sand, prompting him to move in that general direction.

"Do you think you can survive?" Erich Liudolfings questioned from afar. "I have survived worse than this..."

Derby did not respond at this taunt. He attempted to focus on the location of his voice, pausing again to wait for the sound of movement. He moved towards the right and then stopped at a corner. He came around to the exit of the ruins and decided to go around to where the guard was shot. He found stains of blood in the sand, met with the sight of the guard that he had shot passed out with his back against the wall. His rifle was at his side, and around his grazed thigh was a belt that had stopped the bleeding. A bloodied handprint could be seen on the trousers in the reverse direction. He could hear some murmurs from around, speaking in Italian. From nearby, Derby could see a trench ahead where the tops of tents could be seen.

From within the tent, Derby could see a few of the archeologists huddled down. Upon sight of Derby, they huddled even more, hands on their head and sheltering in place. Derby looked at them, dressed in cloaks like Father Williamson. He then passed them and came out to another tent next to it where there were more of them. Just as Derby had estimated, there were five of them in total (not including Williamson), hiding in the three tents. Derby continued downwards into the trenches. A shout from within the tents in Italian prompted Derby to look annoyed. He carried forwards into the trenches, reaching a junction and looking both ways. He went to the left and continued forward, reaching another junction, but before he could look both ways and approach closer, Liudolfings ambushed him.

Derby moved out of the way as Liudolfings attempted to take a swing at him. Derby dropped his AK-47 and then shot into the cloud as he made his escape. He then took a step back and hid into cover as gunshots came through in return. He stayed put and waited for them to pass, but rather than continue forward, further fire came through, sporadically. Derby climbed up the side of the trench and carried on forward from above, dropping down and going another direction. He passed through a tunnel and came out to the other side, reaching the point where Liudolfings was positioned. Quickly, Liudolfings reacted to Derby's appearance from his right and pointed his rifle. Derby moved into cover and took a shot at Liudolfings, grazing him at the arm, but not causing him to relent.

The gunfire came towards Derby and after wasting the rest of his magazine, prompted him to retreat. Once Derby was sure he was gone, he stepped forward and came around to where Liudolfings had been. He stayed in cover around the corner in case he opened fire at him from ahead. As Derby waited, he looked down at the ground and saw a splatter of blood. He then came out from around the corner and with careful steps, followed the trail of blood. He came into another tunnel and stayed behind a crate. Suddenly, Liudolfings rose from behind a crate and opened fire towards Derby, hitting the crate, walls, and shattering a lamp to turn the tunnel into darkness. The gunfire came over him for nearly a whole minute until Liudolfings was out.

At that moment, Derby moved out from around the corner and stayed low. He crawled forward to reach another crate ahead.

"Where are you?!" Liudolfings shouted.

Derby rested his back against the crate. He controlled his breathing to stay quiet and then peeked around the corner as Liudolfings looked out from all ends of the junction. Liudolfings then fled back outside, but Derby was able to track him by the stains of blood. Ahead of him, Derby could see Liudolfings resting around a corner, arm at his wound. He saw Derby approach, but rather than open fire at him, decided to run. Derby took cover just in case at the corner where he was, waited, but nothing came. He climbed up and proceeded up, looking down at the blood as the sandstorm tore at him. At the next junction, Liudolfings stood with a hand at a post as though he was catching his breath. He then carried on forward without his rifle which he left on the ground. Derby followed from below at his disarmed enemy, reaching him at the end of the trenches where he was on his back against the slope. Liudolfings rested with a hand at his wound, his hand trembling and Walther pistol he had taken up on the floor.

As Derby approached, Liudolfings flexed his index finger as though he still held his pistol. Derby continued to point his own handgun at him.

"You don't look well at all..." Derby expressed.

"A hunted animal can only go so far when he's wounded..." Liudolfings expressed. "You've killed me, so let me die now."

Derby looked at him. Liudolfings had tired light blue eyes that looked past him. Around his neck, he could see a golden cross on a chain, poking through his scarf with blood on it, as though grasped recently. Derby looked at him as he held his pistol towards him.

"You've killed so many innocent, haven't you?"

"We've all killed, us who fought in the war," Liudolfings expressed.

"Innocent lives though…"

"Innocent? What is innocent in a partisan who aids the enemy? Who willingly corresponds with forces hostile to our Fatherland? Who willingly conspires with the enemy to undermine the stability of the nation? Who willingly seeks to terrorize civilians? An innocent life is one who had no involvement in the conflict in question. The Jews will have you believe that nobody is innocent, except their own, as they justify the atrocities they themselves lavash the blood from, doing the same to their neighbors in Palestina and around. Always and everywhere are they the victims. A civilian has no choice but to obey his government, and a soldier to follow their orders, even if the ideals of their government are not agreed upon, what choice do they have but to join the enemy than not comply. They are the victims of war, collateral damage they call them, the truly innocent in war, whether English, German, or French."

"You killed men, women, and children…"

"And you believe them?" Liudolfings questioned. "I say to you, Englishman, I touched not even a hair upon the life of those who were already victims of the war between European brothers. I say this to you as a dying man who will say the same to his maker… If you truly believe that I am the evil man so many will have you believe, then kill me now. I did not run to hide from what were perceived crimes, but an assured death to be silent in the new world that was to be made from the old. The end of the war… it was death of the old world, and Hitler and his armies like Odin and his, marched towards the end so that they may be joined in Valhalla, except there is no such fate… It was all… a trap… there was no way in which Germany could have won such war, but it was done so that the end of not just our ambitions, but the ambitions of an entire now ancient world could die in that same war. In that war, Germany and Italy lost the conflict, Britain and France their empires, and the United States and Russia their spirit. There were no victors in that war, but the Zionist tyrants who have claimed a state for their own and wage an even more terrifying war on their neighbors, with endless support from both the United States and Russians, without condemnation or consequences... Does that not sound like the true victors of a war? You fought, I fought, so that they could be raised up..."

"Be quiet," Derby warned, continuing to point his rifle.

"And even now, you point your gun at me, a stooge of them no less... to hunt me down. So what are you waiting for? Kill me now, so that I should join my brothers in paradise..."

Derby's hands trembled. He put his handgun into its pouch. He then paused as he heard the sound of trucks arrive. He then looked back down upon Erich and reached over to grab his unwounded arm and raise him up.

"I'm not a killer, Herr Liudolfings," Derby expressed. "I'm done being soldier to one side or another. I fight only for God..."

Derby helped the Liudolfings out of the trench as the sands continued to rage through the dig site. He could see the headlights of the trucks that arrived ahead, and so he walked towards them to see men in uniform scattered around with rifles in hand. They approached Derby and he could see the flag on their uniforms were American. They took hold of Liudolfings and began to carry him for Derby, allowing him to walk on his own and approach the trucks.

A man then approached Derby and he recognized him – Kory. He was dressed in a suit.

"Well done, Mr. Cabernet," Kory expressed. "You did what we thought would have been a near impossible task."

"It took a bit of effort, but the job is done. He's yours to take to the Hague, or wherever his trial is to be held."

Derby looked over to where they had sat Liudolfings in front of a rock. Meanwhile, the U.S. troops gathered the rest of the archeology team members and sat them down on their knees near the trucks. Derby noticed that some of these men were priests by their Roman collars.

"How did you and your men reach me?" Derby questioned. "Are we near the Turkish border?"

"Indeed we are, but at the same time, after we lost you in Israel, Secretary Clayton organized a search party that I took to carry on from where you left off. Later did I learn that you were in Iraq, so I put the pieces together and here we are..." Kory expressed. "Many thanks are owed to you for this service to your country."

"Not country..." Derby muttered, pausing for a moment. "It was you then who sent the Kurdish rebels to the monastery, equipped them with that American-made tank..."

"Yes, and it was they who followed you here..."

Derby looked at Kory and then to some of the Kurdish rebels who were with the U.S. troops. He frowned more and then looked over to Kory.

"Your work here is done, Mr. Cabernet," Kory expressed, turning to an army officer. "Torch this place, and kill them all."

"What?" Derby questioned.

Kory climbed up to the side of the truck he came in. "Oh yes, there will be no trial, Mr. Cabernet. Travelling with these fugitives is too dangerous, and they would only receive a sentence all the same."

"What about learning what information Herr Liudolfings knew, or shared?"

"Everything that he knows is here with him," Kory expressed. "The rest of it is no concern to me..."

The truck that Kory got into then drove off. The troops that remained began to torch the tents while U.S. soldiers pointed their rifles at the backs of the heads of the archeologists.

"Stop! You're making a grave mistake!" Derby expressed, taking his handgun out.

"Restrain him!" the army officer commanded.

Derby was grabbed by two nearby soldiers who held him in place. His pistol fell to the ground. The archeologist team members were executed first, and then the guards that were unconscious and nearby too. The army officer then came around, picked up Derby's pistol, and then took it over to a wounded and defeated Liudolfings. Derby flinched as the gun shot fired and killed Liudolfings.

"No!" Derby shouted, increasing strength as the soldiers held him. "You animals! Savages! Every bit is right about you lot! Bloody yanks!"

The army officer threw Derby's pistol at his feet and then left. A third soldier came around and hit Derby across the face with his rifle, causing him to fall over.

"Leave him," the army officer remarked. "Kovner said no survivors, that includes him. Goodbye, Mr. Cabernet."

Derby looked around and was unable to steady himself as he fell over. The rest of the American troops got into the remaining trucks with the rebels and then drove off. He came onto his back and closed his eyes for a moment to rest, eventually standing up and looking out around him. The dust had settled down and passed over, but it was now twilight and increasingly darker as time passed on. Derby looked over to the corpse of Liudolfings, and then to the others, and to the burning tents.

From a distance, Derby could see a man on a white horse look towards him from afar. He looked out to this man and then saw him ride off into the horizon. Derby sat down to gather himself, picking up his pistol, and then going around to pick up a Sturmgewehr 44. He paused for a moment as he sat on a rock.

"What a fool I've been..." Derby expressed, standing up.

Derby proceeded to search the wreckage of the tents, finding only charred remains and ruin. He came to the priests, searched their pocketless bodies, and then one by one took them to pits to bury them each. Finally, Derby came to the soldiers, but found little on them, returning them to the earth, he then came to Liudolfings. Derby found a journal in his possession, opening the inside, he found a photograph of women and children on the inside. Derby proceeded to read through the journal as it became dark, but the skies were now clear and moonlight gave him ample light to read through the journal that spoke on the investigation here in the Levant.

When Derby was finished, he took the corpse of Herr Liudolfings and set him in the last pit. He then poured what gasoline remained, set the bodies ablaze, and left the dig site to return to his black horse and leave to return to the monastery.

Act 5, Prologue

Derby travelled in the back of an army truck, kept dry underneath the canopy cover as rain poured down heavily. He was sat the edge of the truck, looking over the gate to the countryside road behind him where the winter snowfall was replaced with green pastures. Likewise, Derby wore his regular battle dress, except the weapon at his side was a Lee-Enfield No. 4 bolt-action rifle. Inside the truck with Derby were some of the men of his platoon, including those that had served in Lt. Murdoch's platoon and were transferred under Derby's leadership. At least two-thirds of the men in this truck were British soldiers, while the rest consisted of American infantrymen. The American army uniform was significantly different than the British battle dress. The American battle dress consisted of olive-green trousers, boots, and a jacket with the round helmet. The weapons that the British soldiers wielded were different than those of the Americans. The British wielded Lee-Enfield rifles, Sten Mk.2 submachine guns, and Bren light machine guns, whereas the Americans wielded M1 Garands, Thompson submachine guns, and Browning Automatic Rifles (BAR). The British troops made light banter with the American troops, but otherwise the two groups minded their own business as the truck continued to drive them through the countryside, passing blown out signs in German that had some city names, Munster, Essen, and Dortmund. Behind the trucks travelled both American tanks, Shermans and Pershings, and British tanks, Crusaders and Churchills. The convoy travelled along the German countryside at a slow pace, faster than if they were to march, but still slow and not made easier with the weather that turned the roads to mud.

After an hour, the rain settled down and a march going the opposite direction could be seen along the side of the road, supervised by American troops. Derby looked out from the side to see the march of German prisoners of war, many of them, nearly a hundred plus men being taken away from the frontline and towards temporary shelter. The disarmed enemy combatants wore wool coats rather than their uniforms.

"If it were up to me, they should all be shot dead," an American troop remarked across from Derby.

"You'd shoot anything that moves, Perry."

"They're animals, all of them," the American troop reiterated. "What are you supposed to do with rabid dogs?"

"Very well may be," Derby expressed. "I've never had a fondness for krauts, but the most savage of beasts are better kept in captivity than shot…"

"I've hardly heard you speak, Cabernet," the American troop remarked, "and that's what you have to say…"

"Apologies if I've given the impression that I adore the Germans."

"I never had that impression," the American responded. "I think we all hate the Germans. Otherwise, why would we be fighting out here?"

Derby did not respond. The truck continued to drive towards the frontline as they finally reached the outskirts of a town and the truck came to a halt.

"Alright, everybody out," a voice cried out from nearby.

The truck gate opened and Derby hopped out to stretch his legs. The tanks drove forward and teams were organized into parties, each with a tank, assigned to sweep the streets of the town. However, even before the teams could set off, gunfire erupted as they were met with resistance. Derby stayed put as American troops ahead returned fire. Rather than join them from afar, he stopped to look around at the desolate and already ruined German town that they had come into.

Nearly all the buildings in the town were already destroyed to some extent. All that remained at some properties was rubble. At some, some walls still stood, and very seldom was there an entire building intact. The most common sight was either an entirely destroyed building, or a collapsed and partially ruined building. The German resistance shot from buildings on the road ahead, from one of the partially destroyed building. Suddenly, Derby flinched as he heard the American tanks ahead fire their cannons at the building from where gunfire came towards them and obliterated the building. The gunfire stopped, and the patrols resumed as teams split up.

"What're we doing, leftenant?" a British troop asked.

"Everyone in their squads," Derby expressed. "A tank to each of you. We take the left, and clear each street as we can."

"Yes, sir."

"Any prisoners, you let me know to transfer back."

"Yes, sir."

Derby went with his fireteam and followed a Crusader tank as they went to the left of the city. They walked along the sides of the road rather than in the middle, while the tank rolled down ahead of them. There was very little to screen, and the fireteam passed the occasional civilian, German woman, child, or children. Eventually, the squad reached the city center where they noticed some gunfire nearby. Derby went forward to take a look and saw American troops engaging with some hostiles ahead.

"Shouldn't we help them?" a British troop asked.

"Of course we should," Derby responded. "Careful steps, lads. Let's go see what all the ruckus is about."

Derby led his men around the city streets and towards the American Pershing tank as it engaged hostiles in nearby buildings. The tank fired its cannon towards one of the buildings, demolishing the building from where gunfire was supposedly coming from, but the shots continued to come around. American troops hid behind whatever cover they could keep low behind. Derby joined them and took cover behind their tank.

"What's going on here?" Derby questioned.

"These krauts are giving us a headache," the U.S. troop complained. "They've been ahead of us at every street, likely partisans and stragglers yet to surrender. Nothing here you can do..."

"I wouldn't be so certain. If they're moving ahead of you, then we can move behind them. My men will push in with you."

The Crusader tank moved forward and began to go down the street while Derby and his fireteam stuck to the side. They approached the approximate position of the building the gunfire came from. Derby and his fireteam took position around the doors of the building while their tank aimed the turret at the doors. Meanwhile, the American fireteam and tank moved forward and around the corner, while another British fireteam and tank moved forward on Derby's direction and continued around the other corner to prevent the German resistance from escaping.

"Right, let's breach," Derby remarked.

The fireteam opened fire into the windows, while another soldier threw a grenade into the building. The grenade set off, and then Derby and the soldier with him kicked down the doors and looked inside. The room was empty. Derby led his team inside and around the corner to a stairway that went upstairs. He then carried through and came out to an alleyway. From around the corner, Derby spotted German soldiers escape. Derby rushed forward and took cover around the corner. He stayed put and turned to peek before he called his men to join him. He then went inward down the side alley to the streets where the American unit arrived. The fireteam opened fire as the German soldiers fled into another alleyway.

The American unit caught up with Derby. An American officer, a captain, approached Derby and said, "No way of catching them that easy."

"What a nuisance," Derby complained.

"We've been lucky now, but sooner or later they'll be real thorn in your side," the sergeant expressed. "Eventually we'll catch 'em."

"Right, continue your search on this street. My men and I will take the ones perpendicular."

"Whatever you say, partner."

The American continued to patrol the street, while Derby took his unit and went left again, while the other British unit went right. They continued to go street by street, occasionally engaging unknown hostiles that were either civilian partisans or Wehrmacht units. By high noon, there was still more than half of the town to comb through, but as Derby's unit arrived at a bridge into the other half the town, the hostiles from within the ruins opened fire at them again.

An American tank shot its cannon at the building before Derby could even open fire, and the building collapsed. The gunfire stopped, and Derby signalled his men to follow him towards the street block. As he approached the building, it was certain that whoever was within, did not survive, if anyone was.

"Over that way!" a British troop remarked, opening fire.

Derby quickly turned and took a shot over as he saw the iron helmet of a German troop pass over the crest of a bridge.

"Did you see that? Damn krauts…"

"Wehrmacht," Derby remarked, "what are they planning… Let's move in on the other half of this town. They must be on the eastern side of the town."

"Yes, sir."

The tank moved forward and they proceeded through to reach the top of the bridge. At the bottom half, sand bags were set up with barbed wire. The tanks approached them crossed the defenses with each, while Derby saw the Wehrmacht troops disappear into a building further.

"Right there," Derby expressed, pointing, "fire at the flats to the left, perfectly intact."

The turret positioned itself and then the cannon fired at that building, causing a cloud of dust to shoot out from the ground floor. Derby observed the wreckage of a panzer nearby. They crossed the bridge and went down the lane when a German soldier appeared from the attic of an apartment building and fired a rocket at their Crusader.

At the same time, German soldiers in position ahead opened fire from their defenses, prompting Derby and his fireteam to take cover. The rocket from the panzerfaust hit the turret and destroyed the cannon. The tank drove backwards and parked itself at its side to provide additional cover while the troops shot towards the building. An anti-tank gun shot from the enemy side and hit the engine of the tank as it was reversing, hitting the back of a building. The tank crew escaped from the turret and joined them on the street.

"Everyone take cover and hold your positions," Derby expressed. "Anyone wounded?" he cried out to the tank crew.

"We're fine, just a little razzled."

"Right, well keep it together," Derby responded. He continued to return fire with the hostiles from afar. Little progress was made on both sides, but they held the line until the American troops could arrive with their Pershing.

"Stay back," Derby warned, "they've got an anti-tank gun ahead, and who knows what else."

"Is it manned?" the captain from earlier questioned.

"No, but it wouldn't take much for one of them to run to it."

"I don't see the threat then," the captain responded. "We've got to clear this town before sun set. Everyone on me…"

The Pershing tank moved forward and began to go past the Crusader and down the street, over the sandbags set up and traversing the dents and blown out portions of the street. The Wehrmacht soldiers began to retreat into the buildings, which prompted fireteams to set up and proceed to clear each building.

The tank continued forward until it made a good distance, and Derby moved up to join the sergeant.

"That's the problem with you, Brits," the captain expressed. "Always too careful... my men often complain about being stuck back when other outfits are halfway to Berlin, and all I have to say is that someone's got to hurry them."

"We have our reasons to be cautious," Derby expressed. "Not as keen to rack up losses. We're just one island nation over an entire continent."

"There's finesse to it, Cabernet. Germany isn't much larger of a country, and they were halfway up the Soviet's ass."

"They took a quarter of a million casualties in a fortnight. Besides..."

Derby flinched and ducked as he heard a loud gun shot towards him. He looked ahead and saw Captain Williams was shot in the head, collapsed and dead.

"Sniper!" Derby shouted. "Stay down!"

"Son of a bitch!"

The Pershing tank began to move forward, forcing Derby to stay behind it with some of his men and the American troops as they moved closer to the hostiles. The Pershing tank then came to a stop and moved its turret towards the apartment building the sniper fired from. A shot fired at the tank, but barely made a dent. The cannon positioned itself and fired, obliterating the wall of that part of the apartment. The Pershing tank then began to move forward again, but not before returning fire was launched from the German soldiers to engage the infantry, including Derby. The tank came to a stop, moved its turret, and then a shot was fired, but not from the cannon, but from the anti-tank gun. A shot hit the turret cannon and destroyed it. The hatch opened, but the troops did not step out as gunfire hit the top of the tank. The Pershing tank began to move forward slightly.

"Keep that anti-tank gun under check!" Derby shouted as his vision was obscured as the tank moved in front of him.

"It's clear!"

Suddenly, a rocket hit the side of the tank and caught it ablaze. Derby could hear shouts from inside the tank. He put his gun at the side of the tank and climbed up it, using the turret for cover, he shot towards the rocketeer on the attic, but another of his men was able to eliminate him. Derby then focused on assisting the men in the tank out. Once one man was out, Derby and him helped the other, a wounded soldier, and then the last helped raise one who was killed in action, and then the last soldier.

"These bastards," an American soldier expressed, "they'll pay for this..."

Derby looked at the sergeant and then dismissed his comment as he hopped down to join his own men.

"We've got them on the run, sir," a British soldier reported.

"Good lads."

Derby joined his men as they continued forward, and not too far within, they were joined with more troops who had the German soldiers at surrender. As the day came to an end, Derby oversaw the disarmament of the prisoners alongside an American leftenant. Behind them as they saw the prisoners marched off, some American soldiers, including the sergeant from earlier were seen taking amongst themselves.

Meanwhile, a British patrol returned with some additional prisoners, one of whom appeared less like a soldier as he was dressed in civilian clothes.

"Who's this?" Derby questioned.

"A civvy," the British troop responded, "or did you mean what the little bugger's name was?"

"Calm down," another British troop remarked. "He's just a kid, look at 'im."

Derby looked at him and sure enough, he appeared to be a teenager, at least six years younger than Derby. The young adolescent had blonde hair and blue eyes. He looked the civilian with annoyed eyes and then over to the troop.

"We found him with one of these," the British troop stated, holding a Gewehr 43 fitted with a scope. "Reckon he's the one that's been poking holes at everyone all day."

"Are you being flippant, private?" Derby questioned, looking at his own soldier. "Suggesting that our dead have had holes put in them?"

"Apologies, sir, just trying to stay light-hearted."

Derby looked at him more annoyed than he looked at the German civilian. The civilian began to speak in German to Derby.

"I'm sorry, but I don't understand you," Derby expressed, tired. The German civilian attempted to reason or beg with Derby.

"What's he blabbering about?" an American questioned from behind.

"Never you mind," Derby remarked to him.

"Kid's our sniper from earlier today..." a British troop stated. "You wouldn't believe it..."

"Really...?" the American troop replied.

Derby ignored them. He looked at his men and said, "Get this kid out of here along with the other prisoners."

"Come on, mate," the British troop said, grabbing the boy by the arm. "Let's go..."

Derby resumed processing prisoners with the other officer while he kept an eye on the American troops who continued to discuss amongst themselves as the sun continued to set. When the job was done, Derby was joined by some senior officers who invited him to dine with them.

"Sorry, but I'll be with the men tonight," Derby expressed. "Perhaps some other time."

The senior officers, both American and British, left with the American leftenant, who went off to celebrate the life of the fallen captain. Derby went to return to his men nearby when he realized he lost sight of the American troops.

"Alright then, lads," Derby said to his men. "Well done, all around."

"Shame about Captain Williams," a British trooper expressed.

Derby nodded and replied, "We've had our fair share of losses, it seems as though it'll never end before the war is over, and even then... who's to say it won't stop with these partisans about..."

"What if we lose you, leftenant?" a soldier questioned.

"Never you mind that... the odds that I should perish are just as well the same odds as everyone else. It's best not to think of what if, out here, Perkins," Derby expressed. "Best not to think of a lot of things... Although, speaking of which, did you see the young boy transferred out with the rest of the prisoners."

The soldiers were quiet as they looked at each other.

"Donald..." Derby said, looking at him, "did you see the boy transferred out..." he reiterated. "I'm speaking to you."

A British soldier nudged him.

"Alright, alright..." Donald answered. "Yeah, I did, but listen, I gave him to the yanks. They weren't happy with 'im over what happened to their captain and other men."

"Dammit, son," Derby cursed. "What have you done?! Where are they?"

Derby ran off, some of his men joined them. However, as they ran into the ruins of the German town, suddenly, a series of volley fire was heard from the distance. Derby ran towards the approximate location and found a half-platoon of American soldiers stood in a line with their rifles.

"My God..." Derby expressed, looking ahead at what they faced. A dozen Wehrmacht soldiers laid own the ground, lifeless, and at the end of that line was the civilian boy. His heart stopped for a moment, his hand at his side turning to a fist, and then his eyes fixated on the sergeant. "What in God's name have you done?!"

The American troops look annoyed at Derby as he confronted them. They lowered their guns while they didn't respond.

"It's not what it looks like…" the sergeant finally said.

"I suppose then you didn't just execute prisoners of war, a civilian – a young boy…" Derby remarked. "What the bloody hell wrong with you lot?!"

The American soldiers stood around, even more annoyed.

"For what? For what are we fighting for if we treat our enemies without any decency, any virtue? When these past years it's been this exact sort of tyrannical behavior from our enemies that we've always fought against? For what cause? For what reason have we been fighting for when our actions are no better than that of our enemy?" Derby questioned. "Answer me, for what have we been fighting for?"

"For the fact that they're under a tyrannical dictatorship," the sergeant answered.

"You say that, and yet even Adolf Hitler was voted into power," Derby expressed. "A democratic process, just like your president, President Roosevelt, was elected into power twelve years ago."

"Are you suggesting the United States is as bad as the Nazis?"

"I'm suggesting that at its core, the people are what make up the nation, and if the people are savages like the barbarians we fight, then it has been a vain war indeed," Derby remarked. "I expect this act from the Germans, from the Russians, but American…?" he paused for a moment as he saw some of his own men with them… "British…?"

"Listen, a little blood lost on their part is nothing compared to the innocent lives they've taken," the sergeant expressed. "Think of all the innocent people they've persecuted, racial minorities segregated from their own people, their own citizens thrown into internment camps and designated enemies of the state, all the brainwashing and all of the arrests made for having wrong views, and worst of all, the millions of lives that have perished all in one location, an entire genocide of millions of innocent people, Jewish lives. If you want to compare country to country, I don't see a fair comparison."

Derby looked at the sergeant without a response.

"We've come to Europe to liberate Europeans from themselves," the sergeant expressed, "and their antiquated, imperialist ideas that started this war in the first place. Think of the kind of world we could have in the next century, the American century, of peace to come... This is why America joined the war, not to save your sorry asses, but to bring justice and peace to like you said, a savage people."

Derby still didn't respond.

"Are we just going to let these monsters take what's due to us?!" the sergeant questioned. The soldiers responded in the negative. "Then I say to you, if anyone speaks out against what we've done here, then they're an enemy of the United States of America." The soldiers cheered. "And if you say anything that we've done here, then you better sleep with one eye open, Cabernet."

Derby looked at the sergeant. He still didn't respond and instead walked away with his soldiers, at least those that stood with him, while others stayed behind. Angry, but defeated, Derby instead stayed to himself that night and bitterly smashed the butt of his rifle into the side of a building to let out his anger before he returned to his men. Derby looked towards his men and took position to sleep for the night, rifle in his hand, and a spirit of hope that the war should soon be at its end.

Act 5, Scene 1

Derby woke up in his passenger seat aboard a commercial aircraft. He looked around as though suddenly woken up with a jolt, looking at the men, women, and children around him. From the distance behind him, he could hear a baby crying. A man beside him, also in a business suit, lay apathetically to what was around him with his head back. The stewardess walked down the aisle, attending to people, and Derby, holding his journal close to his chest, reclined forward as he came to. He put the journal back into his suit pocket and then looked out the window.

The aircraft window looked out to the Argentine Sea in the South Atlantic Ocean, stretching for miles without interruption and demonstrating cool blue waves. Closer beneath the airplane was the body of water known as the Rio de Plata, sometimes considered a river between Argentina and Uruguay, while at other times an estuary where the Parana River and Uruguay River emptied out, and other times a gulf within the continent. In contrast to the cool blue waves ahead, the Rio de Plata's waters were not a silverline blue, but murky and greenish-brown, not that color due to pollution contrary to popular belief, but due to sediments carried from the respective rivers that emptied out into this body. The merging of the bodies of water, the Rio de Plata with the Argentine Sea, was smooth and gradual, demonstrating the mixture of fresh and salt waters. The aircraft window began to show the Argentine coastline as the plane turned west, and before long showed the city of Buenos Aires.

Buenos Aires was a large metropolitan area on the coast of Argentina, on the southern shore of the Rio de Plata, that stretched for miles in every direction of its coast. Like the cities and towns in Italy, Israel, and Iraq, these buildings were typically rectangular and consisted white, but also grey colors. The organization of the streets and roads in Buenos Aires was uniform, set up in a grid-lick pattern with rectangular blocks.

The size of the buildings varied, some large apartment buildings setup in the midst of these blocks. Around the perimeter of some of these blocks were tall green trees that added borders, boundaries, and color to the blocks and cityscape. The airplane made its descent over the city, looking eastward still, and closer to the coastline, Derby could see a wide avenue with an obelisk at the centre. The plane continued over the city, beginning to pass it outright and make a turn around as it descended towards the international airport. Buenos Aires International, known formally as Jorge Newberry International Airport, was a small aeropark on the coast of the city and from there Derby emerged to enter into the Argentine city.

From the airport, Derby took a cab into the city and to a hotel where he checked in, and then left shortly afterwards by foot. The streets of Buenos Aires were clean and modern, much larger than the ones in Italy. The sun shined down hard, and it was very warm, but Derby persevered through that summer heat as he wore his beige blazer jacket and trousers. He covered his head with a panama hat. The pedestrians on the sidewalks were no different than those he encountered in Italy, tanned skin and dark hair, to fair skin and dark hair, or light hair, on occasion. The clothing that pedestrians wore varied with the majority of men and women dressed up while the youth in casual clothes. The buildings on the streets were mostly grey, built out of stone, and others beige. These buildings were tall, taller than the ones in Italy and Israel. What was more apparent than any location that Derby had visited in the past month was the presence of advertisements on billboards, bus benches, and posters; all in Spanish, but most of the brands of which were American brands. There was also an abundance of signage throughout Buenos Aires. Derby took a left around the city corner and approached a café where he entered through.

From that café, Derby sat down and ordered coffee, picking up a newspaper, and waiting in place. He looked up on occasion to the ringing of the bell at the café door, looking at whoever entered in. Only once did Derby catch the sight of someone looking back at him upon him raising his sights, an older male with a grizzled face and faint tanned skin with dark greyish hair like wool. He wore a suit and looked over to Derby as Derby raised his sights at him, and then after he passed, without any sort of reaction, went to sit down at the other side of the café. Derby looked back down at his newspaper and then to the side. Suddenly, the door rang again and he looked forward to a familiar sight.

"Jean-Baptiste!" Derby remarked, setting his newspaper down and standing up.

"Monsieur Cabernet!" Dr. Dumas remarked, approaching forward. "My apologies, my friend, for my being late."

"Not at all, my dear boy. Sit down."

Derby and Dr. Dumas sat down at their table together. Jean-Baptiste called for a coffee while Derby folded the newspaper and sat it aside. Dr. Dumas wore greenish-brown trousers with a beige-tan collared shirt with the top buttons open to show the white undershirt underneath.

"How have your voyages been, Mr. Cabernet?" Dr. Dumas questioned. "What is the grand discovery you have made that you have me come out to South America?"

"Not here, son," Derby answered with a hush. "I will tell you shortly…"

Derby instead began to explain his meeting with Secretary Clayton in Naples, his trip to Rome and audience with the Pope, and then his trips to Israel and Iraq in pursuit of Erich Liudolfings. Finally, Derby spoke about his final confrontation at the ruins.

"What these archeologists have been up to… it was unanticipated, but it appears as though I've been played," Derby quietly reckoned, looking around the café. "Come my friend, let's walk and talk."

Derby and Jean-Baptise stood up, paid for their drink, and then left the café. On Derby's exit, he looked towards the strange man that had made eye contact with him to make contact with him again. They left the café and began to walk down the street, Derby turning around to see that nobody was following them.

"I understand that the brunt of your research is in European histories, anything between mid antiquities to late and medieval works," Derby quietly expressed, "but I need to appeal to your expertise on this matter nonetheless because it appears as though that archeological team in the Levant was on to something of immense proportions."

"What do you mean, Mr. Cabernet?"

"I mean," Derby said, stopping in the midst of the sidewalk, "what they had uncovered had not been uncovered before. We're talking about giants, Jean – real giants, just like those from the Bible, with recovered bones belonging to humans eight to twenty feet tall."

"What does the assassination of a former Nazi officer, and an archeological team that he was hired to protect, have to do with giants?"

Derby continued to walk with Dr. Dumas before he said, "Let me explain from the beginning – that's where it does begin, at the start of civilizational history in the days of the Book of Genesis. According to the good book, before the flood there were giant people who walked the earth alongside humans, but these humans had a nefarious origin, being the Sons of God, angels, more specifically fallen angels, who had sexual relations with human women. In some translations, these offspring between fallen angels and women are simply referred to as giants, but in Hebrew that word is *Nephilim*. The Nephilim were thought to have been all wiped out as a result of the flood, which allowed for the repopulation of the world by the three sons of Noah: Japheth the eldest, Ham the middle child, and Shem the youngest, populating the three corners of the ancient western world. Are you familiar with the bottleneck effect?"

"No."

"The bottleneck effect is a phenomenon in which a sudden reduction in a population causes a loss of genetic variation. If the Nephilim were in greater numbers before the flood, they would struggle to reach that dominance and be now in dwindling numbers, forced to breed with human women to survive as a people and in turn be subject to genetic alterations more common with humans than in their own kin. The result would be less height, which is an ongoing trend that occurs according to the research I recovered.

"After the Great Flood, the giants came to inhabit the savage lands of the Canaanites, the Promised Land, having dominance in this land years after the migration to Egypt. In the Book of Joshua, we have the next cataclysmic event come onto the giants; their massacre at the hand of the Israelites, and their survivors fleeing to Philistia. From here, years later, a notable giant known as Goliath comes from, defeated by a young boy, David, and after much conflict between the Israelites and Philistines, by the time of the Great Exile, so too are the Philistines massacred once more and their survivors integrated into Neo-Babylonian society (full circle, as early Babylonian civilization is suggested to have been dominated with giants too, where the great-grandson of Noah through Ham, Nimrod, was also a giant). In conclusion, I've been able to identify three cataclysmic events in which a bottleneck would have occurred and required interrelations with humans to survive, reducing their genetic purity and size, which is consistent with expeditions completed in Ashkelon (Philistia), Ai (Canaan), and Mosul (Babylonia).

"The sources I was able to retrieve, only one of which is in English and other in German (which I was barely able to make sense of) describes bones collected in these three sites to be increasingly larger, from eight to ten feet tall in Ashkelon, to eleven to thirteen feet tall in Ai, to fourteen to eighteen feet tall in Iraq. An entry in the journal I retrieved in German draws a comparison with bones taken from right here in Argentina, in the Patagonia region, that measure between twenty to twenty-two feet tall (two-stories tall).

"Really?"

"So it says according to their research, but what puzzles me and is not all that clear in what I was able to recover is how these giants went from Argentina to the Middle East. Nonetheless, we have a timeline, even if there is a gap and a missing link. From Argentina, they reached the Old World (possibly even a founder effect took hold)."

"What then? After the Babylonian exile, I mean."

Derby stopped and turned to face Dr. Dumas as he said, "According to a manuscript I recovered from a stronghold of a secret society (this society of which is modern in comparison), they speak of servitude of ancient giants to the Canaanite deity Moloch-Baal, referring to these giants as their ancestors. I didn't mean to uncover this secret society and their stronghold, in truth, I was searching for Erich Liudolfings when I was brought to it, but it was peculiar... almost as though I was guided there. In Rome too, I received an invitation to a similar stronghold on the other side of the city where I found a symbol, an amalgamated symbol to one known as the Star of Moloch, and the same one seen in the stronghold in Iraq. At the stronghold in Rome, I uncovered a meeting of gentlemen that I believe I was not supposed to uncover, and after I escaped, I met with a man in Israel."

Derby told Dr. Dumas about his encounter with the stranger who hijacked his escort to the Tel Aviv University.

"I am unable to confirm who that man was, but based on photographs of possible suspects, I believe the man I had talked to was none other than Mortimer J. Schildsman."

"I don't understand – who is that?"

"Mortimer J. Schildsman, a less than well known figure, is an American financier and majority shareholder of Blackmore industries, considered to be one of the wealthiest companies in the world due to this company's financial activity at the end of the war, and recent investments in military weaponries. At the end of the war, Blackmore also became the U.S. government's largest creditor when they provided financial aid to European countries under the Marshall Plan; the agreement of that plan Blackmore also profited from. According to Mr. Turner, my executive advisor, the Marshall Plan provided opportunity for Blackmore to assert financial control in a war-torn Europe through investment banking (Blackmore & Co.). The use of that capital was then to buyout independent banks in the United States, which Blackmore has done for the past decade. In the last ten years, the numbers of independent banks in the United States has dwindled so much so that it is estimated in forty years from now, there will be fewer than a handful of major banks who control a supermajority of the world's wealth. The banking sector is not all that Blackmore is involved in; the Blackmore family started out in the petroleum business from where they initially garnered their wealth, and aside from banking have also had prominence in real estate, going so far to even buyout the Rockefeller Centre."

"He is wealthier than you are then."

"Blackmore is perhaps ten times as wealthy as Cabernet Industries, and several times over more powerful... He threatened me – well, at first, he hoped that I should join their cultic affairs, but I refused, and upon realization that I was a Roman Catholic, his hands tensed and he lurched back in his seat as though in disgust, and that was the end of our conversation. Next did I know, in the West Bank, I was running for my life, and later on previously thought to be friends turned to enemies when American units and their allies became enemies."

"So, what does it all mean then, Mr. Cabernet? Are you afraid?"

"No… not for myself. I haven't returned to England because I don't know what sort of heat is on my tail end. I wasn't supposed to survive being left behind in Iraq, and there is a peculiarity to me in what this archeological team was investigating, almost as though the interest was not merely in Liudolfings, but in the archeological team themselves. I was never sure of what Liudolfings role in the archeological team was, and when I met him, I was certain it was a protective role, but based on this journal of his, he seems to have been more than a partner in the research led by Fr. Tristan Williamson, an Athanasian priest of a disavowed order who disappeared from the scene. There is some sort of connection between what was being investigated in that desert, what was found in Argentina, and this secret society I suspect to be led by Schildsman."

"Is there any connection between Mr. Clayton and Blackmore? This secret society?"

"I'm not sure. I researched a bit on Secretary Clayton, he was recently promoted to the role of Secretary of Defense in the last year after Robert McNamara took a role in the World Bank. He's been quite involved in President Lyndon Johnson's cabinet, an avid Zionist, but not one I would suspect to be in this secret society."

"Did he provide you with the invitation in Rome?"

"No, impossible. The invitation must have been put in that book by a Vatican official, which is more disarming than if it were him. I am interested in his assistant though, Kory, or Korah Kovner, as he knew somewhat about the symbol of the cult, its full form at least. He informed me that the full form was referred to as the Star of Moloch but denied knowledge of the partial form I had drawn in my journal. Although it was him who abandoned me in the desert and had Liudolfings and the others killed, I don't believe he's a part of the secret society either although there must be some sort of connection… Schildsman did have access to my car and knew where I was…"

Derby looked around as they stopped again. He put his hands on Dr. Dumas' shoulders.

"Listen, we're in Argentina, and it's to continue the hunt. We need to search for this excavation site Liudolfings and the others uncovered, as referenced in his journal. The little research I've been able to do tells of ancient giants believed to have lived Patagonia and themselves known as Patagons. However, to find this site, we will need to find where Liudolfings lived. His journal had a photograph, of a family…"

Derby removed the photograph from his blazer and looked at it. The photograph depicted a young woman with fair skin and light brown hair and two children, both of whom had fair blonde hair, a daughter at least ten years old and a young son at least six years old.

"His family… they live in Argentina where Liudolfings escaped to after the war, but I'm not certain where they live. The former Nazi underground in Argentina is a single network connected together…" Derby said, putting the photograph away. "We'll need to find them."

"Yes, and I did what you asked me to, Mr. Cabernet, or at least what Mr. Turner informed me that you had asked me to," Dr. Dumas responded. "There is a bar on the outskirts of town, known as the 'German Club' because German-Argentinian frequent it. I was at the bar once already, put my German to use, and there's a man there who may be able to help us."

"You've done excellently then," Derby acknowledged, patting the sides of Dr. Dumas' shoulders. "Good work…"

Derby looked beside Dr. Dumas as he noticed a figure behind. His eyes focused closer to see what he thought to have been the man from the café, but as he looked again, the figure was gone.

"Mr. Cabernet," Dr. Dumas remarked.

"Sorry, what did you say?" Derby questioned.

"I cannot stay very long in Argentina. No more than three days…" Dr. Dumas stated. "My wife… she will kill me if I stay ever longer."

"Very well," Derby remarked, "I won't keep you long. You have your commitments to Marie, Jacque, and Manon. I hope that I may be done here soon so that I can return to my family, to Ophelia and Charlemagne…." He paused for a moment and then said, "At any rate, let's get out of here. You'll need to take me to this club."

•

Derby left the city streets of Buenos Aires later in the evening to take a taxicab from the city center to the outskirts of the city, in a municipality known as Martinez. Jean-Baptiste told Derby that this region was the largest and most populous with Germans and Argentinians with German backgrounds. The municipality was attached to the capital city, but in a less dense area of the provincial region. Immediately, Derby noticed the streets become smaller, buildings usually only a single floor in height aside from the odd apartment block here and there, and the architecture to be consistently colonial Spanish. The walls of most buildings consisted of stucco and terracotta sloped rooftops. The material of the streets varied by road, some made of concrete and others of stone bricks. Likewise, the apparent wealth in the neighborhoods varied too, some appearing cleaner and well-maintained compared to others where vandalism, graffiti, broken and barred windows, and the sort were too common. Likewise, the people in this town varied in dress compared to those in the city capital, most of whom wore casual everyday clothes rather than formal wear. The taxi driver brought them to the bar in question, the Alpen Club, a dive bar in the midst of an unsavory neighborhood where the sound of dogs barking in the distance was also met with suspicious eyes from locals at the two of them. Derby left the taxi and looked at the façade of the building, consisting primarily of stucco, barred windows, and a single entrance point with A sign in German blackletter that read the name of the club in Spanish, *Club Alpen.*

The interior of the Alpen Club was about as much as savory as the exterior. The floors consisted of red terracotta tiles. The walls were the same stucco material, and the windows at least translucent enough to not show the bars on the other side of them. From the entrance, on the either side were arches that led into private nooks. On the left and right were seats where patrons could sit in private, while on the far left and right were more secluded seating arrangements. In the center back of the bar were wooden counters with shelves of liquor behind and taps at the front. A single exit point behind the counter led further back. Above the archways on the right was an imperial German flag, the former tricolor of red, white and black, hung vertically. On the other side of the bar, hung atop the pillar of the arches was a portrait of the late but revered Argentinian president, Juan Peron. The lighting in the bar was dim and in the early evening there were few people.

Derby and Jean-Baptiste approached the bar from the entrance.

"Here's the man I was referring to," Jean-Baptiste remarked. *"Guten abend, mein Herr."*

"Pipe down, son," Derby remarked. *"Hello,"* he greeted in Spanish, *"my friend here recommended to me that I speak to you."*

The bartender looked at Jean-Baptiste and then to Derby as he washed a beer mug.

"Yes, I remember your friend," the bartender responded in Spanish. *"He was asking a lot of interesting questions for a man whose German is so bad."*

"I'm sorry, but my Spanish is not any better," Derby stated, *"but I am here because he told me that you could help me. You*

see, a friend of mine recently passed away, you may know him –
his name is Erich Liudolfings," he said quietly. "Do you know
him?"

The bartender shook his head at Derby and replied, "I don't
know him. He comes here?"

"I'm not sure," Derby responded, looking at Dumas. "I am
trying to find anyone who knows where he lives... or lived. Erich
died not long ago... during a trip in the Middle East. I want to
let his family know, or at least his wife, that her husband won't
return and what had happened to him."

"What happened to him?" the bartender asked.

"Sorry, but I want to let his spouse know. Perhaps if I show
you a picture of his family..."

Derby took out the picture of the Liudolfings family and
showed it to the bartender. The bartender looked at the family
and then shook his head.

"Sorry, but they don't look familiar to me. We don't get many
families here, and the men that come here don't talk much about
their families either."

"Okay..." Derby responded, looking around, "and if I can
ask, what type of German men come here?"

"All types..." the bartender answered with a shrug. "It is a
German restaurant..."

"The sort who celebrate the flag of the Kaiserreich? Juan
Peron?"

"Most immigrants that come from Germany are not from East
Germany, or West Germany, or even Weimar Germany, but from
Old Germany."

"Before the war?"

"What do you want?" the bartender questioned. "You and
your friend come here, like tourists, asking about my patrons?
I've had others come asking the same questions, but less stupid
than you pair. Please don't harass my clients, they come here to
drink, not wage war or commit crimes."

"You think I'm here because I am a hunter, or murderer," Derby expressed. *"I'm neither of those... I just want to know where Mr. Liudolfings family is to deliver them the news that their father is not coming home from the Middle East. I don't mean them any harm..."*

"Did you kill him?"

Derby did not immediately answer as he put the picture away and looked at the bartender with a frown.

"No, I did not kill him," Derby answered, *"but I did see who killed him."*

"Who?"

"Nobody special, but he was hunted and he was killed. If you'll please, I want to let his wife know about the news. I'm not interested in any of your other clients, and it would make my quest to deliver this news a whole of a lot easier because if I don't find him, I'm going to have to go looking for his colleague instead."

"Who is that?"

Derby looked at him intently and then replied, *"An Athanasian priest, Father Tristan Williamson."*

At the sound of that name, Derby turned around as he heard the scratch of a wooden chair leg run up against the tiled floor. He looked around but saw nobody of apparent notoriety around him. He turned back to the bartender who was looking aside for a moment. Dumas noticed too and began to look around while Derby faced the bartender.

"I hope you can understand," the bartender remarked, *"but these people you search for, they don't want to be found..."*

"I hope you can understand the need to let Mrs. Liudolfings know that their husband is dead, and how he died."

"For sure, but I don't know a man by that name," the bartender remarked, *"and if you don't want to draw attention to yourself, I would suggest you forget that name and don't ever mention it or the other ones again."*

"Why?"

"You should know why – you're not the only clients who come here asking for certain people. Every week, it's one bounty hunter or more..."

"I'm not a bounty hunter..."

"I didn't say you are, but I can't help you regardless of your intention. I have never heard of a man by that name before..."

"Sure..." Derby remarked, looking at the floor for a moment in silence, *"and what if..."*

Derby was interrupted as Dumas pattered him on the shoulder. He turned around and saw a cloaked figure pass him. He was briefly able to see the outline of the man's face, very fair skin with a Nordic nose. The man in the black cloak had his hood raised over him, concealing the rest of his head and the robes went down to his ankles. The two watched the figure leave the bar and exit out.

"What?" the bartender questioned.

"A moment, please..." Derby mentioned, looking over to Dumas next. "Stay here..."

"Certainly, *ein Bier bitte*," Dumas remarked, sitting down at the stool.

"Hold on to these for me..." Derby said, passing him his journal and Erich's. "Do not give them to anyone else, understand?"

Derby left the bar and looked down the street towards where the cloaked figure was walking and turned the corner. He moved forward to catch up to him, at a faster speed, turning around the corner to notice the cloaked figure up ahead also increasing speed. The cloaked figure jaywalked across the road and then disappeared into an adjacent street. Derby gave a light jog to catch up to him, reaching the sidewalk and then slowly walking up behind him to see where he went. During that walk down the street, suddenly Derby was met with the barks from a dog behind a steel chain fence, causing Derby to jump. The cloaked figure turned around, but Derby was unable to see their face. The cloaked figure nonetheless began to run from Derby, prompting Derby to shout, "Oy, you there! Stop!"

Derby ran forward towards the end of the street, seeing the cloaked figure to the right with his hood pulled back. The short blonde hair of the figure was revealed, and Derby was assured that this person was Fr. Williamson. Derby ran towards the priest as he disappeared into another street. He chased him down this street, and then to the right down another wider street with more pedestrian and car traffic. The road went slightly to the right on a bend and continued forward, and Derby chased him around, losing sight of him as he came next to an alleyway. Derby looked around momentarily and then went into the alleyway, slowing his pace to a light jog and then reaching a courtyard.

"Where did he go?" Derby questioned a group of locals in Spanish.

"*That way,*" a local pointed.

Derby walked past an archway and found Fr. Williamson hidden behind a plant. He then moved out of the way and ran towards an exit. Derby caught up with him, and they came to a smaller road where there was more car traffic that forced the priest to go down the sidewalk before cutting through traffic and causing the cut-off car to honk at him. Derby rushed past this same car and went into the alleyway Fr. Williamson had gone into, reaching the quieter street at the end where they ran right and then entered another. Fr. Williamson turned right on the alleyway, going down a junction and then through an archway on the left where he closed its gate. He then disappeared around the corner, prompting Derby to climb over the side wall and jump down. On the other side of the wall was a marketplace, full of people and stalls, and lost in the crowd was Fr. Williamson somewhere.

Derby proceeded to look around the crowd to identify where Fr. Williamson had gone. He proceeded to look around slowly, catching his breath as he felt a mild wheeze in his lungs. Some passerby locals looked at him strangely while others spoke in Spanish amongst each other. Derby looked carefully around the marketplace, seeing the various shops and merchandise for offer. Suddenly, Derby caught the attention of some people speaking to each other as though caught by surprise, so he went towards them, and they looked at him. He then looked to the side where saw the priest hiding behind a barrel. Derby proceeded towards him, and he pushed the barrel he was behind forward and then ran over the contents.

Fr. Williamson made his escape from the market, while Derby took a step onto the fruit that was before him and slid onto his side.

"Dammit…" Derby remarked under his breath, standing up. He growled and continued his pursuit.

Fr. Williamson came out to the street and ran down towards a park where he ran through to the other side. He then went into another alleyway, climbing up a set of stairs to a balcony, going around to the other side and then skipping over onto the rooftop of an adjacent building. Derby climbed onto the tiles, seeing that they were not very secure, he tread carefully with his body weight, sliding down the other side and continuing down the road as he saw Fr. Williamson approach a church not too far off. Fr. Williamson came into the church and closed the doors behind Derby, and Derby entered through and found himself in the narthex of a large church as bells rang to signal the start of Mass.

Derby stepped forward into the church proper and saw the congregation rise as the priest came out with altar servers for weekly Mass. He looked around the congregation and did not see any cloaked figure, nor did he feel it appropriate to survey the large church and all its pews for Fr. Williamson. He dipped his hand into the holy water, made the sign of the cross, and then walked forward to the end one of the aisles to look left and right into the transepts, but nobody could be seen. Rather than genuflect and sit down to join the service, Derby retreated. Derby stepped out of the church and looked around the church grounds, hoping to find Fr. Williamson, but he was gone.

"Dammit..." Derby muttered, leaving the church, and retracing his steps. He walked with a mild limp and still catching his breath.

Within half an hour, Derby arrived at the bar again and met with Dumas at the bar.

"*A beer, please,*" Derby expressed in Spanish, sitting down at the stool. "No luck," he said to Dumas. "We're at a dead end."

"Perhaps not," Dumas expressed, flipping through the book. "When you looked through this book, did you translate it on your own?"

"Of course not, I barely understand the fundamentals of that barbaric language," Derby expressed. "All I did was translate some captions at the sketches with a dictionary."

"I've had a read through and it's impressive stuff, very detailed and specific," Dumas remarked. "Just about all you've told me, but I don't believe this book belonged to that man you said. What did you say his name was? Erich Liudolfings?"

"Yes? Why do you say it's not his?"

"The name on the front, it reads Rudolf Engstfeld."

"No, no, that's his pseudonym," Derby expressed... "although..."

The bartender served Derby's beer, and he signalled over to get his attention afterwards.

"*Sorry to bother you again, but maybe you know the man I am looking for by another name: Rudolf Engstfeld?*'

The bartender looked at Derby, stretched out his arms across the counter, and then lowered his head as he nodded. He then looked at Derby.

"*Yes, I know a man by that name. I thought he was who you were talking about, but I did not know him by that other name.*

Also, he was not the only one I knew who had left Argentina on that trip. He left with a few other patrons…"

"*I regret to inform you that they're all dead,*" Derby informed. "*I do not know all of their names, but if you knew them…*"

"*I'll let their wives know…*"

"*What about Rudolf's wife?*" Derby asked. "*Please, you see what my friend holds… these are his notes, and he was working on something important. I'm trying to finish his work, and if I can find where he lived, his wife, I may be able to learn more about what he was doing before he left Argentina.*"

The bartender looked at Derby and nodded. He then said, "*How can I be certain that it was not you who killed him, or that you don't intend to do the same to those in that village? His family?*"

"*I am not a murderer,*" Derby repeated. "*I only want to know what Rudolf was doing with the archeological team.*"

"*Not you then, but others?*"

"*We'll travel alone,*" Derby assured him. "*We won't stay long either.*"

The bartender sighed, stepped aside, opened a drawer, and then showed them a map of Argentina.

"*You'll want to travel here,*" the bartender expressed, "*It's a remote village known as Santa Reina in the Valle de Lágrimas region of Mendoza.*"

Derby took his notebook back from Dumas who continued to read the one in German. He took a note down of the approximate location of the village.

"*Travel with caution, the villagers will protect each other if you mean to harm them. I will let them know that you are coming, but without guarantee that you won't be friend or enemy.*"

"Good," Derby remarked, "*let them know that Derby Cabernet is on his way then to meet with Mrs. Engstfeld to tell her about her husband.*"

Act 5, Scene 2

Derby and Dumas rented a white pickup truck and drove from Buenos Aires, across the country to San Rafael over the course of one day, and then from San Rafael the next day to the secluded village of Santa Reina. Derby drove the entire way, hands on the wheel while Dumas studied the journal more intensely.

"There is so much more than what you had thought to even uncover, Mr. Cabernet," Dumas expressed, turning the page. "You only translated short snippets, but I can read entire paragraphs of their methodology, what led them to these locations and for what reason. Between the lines, it seems to suggest something more than just archeology behind their intent. There is continuous reference to both the Patagonia expedition as you referenced, which in itself is not in this journal as the first entry begins with their departure from Argentina to Spain, but also another expedition that has more mention than the former – an expedition to Antarctica."

"You know I can't read German. I only translated the captions," Derby expressed. "If you can translate all of that, then I can have a better understanding of what they were thinking too… What does it say about their expedition to the Antarctic?"

"Very little, except comparisons of the specimens they find in their expeditions to that of an initial specimen, or '*das Ding*' as he refers to it, found in Antarctica."

"Ding?"

"Liudolfings uses that word once, and otherwise uses neutral pronouns to refer to it elsewhere."

"Interesting…" Derby expressed.

"I will take this journal with me back to Europe, but I can't stay with you another day longer," Dumas replied. "When we are finished here, I will need to return to Europe at once or else I will have Marie put me in my own grave in the desert."

"We're just about there," Derby assured him. "I'll gather what I can from the Liudolfings home, if the poor widow permits me to, and then you're free to return with those documents to Europe to continue to translate them."

"Mr. Cabernet, there is a bit of underlying tone in these entries too – not just in reference to what they had found in Antarctica, but references to this... thing as being the predecessor of a group of people."

"Of whom?"

"Mr. Liudolfings uses only one word to describe them, but its usage is just as strange. He uses the German word '*die Kinder*' multiple times, referring to the Nephilim and giants as being the ancestor of *die Kinder*. This word in German means children. What children is he referring to... it's unclear..."

"Perhaps there is..." Derby paused for a moment and then said, "Perhaps somewhere there are live specimens, children, great descendants of these primordial beasts."

"Nothing to suggest that theory unfortunately..."

Derby continued to drive along the road in silence as Dr. Dumas continued to forage the journal for information, making reference to Derby's journal and notes too. He passed a small town in the midst of the countryside, making his way into a forested and hilly area with tall evergreen coniferous trees and green grasses. The road became narrow at some points, had wide turns, and steep cliffs at some points, but eventually after another hour, they reached a point that demonstrated the breathtakingly large lake in the midst of the valley, *el Valle de Lagrimas*. At the coast of the lake nearest to them was a small settlement of houses grouped together, while further back to those houses were farmsteads. Perched atop of a hill on the other side of the valley from where they entered was a small compound with a tall bell tower and adjacent buildings with barns around. Derby continued to drive along the road and made his descent into the township of *Santa Reina*.

"What a breathtaking view and land," Derby acknowledged, "so familiar to the Pacific regions of British Columbia and western Alberta. This town… much like Allabrese."

Suddenly, as the pickup truck made it down the hill and adjacent to the farmlands, he took notice of some figures in position behind a signpost they had just passed. He heard them blow a whistle and saw that these males were armed with some sort of assault rifles.

"Oh no…" Derby expressed, looking in the rear-view mirror, "looks like we're going to have some trouble…"

"Trouble?" Dumas questioned, looking up just as a group of people stretched out spike strip across the road.

Derby immediately hit the breaks as they were about to run into the spikes. The car came to an immediate halt nearly an inch away from the spikes, and both men put their hands up as the locals raised assault rifles towards them. Derby looked at the rifles they carried and they were Sturmgewehr 44 automatic rifles.

"*Out of the car!*" a local yelled in Spanish.

"What did he say?" Dumas questioned.

"He said get out of the car," Derby remarked, opening the car door and stepping out.

Two of the militia members went to each of them as they stood adjacent to the car. They began to search them, patting them down before the fifth one, an older male approached them and looked them. Derby looked back at them, most of these men had fair skin, one on the tan side and with darker hair, but the others with medium to light brown or blonde hair. They wore regular clothes, cargo pants and collared canvas shirts.

"Hey, I need that," Derby expressed as one of them took his passport from his jacket.

The local provided the passport to the older male, the undistinguishable militia leader, who looked at it and then passed it back.

"*So, you are Derby Cabernet,*" the older male remarked in Spanish. "*You bring sorrowful news to us of a fallen comrade.*"

"*Yes, that is correct.*"

"*Then, tell me how and why our brother, Erich, is dead.*"

"*Certainly,*" Derby answered, "*but do you know why Erich had left you? Who he had travelled with?*"

"*That crazy priest,*" the older male answered, "*Erich was always talking to him at the monastery since he came here. He said he left to do some important work, for all of us.*"

"*Yes, Erich left with Fr. Williamson to go to the Middle East for some important work, and while he was in the Middle East, he and the entire team was killed by the Americans...*"

"*Americans? You mean to tell me the Americans killed him? Why did they kill him and the others?*"

"*Because... and I am not sure, but I think it was because of the work they were doing,*" Derby explained. "*They were investigating something...* oh how do I say this in Spanish... *something dangerous.*"

"*What dangerous thing?*"

"*I don't know how to explain it in Spanish,*" Derby remarked. "Jean, do you know how to say it in German?"

"In German? Yes... uh... die Kinder, das Ding..."

"No, not those," Derby replied. "The secret society... the giants..."

"Ah yes," Dr. Dumas responded, clearing his throat, " *Mein Freund glaubt, Erich und andere seien von einem Geheimbund getötet worden.*"

"*What secret society?*"

Derby scoffed and then said, "*We don't know who, but whoever they were working under is connected to a secret society, which in general Erich and the others were researching more and more... I'm sure that in some way it is all connected to the United States, to Israel, and to Mossad. Mossad and Nazi hunters were already looking for Erich at this time... What else do you want us to tell you?"*

The militia leader looked at Derby, unimpressed, and then asked, *"Why do you want to visit Mrs. Liudolfings? I will tell her what you have told me..."*

"My friend and I are continuing Mr. Liudolfings work," Derby expressed. *"I need to know more about his research, so I wanted to not only tell Mrs. Liudolfings the bad news myself, but also to see if there are more notes in his home...."* Derby said, not receiving an immediate response. *"Please, do not let his death... be in vain."*

The older male looked at Derby and then over to Dumas. He nudged for his men to lower their weapons.

"I will take you to his home," the older male remarked, walking towards his vehicle on the side of the road. *"Follow me."*

Both Derby and Dumas lowered their hands and got back into their pickup truck. The militia members pulled the spikes off the road and they proceeded to follow the sedan ahead that took them into the township and towards one of the houses in the midst of many.

"Well, here we are, Mr. Cabernet. What are you going to tell the widow?" Dumas asked.

"What do you mean what am I going to tell the widow?"

"Are you going to tell her just as you said to these men? Were you not a witness to what transpired? Did you not lead the Americans to the camp?"

"As I mentioned," Derby grunted, "they would have found them with or without me. Why do you want me to compromise myself as a subject in this when we need Mrs. Liudolfings to tell us the truth about what her husband was up to. I don't want to spend anymore time in a land of former Nazis than you do... no doubt, the regalia in their home will be damning for a former war criminal, no doubt indoctrinating his children like the rest of them in the hateful ways of the Third Reich."

The sedan pulled up to a small, modest house, a single story tall made of stucco. It did not have much of a front lawn aside from the sidewalk and a bit of grass in front of it. The windows on the front of the house had bars installed on them but one could not see inside due to very translucent white curtains on the other side. The rooftop consisted of terracotta tiles but at a very flat angle. The side of the house were narrow although it seemed that the property was lengthy.

"Shall I wait here then?" Dumas questioned.

"As you wish, mate," Derby expressed, annoyed as he exited the vehicle. He closed the door behind him, seeing a car pull up behind with some of the militia men. The leader stood next to the front door, unarmed.

Once Derby joined the militia leader, he went towards the door and knocked hard on it. Within a few seconds, the door opened and on the other side of the door stood a short woman, less than a couple inches over five feet, dressed in a dress with floral patterns on it. She had tanned fair skin, but her hair was medium blonde and her skin smooth. She was young, appearing to be in her late twenties to early thirties. Her hair was tied in a ponytail and there was grimness in her eyes.

"*Mrs. Engstfeld, Mr. Cabernet,*" the militia leader greeted.

"*Thank you, Luthor,*" Mrs. Engstfeld replied, looking at Derby with a displeased look. "*Does he speak Spanish, or...*"

"*I speak Spanish,*" Derby answered. "*Can I come inside?*"

Mrs. Engstfeld looked to Luthor, and then back to Derby. She uncrossed her arms and nodded. "*I'll be right here,*" Luthor said as Derby stepped forward. The door closed behind them.

Derby looked to his left and found a small living room with a television in the corner. In the immediate space he was in, on the left, was a dining table, and behind a kitchen. Further ahead was a corridor that led down to some additional rooms. Derby looked around himself in astonishment, but not in the smallness of the living quarters, but in the vast amount of fanatical decorations planted upon the walls and furniture. From the living room, Derby saw a crochet blanket of the Virgin Mary, a tapestry on the wall, religious statues of not just Our Lady, but of saints and a nativity scene on the fireplace mantle, a statue of the Good Shepherd next to that, and then a larger statue of the Virgin Mary before the fireplace. In the dining room, behind the head of the table was a depiction of *Theotokia*, a Byzantine depiction of the Virgin Mary with a child Jesus in her arms. Next to the main door on the side of the dining room was a crucifix, and there were many more crucifixes throughout the house, and rosary beads laying about almost everywhere. There were as many religious items on the walls than there were family photographs, most of which were photos of one of the two children, or Erich and his wife, or the entire family. A photograph on the fireplace mantle showed Erich Liudolfings in his SS uniform, out in the open. Derby looked finally towards the grieving widow who stood next to a wooden chair in the dining room, opening it and taking a seat.

"*My dear*," Derby expressed, a nervous tone in his voice, causing him to clear his throat, "*I... I have some unfortunate news about your husband.*"

"*I know... what happened to my husband?*" she asked, anxious.

Derby stepped towards the chair on the opposite side of Mrs. Liudolfings.

"*Before I say anything more, where are your children?*" Derby asked.

"*They are with my mother, near here,*" Mrs. Liudolfings answered.

Derby nodded and then sat down. "*You know what kind of life your husband lived before he came Argentina?*"

"*Of course*," Mrs. Liudolfings.

"You know that your husband is a wanted man who escaped captivity? Who escaped his punishment for crimes that he committed during that war?"

"Who is truly innocent that has fought in that war, sir?" Mrs. Liudolfings answered. *"Did you fight in the war?"*

"Yes, I did, but for Britain. I'm English."

"Do you believe yourself to be innocent then?"

"I…" Derby hesitated to provide a full answer.

"The only difference between you and my husband is that your country won the war, and my husband's lost."

"Ma'am, there are lots of differences between my country and your husband's."

"The differences not being the negatives…"

Derby did not respond as he looked at Mrs. Liudolfings, took in a deep breath, and then said, *"You understand in the least that there was a bounty on your husband's head, so I won't say more than that. All sorts of people wanted your husband, dead or alive, and unfortunately that happened during his trip to the Middle East."*

"How? He told me he was going to be safe… He was with Fr. Williamson, they were travelling together with others…"

"Someone was looking for him…"

"Who? Was it a bounty hunter, or Israeli spies?"

"Something of that sort…"

Mrs. Liudolfings looked at Derby closely and then asked, *"Who?"*

"The technical details, ma'am, are that American officials hired a bounty hunter to kill your husband. This bounty hunter tracked your husband down to Israel, and then to Iraq, where he was killed by American soldiers that had entered into the country through Turkey. These soldiers were led by an assistant to the Secretary of Defense, Korah Kovner, who upon your husband's capture, had him executed."

"*You can tell me what the name is of this assistant, but who is the bounty hunter?*"

Derby looked at Mrs. Liudolfings as he held both hands in a fist. He gritted his teeth and then released his tension as he said, "*It was me. I was the bounty hunter... I had tracked your husband down from Israel to Iraq, but please... understand that...*"

Mrs. Liudolfings immediately stood up and slapped Derby across the face. She attempted to slap him again, but he protected himself, causing her to pick up a candleholder instead and wack him with it. Derby took it off her as he stood up.

"*Enough, it was not my intention to get your husband killed. He had killed innocent people, or at least that's what was told to me, and I was told he would be put on trial.*"

"*You murder! You swine! Get out of my home! You British are all pigs! Get out!*"

Mrs. Liudolfings picked up the other candleholder as Derby backed up, stepping out of the way as it landed beside him. She burst into tears as Derby stood back and the door opened for Luthor to look inside.

"*What's happening?*" Luthor questioned.

"I... I don't think I'll get to see Herr Liudolfings study," Derby expressed, looking around the home. "Come to think of it, I don't suppose he would even have one..."

Luthor walked over and led the widow to the living room to sit down.

"*Do what you need to, and then get out of here,*" Luthor expressed.

Derby nodded and then stepped forward, towards the corridor. He quickly made his way into the corridor, looking into the bedroom on the right behind the living room where there was a master bedroom, and then to the one after that where there were two children's beds. A door at the end of the hallway went into the small backyard which at most had a shed and a chain-link fence behind. He looked into the final room behind the kitchen on the left and saw that it was a small study, a shelf with more religious icons and items, and a framed Iron Cross medal on the wall with photos from the war, of Erich Liudolfings with other officers and groups of soldiers. A smiling photo of Liudolfings has him receiving his Iron Cross medal, considered one of the highest merits in Old Germany. On the right was a desk before the window with a few papers around. Derby nodded and rather than pry, he decided to retreat back and simply leave the house as the widow continued to cry.

Dumas looked at Derby as he held a sunken look on his face. He stepped into the cabin of the pickup truck, turned the keys, and then drove off.

"So, how did that go?"

"Awful," Derby expressed, "absolutely awful, I... I think we ought to visit the monastery on the hill before we leave."

Dumas nodded to his mentor, and they drove out of the town and back into the countryside to go towards the east side.

After a few minutes, Derby drove up the hill and reached some iron gates at the front of some hedges. A sign above the gate read, '*Terrae Sanctum*,' and another sign in front of the hedges read in English, Spanish, and Latin, 'Abbey of Our Lady of Sorrow.' Derby exited the truck as the engine still ran and went up to the gates to open them. He then drove up to the front of the abbey and shut off the engine.

Without a word, Derby left the truck and went up to the front of the monastery to enter through the open doors, marched forward towards the church doors inside, and pushed them open. He quickly walked down the aisle and came to one knee before the altar and then the other as he gritted his teeth, fists in both hands at his side, clenched and knuckles on the floor. He beat down at the floor with his right fist and then took it to his breast, beating it and saying, "Lord Jesus Christ, Son of God, have mercy on me, Lord, a great sinner." He repeated those words three times and then the tension released in his fists and his face was wet with tears. He bowed forward towards the tabernacle in worship and let it all out.

Suddenly, Derby came to one knee as he heard movement behind him. He stood up, pivoted, and saw a figure emerge from the right side. The figure wore a black cassock with a Roman collar around his neck. It was Fr. Williamson.

"Let it all out, Mr. Cabernet," Fr. Williamson remarked. "Offer up every tear, for where there are tears there is certainly mercy."

"What do you want?" Derby questioned.

"It's not what I want, it's what I can do for you, I believe," Williamson remarked in his English accent. "Seems as though you're here for a reason, not to hunt more former members of the NSDAP, but to put the dots together so to speak on what we've been up to. Have you figured it out yet?"

"You've been excavating sites in the Levant and uncovering giants of varying sizes, comparing them to one you uncovered in Patagonia. Is it all true? You found one close to twenty feet tall south from here?"

"Oh, it's true all right," Williamson answered. "Do you know what all that means though?"

"Nothing of which our faith hasn't already told us to be true."

"Evidence turns faith into certainty though, so these objects of faith are now objects of certainty, of knowledge."

"What about the thing you found in the Antarctic?"

"A mystery to be certain of still, but further genetic studies are necessary to pull the seams together on it all. I shan't pursue it any longer though, but you... you seem to be perfect for the job, Mr. Cabernet, a perfect penance to take what was Erich's ambition to become yours, and it should fit right alongside your other work."

"I... I don't understand. What about children?"

"What about them?"

"Where are they? The children of the giants? Are they here?"

"The children of the giants...?" Williamson questioned. "Let me explain that bit. The Children are not young children, but offspring in a certain sense (as we are trying to prove), but a shortened form of a full name, the Children of Moloch, a secret organization with increasing influence across the world and consisting of members who refer to themselves as Children, but also by another ancient name, the Chosen."

"Chosen?"

"The Chosen are a small elite group of men and women, most of whom are Sephardic or Ashkenazi Jews. The expedition that my team set upon was to prove the origins of these so-called Children, but also to clarify the relationship between the Children and Chosen. What we've uncovered is... still inconclusive, but to generalize, the Children exist within the Chosen as the most powerful and nefarious of these elite. The Children are the descendants of the Nephilim, or giants, and it is they who are the true enemy of all human people. In Biblical times, these were demonic Canaanite kings that ravaged the land with bloodthirst and savagery, and we have traced their existence clearly by their size as giants to the collapse of the Neo-Babylonian Empire. What is left in our research is to where they went, and there is much work still to be done too on how they came to the Near East from South America.

"My working hypothesis is that from the Neo-Babylonian Empire, they came to the lands of Judea as well as other neighboring lands as they assimilated with other peoples, consolidating power among the most powerful groups of the time. By Roman times for example, these people were the chief elders and scribes of the Pharisees and Sadducees, and who knows where else among the Persians and Greeks that came in conquest after the collapse of the Neo-Babylonian Empire. What is certain though is that they nested within Jewish communities at least by the time of the diaspora, and who knows if they too extended their subversion to Roman peoples. I say with certainty that they must have nestled within Jewish communities because of the existence of this inner circle within the Chosen of those referring to themselves as Children of Moloch, many suspects of whom happen to be of Jewish descent."

"What about Mortimer J. Schildsman?"

"Yes, with certainty he must be one of the Children, but so too many a majority of whom are Zionist leaders, their high-command, as the State of Israel has become like a hornet's nest of these people who are ultimately not Jewish, but Nephilim, or descent of the Nephilim and taken host among the Jewish people. Who knows for how long and to what extent the parasitic relationship has been of the Nephilim among the Jewish people, or to what extent it could even be called parasitic, and the former not assimilated into the latter. Are the entire Jewish people in modern time descendant of the Nephilim? I'm sure you would be intrigued to know, Mr. Cabernet, for your own work."

"Don't be outrageous," Derby rebuked. "You are just being antisemitic now – to label and entire people as not their own people, but subverted by the Nephilim, and wearing their identity like masks."

"Was that not the premise of your work? To discredit the identity of the modern Jewish people?"

"I did not say that they were not descendant of the Israelites – I simply drew a distinction in cultural traditions and religious practices of modern Jewish people, as well as clarity in them as descendants from the Pharisees and Scribes to become the three major communities of Ashkenazi, Sephardic, and Mizrahi Jews. I concur with your analysis of the situation, and hypothesis, and in my heart do I know that the Jewish people are innocent and blameless, even if there be bad men among them that have lusted and killed – who is to say that these were even their men, but not the Children among them? If so, that would provide the hypothesis that the Jewish people are truly innocent and have been subverted – they would truly be the victims of not just persecutions aimed towards them at the hands of the Children, but victims of the Children themself – of that cabal!" Derby paused and then said, "Theories aside, you and Erich sought to prove the ancestral ties of the Children of Moloch, this inner circle who claim to be the descendants of Moloch-Baal, to be legitimate? To say for certain that they are descendants of the Sons of God, of fallen angels?"

"Yes, and to add to my hypothesis that all Jewish people are somehow descendant of the Nephilim, I say that it was Jews who chose over God, the Devil, their self-proclaimed father as it is said in the Bible, so that they crucified Our Lord on the Cross for that reason and took that blood onto their hands and the hands of their descendants. Just as many Israelites were subverted by Canaanites to embrace idolatry through the course of Salvation History, so too as the Old was replaced with the New, the Jews who were Old and refused to come to the New became enemies of God rather than his people, and cursed to wallow in that livelihood. They have replaced the Canaanites the Israelites once faced, and become the Canaanites us Christians must face. The entire Jewish faith is based not upon the Mosaic Law, but the Talmud whose own pages recount how after the crucifixion, no sacrifice would be received in the Second Temple afterwards up until its destruction. Although I cannot doubt that some Jews worship God the Father, the Chosen, these elites, do not, and have been instrumental in anti-Christian behavior from the persecutions and blood sacrifices in the past two-thousand years, to the revolutionary impulses and rebellions led on in the modern century that you so describe yourself in your book.

"The Children of Moloch is not a new organization either, but it certainly is one that has become increasingly more powerful and continues to lead revolt (fittingly like their so-called father before). Moloch and Baal, both Canaanite idols, are interchangeable words (even able to be put together), for Satan, a more accurate term of which would be Beliyal, the incarnation of evil and malice itself that is the adversary to what is good, beautiful, and true; an ancient evil seen in flesh through Lucifer, the primal fallen angel doomed to wander the Earth upon his belly, and all his minions whose children are the Nephilim, and descendants the Children under belief and mission to carry out the work of Abaddon, their true father. They've existed as an organization for at least the past three-hundred years, as long as the Order of St. Athanasius, but in recent years have expanded and taken over fledgling and diminishing secret societies like the freemasons and illuminati, groups that once held power in the modern world but now of which have become defunct."

Derby scoffed and replied, "Antisemitic nonsense."

"Oh? What do you know about race and genetics? Do you really think that the Nephilim could remain so pure, when even Jewish people struggled to not integrate European blood in Ashkenazi and Sephardic peoples?"

"You should be careful... to much focus on racial differences and genetics will turn you into a Nazi rightfully."

"And what if they weren't wrong to believe in differences in human beings? The bottom line is that the Children of Moloch are more powerful than ever before, and they intend to dethrone Western Civilization unless we reveal them to the world, and for this reason did they have you chase us, chase Liudolfings, to stop us from doing so. You must do what we could not..."

"How do you suppose I do that?"

"You must continue to write your series on Judean people, and write your next chapter on what you truly know about the modern Jewish people. You must speak strictly on their subversive activities in the West from the seventeenth century to the twentieth century, a document of which I'm sure you've already started on, no doubt. From there, you will talk about the Children of Moloch and the Jewish elites self-referred to as the 'Chosen,' their plot to subvert the West, and also clarification on their origins not being Judean at all, but enemies of the Judean people.

"In your third and final chapter, which will take some time, you will compile all the research that has been put together here by me, Mr. Liudolfings, and others, on the Nephilim, and how they continually subverted entire populations as giants, and then later as common people. You will tell of their origin from the Flood to the Babylonian Exile. You will tell romantic tales of how heroes like Samson tore the temple down upon these vampires, or how David as predecessor of Christ our Lord slayed a Nephilim descendant in the form of Goliath, mirroring how Christ slays the great dragon beast. From there, you will then talk about the origin of the Nephilim, here in Argentina from Antarctica."

"I will need to go to Patagonia to see for myself all this that you are telling me, if you expect me to do what it is you think I should do."

"You will do it, and I will travel with you to Patagonia in the least to show you the truth, only because it is safe to do so. Afterwards, I will not. You will take what you have learned, samples and all, and travel to West Germany where there is a state-of-the-art laboratory that will be able to compile data for you show the world the truth about the Children of Moloch and the Chosen. It will be perfect. They may not have ever taken for credibility what myself or Liudolfings could publish, but you with your platform, could do so much more. You could save Western Civilization, if not provide a prophetic warning of what is to come. You will see…"

"I will…" Derby remarked, "I'll go with you to Patagonia, but I'll be writing this my way, with my conclusions and words, and none of your drudgery. Where was this excavation site in Patagonia?"

"In a southern region of Argentina known as *Tiera de la Fuego*, the very tip and end of the world."

Act 5, Scene 3

Derby and Dr. Dumas stayed at the monastery for the rest of the day, eating with the monks and Fr. Williamson. When evening came, Derby and Fr. Williamson saw Dr. Dumas off.

"I will see you in one to two weeks from now," Derby remarked, shaking Dr. Dumas' hand. "I wish I could entrust in you the words of this journal, but I may need to refer to it during my voyage. Fr. Williamson and I will travel to *Tierra de la Fuego*, and when I have seen what I need to see, I will put down in writing all that I have seen in two parts, one I believe I can finish quickly and send to you to peer-review, and the other will take me some time. When I return to Europe, I will need to go deliver the specimens I need to collect, and hopefully we will have some time to put down together what is in Liudolfings journal."

"Safe travels, Mr. Cabernet," Dumas encouraged. "I will wait for your papers and your return with eagerness."

"Take care, my friend," Derby said, embracing him next. "If for whatever reason, I do not return, please have both yourself and Marie be there for my dearest Ophelia, and also... be kind to little Charlemagne, constantly reminding him that his grandfather is not far."

"I assure you, my sir, I will not have it any other way," Dr. Dumas responded. "I will pray for your safe travels, but I am confident that you will return to Europe in one piece."

Derby and Dumas parted from each other, smiling and then letting go. Dr. Dumas got into the pickup truck, closed the door, and then drove around and left the monastery. Derby took in a deep breath and then turned to face Fr. Williamson.

"How will we travel to this place of fire?" Derby asked the priest. "I imagine it will be a long journey."

"We will need to leave tomorrow in the early morning," Fr. Williamson said. "We will drive from here to the eastern coast to a small fishing village where we chartered a boat to take us down south. The journey will be as you imagine, very long, but it should provide ample time for you to write down what you need to."

"It will be just the two of us?"

"Unfortunately, the rest of my team cannot join us, as you imagine, and any resources for this journey will be dependent on your own wealth... although I'm sure a man like you should be able to manage that."

"Yes, yes, and how about defense? I can hold my own with a rifle, and a pistol, but can the militia here provide those for us?"

"For the right price, I'm sure they will," Fr. Williamson remarked. "We can go into town to pickup supplies to bring with us onto the boat."

Derby nodded and then looked out towards the compound of the monastery. The grounds consisted of a livestock farm in addition to the monastery building, including stables with horses and barns. In the midst of the ranch was an open field between these buildings.

"I've been to two other monasteries of the Order of St. Athanasius, a religious order I did not know to even exist a month ago," Derby acknowledged. "Indulge my curiosity... I understand the basic history of the order, but what about this schism from the Church? I've had my disagreements with the modernists in the Church, the new liturgy to be introduced after Easter, and so much more, but I could never think to ever disobey or refute the Holy See. Why then does the order do so?"

"The order has a mandate, to uphold tradition."

"I understand that Bishop Chevalier was killed, and many more put down and your monasteries assimilated into other orders or shut down outright."

"Correct, but don't think that it was the Holy See who had our bishop assassinated. I'm convinced that the assassination was an act of the Children."

Derby stood plain for a moment and then said, "When I first came to the Children in Rome, it was because someone had placed an invitation into a book Pope Paul had given me. Are there members of the Children in the Vatican as well?"

"Very certainly there are," Fr. Williamson replied, "but Mr. Cabernet, we live in a world of darkness. There are bad people, good people, and then there are ordinary people. As you can imagine, the good people prefer the light, while the bad people prefer the darkness. If I were to estimate, I would say that 1% of the population is truly good while another 1% is truly bad. The 98% of people are ordinary people, and these are people who may seem bad, and do live in the darkness and are inclined to do evil, but prefer the light and wish to do good. The Chosen are within that 1%, while those of us who are disciples of Christ, the Children of Light and true chosen people as the new Children of God, are within the other 1%. These are practicing and active Catholics who although not perfect, truly believe. Between those two margins you have secular people, people of other religions and cultures, other Christians, and a majority of Catholics; the people of this world that need leadership to be brought closer to the light. Wherever you go, Mr. Cabernet, you will find mostly ordinary people, but then and now you will also find members of the 1% of either side. The Vatican is no different, although you would be more likely to find disproportionate members of both good and bad people, the same would be true of government and other seats of power and money. There is corruption within the Holy See, because man is corrupted, and this has not been the case just now, but since the very beginning."

"What percentage does the order believe they fall under? What percentage do you believe you fall under?"

"I am a disciple of Christ, even if the Church has disavowed me," Fr. Williamson remarked, "and you Mr. Cabernet, I know are one too. I cannot speak for the entirety of the order, but my gut tells me that a majority of them are the same, true believers who struggle with themselves. The Chosen and evildoers struggle not with themselves, but with God."

"I've heard that the Order of St. Athanasius was infiltrated by Nazis in Germany and in France, and that for this reason the Church shut them down... because they were putting ideology into religion."

"I cannot deny that there has been some people within the order that have let politics and ideology get the best of them, but it is not as bad as you think. The Vatican was too reactive to have shut those provinces down and let their fears get the best of them. The Order of St. Athanasius does not claim to be perfect, no order in their longevity is. The Franciscans have long fallen away from the vision of St. Francis; the Dominicans into degeneracy, both rival orders. It took less than a hundred years for these orders to fall to the temptations of man, how can you expect the Order of St. Athanasius to be any different? We are no different than the Society of Jesus who was surely infiltrated by the Chosen and communists alike, permitted to thrive within the Church and as you have seen, exist in the highest levels of the Vatican. The Holy See has allowed them to thrive, but treats us as though we are their enemies? The Jesuit Order is our primary rival, and they have had us excommunicated because we and our reactionary ambitions threaten their revolutionary ambitions that carries this Spirit of Vatican II."

"The Church has shut you down because you threaten schism," Derby remarked. "I read it in the Vatican archives. In your mandate to uphold tradition, radical belief has come to some of your abbeys that hold that the Pope is illegitimate, the seat of St. Peter vacant, and that the Pope is the spawn of the Devil and a heretic. It defies Church teaching for the sake of a tradition you have upheld as an idol now because of your rigidity and unwillingness to submit to the power of the Holy See empowered by God. I'll say it again, I am not happy about the changes that are being brought about, but it is from the Church and given assent by the will of God to happen, and therefore it must be submitted to. You defy that submission – how can you then believe yourselves to be submitting to God when you won't submit to his magisterium?"

"I've had enough of this squabble," Fr. Williamson remarked. "You are blind to the vision of the Order of St. Athanasius, but let me tell you what, Mr. Cabernet, even if we are persecuted, we hold onto the light of Christ that is truth, and when the modernists have torn down the walls of the revised Church and plundered all it has for the sake of ecumenicalism and reaching out to the world to appeal to them as being modern, it will be us who have survived with the Word of God. I can only say that that is happening now because it is the beginning of the end, there is no changing the path of the Vatican, the Church, in this revolution, I admit it, but to only save the souls of the few that are willing in these final days – in upholding tradition, the Order of St. Athanasius will save the few that seek truth."

•

Derby did not speak to Fr. Williamson for the rest of the night, and even in the morning seldom words were spoken between them. A monk at the monastery was set to drive them from Santa Reina to the coast in a van, after which they would board a fishing vessel prepared to take them down south to *Tierra de la Fuego*. From the village, Derby was provided with a Walther pistol and a Gewehr 43 rifle to take with him. In the next village, they bought supplies for the trip. The drive from Mendoza to the east coast took a full day, and then the next morning they boarded the fishing vessel and set off. During this time, Derby wrote at a typewriter for hours on end, resulting in pages upon pages that would need to be edited, but compiled a narrative for his book. Still, Derby did not speak to Fr. Williamson as they kept to themselves.

On the sixth day, Derby and Fr. Williamson arrived at *Tierra del Fuego* at a small fishing village on the coast from where they hitched a ride inland. The land in this region was simple, consisting of green pastures and rocky cliffs and exposed rocks from the earth. In the foreground of this region were tall mountains with snowcapped peaks, even in the summertime, being so far down south the temperatures were colder than they were in the Middle East. Both Derby and Fr. Williamson were dressed for the weather, Derby wearing his outdoor wear with a poncho, and Fr. Williamson in a durable black jacket.

"Reminds me of Ireland, if Ireland had mountains," Derby expressed as he sat in the back of a pickup truck with Fr. Williamson.

Fr. Williamson closed his book and looked over to Derby.

"You're from England, aren't you, Father?" Derby questioned.

"That's right."

"Where's your order, should I decide to visit some day?"

"We have many chapels in England," Fr. Williamson remarked, "an abbey in North England. My parish is in South London."

"Really? Not the sort of place I'd imagine the order to linger around."

"City folk need the truth as well."

Within another hour, the truck dropped off both Fr. Williamson and Derby in the middle of nowhere where short green grass was beside them on a muddy road. They proceeded to hike into the hills, following a trail that Williamson led them on. Derby looked around the quietness and tranquility of the area around them, the wildlife, and the grey skies above them. Within another hour, the pair ascended to a plateau where there were stone ruins.

"Here we are... here Erich and I discovered the patagon... it should still be in its grave..."

Fr. Williamson rushed forward into the ruins, going around to the back where he climbed up a cliff to another plateau. In this area there were pits in the earth with demarcation lines around them. These pits represented the average size an average person would be buried in, while towards the back was a larger, round pit like a crater. Fr. Williamson gasped and then rushed towards this pit, looking down upon it from over the edge.

"No..."

Derby joined him and looked down at the various round craters beneath the edge.

"They must have used explosives to destroy it all," Derby expressed with a grunt. "It's rained and that's caused some collapses and overlay. If we're lucky a chunk of bone could still be around... We should set up camp and see if something can be found."

Derby went to set up the tent while Fr. Williamson knelt in defeat over the crater. He then came around to join him as he continued to kneel.

"The tents are set up," Derby remarked. "Look, if we don't find anything in this hole, then we still have that thing in Antarctica. You told me it wasn't recovered yet."

"That *thing* in Antarctica is too large to recover, although it would also be too large to destroy..."

"All I would need is a piece to take with you to Germany."

Fr. Williamson scoffed and replied, "It's hopeless. If you hadn't gotten involved; if you hadn't led them to Iraq at the near end of our expedition, none of this would be necessary and we would have had what we needed to expose the Children and shown the world their origins.:"

"You're useless," Derby responded, "that's the problem with you idealists, always pondering upon what-if, and what should, but without willingness to act upon the what is. I'm going down there…"

Derby climbed down the pit and proceeded with the expedition, and after a few hours, Fr. Williamson joined him. They stayed in this region for two days, digging around and recovering a few small shards, but uncertain as to whether this was bone, rock, or porcelain. Derby climbed out of the pit on the third day, looking over to Fr. Williamson near the camp as he packed up his kit.

"Where are you going?" Derby questioned.

"I've had enough of this… As if the origin of the Chosen was all I have to spend my time on, I have a million more projects on my mind and need to recover from the losses I've experienced."

"You haven't finished one project, and yet you want to go and do one more?" Derby asked. "Typical, youth."

Fr. Williamson glared at Derby as he stood up, wiped his hands, and approached the priest. He continued to glare at him.

"You know what your problem is, Father? You haven't yet lived. You haven't been to war to know what it's like to be overseas fighting for those ideals you held close to your heart as a youngster, only to have reality open them and reveal how the world truly works. You think the Order of St. Athanasius can save Catholics, but it will only keep them from growing in love and compassion for others. Your chapels will become caves with campfires, while there exists cathedrals with beacons of light, and entire world of darkness seeking for those with light to shine upon them. Go then, back to your cave…"

Derby turned around to walk away from him.

"You're a loathsome old man, Derby Cabernet," Fr. Williamson stated, "struggling still to cope with the sins of your past, from the war. How many Germans did you kill? How many of those ordinary men did you think to be bad men, and how many of them did you deprive of their life, to expand upon their love and compassion for others? How many heroes of the war did you kill, but from the other side?"

Derby snarled and then immediately turned around to sucker punch Fr. Williamson across the face, knocking him over. "I've had it with you, boy!" he shouted, kicking him gently. "Go on, get out of here! No different than the protestants too, leading good men astray!"

Fr. Williamson picked himself up and then scattered off. He slid down a hill and then turned around to shout towards Derby, "You're a sad old fool! You'll see!"

Derby shook his head and walked around the campfire for a bit. He then kicked over a bucket and shouted, "Damn that boy!" He continued to stand around, shaking his head before he turned around and looked ahead towards the ruins as he huffed.

From across a distance of approximately one-hundred meters, Derby saw a glare from between some rocks. He stepped back and went to the camp to pick up his rifle, and then going over towards some rocks, he took his binoculars to get a better look. However, before Derby could see, a gunshot fired towards him and chipped the boulder next to him. He quickly ducked and grabbed hold of his rifle, binoculars falling over the other side.

"Ugh, what now," Derby groaned, readying his rifle. He came to the prone position and looked through the rifle to where the glare had been, but the figure was gone. He looked around the immediate nearby area to search for the sniper and saw only a trace of someone pass a wall. He focused on the area near there and saw the person lay down, giving him the own chance to fire a shot. The shot did not connect; the sniper fled into the ruins.

Derby stood up and went over to some more rocks on the left to get a wider angle of the ruins below him. He looked around briefly and then got into position to aim. He looked around for a glare from the sunlight that poked through the grey clouds, seeing the sniper at a collapsed portion of wall. He fired at Derby, hitting the rock beside him and triggering a reaction fire back at him. Derby stayed where he was and adjusted his aim, taking another shot and hitting before the sniper. The sniper stood up and retreated, giving Derby an opportune chance to slide down the hill and rush up to the ruin walls. He took cover behind a corner and then looked around the side. He then rushed forward and proceeded inwards, using the cover of the low walls to stay hidden. A shot came towards him from within the ruins. He stayed put and then went around the corner to escape, reaching another position where he looked out and scanned the ruins for the sniper. He only saw the shadow of the assassin. Derby stood up and went forward towards another position where he stayed put and aimed his gun.

Suddenly, the sniper revealed himself at an opening in the wall ahead, rifle pointed outwards, Derby took cover as a shot came towards him and hit the brick wall. He took in a deep breath. Another shot came to him and hit the rocks, causing some of them to collapse.

"I'm not doing this again..." Derby acknowledged, going into prone and crawling through to the other side. He then stood up and began to go into the ruins and navigate himself through. He put his rifle around his back on its sling and took out his Walther pistol.

Derby found the sniper on the other side of the ruins, in the prone position. He quietly approached him and raised his pistol up to crack a shot nearby. The sniper cowered in place and brought his hands to his head.

"Stand up!" Derby remarked. "Drop your weapon!"

The sniper left their sniper rifle as they slowly stood up, but Derby saw them reach for a pistol at their side causing him to fire at his hand. The sniper then went for the handgun with the other hand, but Derby shot at him again, this time in the stomach and causing him to lurch backwards.

"Devilish fiend," Derby snarled, stepping towards him slowly and aiming his pistol at him. "Who are you?! What the…"

The sniper began to lurch backwards from where they lay, moaning and groaning, head going side to side. He then let out gasps for air, increasing in intensity and desperation before leading to convulsions. Derby watched, horrified, as he continued to aim his pistol at him; after another minute, it was over and the man was dead.

When it was over, Derby looked at the rifle and saw that it was an M40 sniper rifle. He searched the corpse of the man and found little on him, leaving it on his person. He looked down at the sniper assassin and took a step back, looking up at the sky as it began to rain. He moved away and then went around to climb back up to the camp as the rain turned to downpour, looking down at the pit where the water accumulated and turned the dirt to mud. Derby looked at the excavation site, shook his head, and then muttered, "Enough of this… to think I nearly died in Belgium in a ditch as my father thought only to come to nearly die in a muddy ditch here… I'm going home."

Act 5, Scene 4

Derby hiked back to the road, and then walked the length of the road to the village, allowing a truck to pass by him without hoping to stop it. He walked the entire length of the road and it took him the entire day. By the evening, Derby was at the village where he noticed a ship anchored afar. He used his binoculars to get a closer look at the boat, seeing it to be a U.S. naval vessel, a little smaller than a destroyer with few armaments and a helipad and helicopter in the rear. At the side of the vessel was the designation, U.S.S. Justice.

"You interested in the American ship?" a man asked him in Spanish. "It's a research vessel, going to Antarctica. Its men were just in town to visit the pub," he said. "The next ship for the mainland will be here in a few days…"

"How long has that ship been here?" Derby questioned.

"Since the early morning," the man said.

"How much would it cost to have a rowboat take me over to that ship?"

"You'd have to be mad…"

"If you've been through what I have in the last month, you would be too."

Derby paid the man and once it was dark, they sailed a boat to the ship and Derby climbed aboard the vessel. The top deck of the ship was quiet, so Derby snuck around and encountered only a single sailor. He journeyed to the lower levels of the ship and came to the cargo container where he stayed put behind some crates, finally giving himself some rest, he fell asleep. He woke up to the sound of the ship horn, falling asleep again, and then waking up to the chilliness in the hull. Derby paid little attention to those around him that came into the cargo hull.

At the sound of the horn, Derby stood up with his rifle and put on some winter clothes kept in the cargo vessel. Unlike the uniform worn by U.S. soldiers during the Second World War, these had winter camouflage on them and weren't green. He then took his rifle, brought it around his back, and then proceeded to exit the cargo vessel to enter into the ship. He walked around with his head down, going upstairs to the surface level where a Chinook helicopter flew a vehicle towards the mainland ahead. At this time of the year, there was perpetual day although it was twilight and the skies were grey. The water on the side of the boat were calm and a steel-blue color. The boat was anchored not too far from the shore where there was not ice, but a grey surface that blended into the ice ahead with a radar tower above. The helicopter lowered the vehicle on the shore where there were some Zodiac speedboats aground and servicemen guiding the helicopter. Likewise, Derby saw some servicemen on the surface deck with radios, communicating with each other to coordinate movement onto the mainland. Once the helicopter brought the vehicle over, they began to transfer cargo that on the side read, 'Dangerous – Explosive'

"Give me an update," a familiar voice spoke.

Derby turned and saw a man in a suit with a wool coat walk towards the work zone with an officers next to him with clipboards. He looked closely at the face of the man to recognize him as Korah Kovner.

"I want one team in to find this place, and then another to follow with the explosives," Korah explained. "Nothing moves off the mainland until I give the word."

"Yes, Mr. Kovner."

Derby walked around to the second vehicle parked, turning around to see some dual-passenger snowmobiles parked on the side. They were being prepared to be brought over to shore. The helicopter returned and they began to prepare to the raise the second multi-person snowmobile over, which prompted Derby to hide behind it and climb onto the side. He opened the door as the helicopter caught the hook and then went inside, lowering himself. The vehicle raised up and was carried over the water.

Derby sat up and looked over to the ship as he was taken away from it, and over to the mainland where he slipped out. Derby walked around to the other corner and stayed put, deciding to slip off and disappear around the cliff side to reach a slope that went up towards the radar station above.

From the perch that looked over the servicemen, Derby sat down and watched as the U.S. servicemen carried more equipment and some prepared themselves to set off into the frozen wasteland. He stayed put where he was until he heard a person exit the station behind him and step down some steps. He turned and faced the man, a young man in his twenties in his winter suit, but unarmed. Derby sat up and looked at him. He went around the side of the base and disappeared, followed by the sound of a motor turn on.

Derby came around the side of the base and stayed around the corner as he saw the young man sit down atop of the Yamaho dual-cycle snowmobile and rev the engine. There was only one of these, so Derby took the moment to step forward towards the man and grab hold of him.

"Be careful… be careful…" Derby quietly remarked. "I'm not going to hurt you…"

The man began to settle down.

"I just want your sled…"

The man began to breathe slowly. Derby took out his pistol and threw the man into the snow behind him.

"What the hell man!" the servicemen cried out, crawling away.

Derby sat down at the snowmobile and began to look at the machine while holding the pistol in his other hand. The man attempted to step forward towards Derby, but he then pointed his handgun at him.

"Don't be stupid, son."

Derby began to roll forward slowly, prompting him to put his handgun into his pocket and then drive forward. He went a fair distance on his own, stopping in the middle of nowhere to survey the land and look at his map. He had a way to go before he reached the research station. Derby began to travel across the snowy wasteland, avoiding crevices in the ice which was easy as the sun came up and clouds parted for the first half of the trip, and then came together for the next half and a wind picked up.

The visibility ahead of him diminished, but as Derby examined his location with his compass and determined where he was, he continued until from a distance through the mist ahead he could see a large compound at the base of some hills. The compound was low and consisted of a few structures put together and tall radar antennas spread throughout. Several flags waved throughout, but one tall one had the Argentinian flag on it. On the outskirts of the compound was a helicopter at a helipad, and a multi-person snowmobile of their own. There were also three smaller buildings, one of which was on struts, nearby the perimeter of the outpost. A hangar at the side of the main compound could also be seen. The visibility was low, but from what Derby could see there was nobody in sight.

Derby came up to one of the entrances of the compound, parked the snowmobile and took the keys into his pocket. He stepped off and went to the door, attempting to open it, but it was locked. He continued around the perimeter of the base, seeing that the main structure was I shaped with few entrance points. He eventually came to a large set of doors, one of which was left open and led into a vestibule. The wind blew into the vestibule, and to avoid any further wind blowing in, Derby closed the door behind him and then stepped through to enter into a dark corridor. This short corridor led into a longer one on the left along one of the far sides of the compound. A door on the immediate right led into an area titled 'Storage Room' in Spanish, so Derby avoided that area and instead took out a flashlight to see ahead of him. Derby came into the room on his right in the longer corridor and saw that it was a chart room with maps laid out.

From this room, Derby went into the next and saw that it was a communication room with radio equipment. He then exited out that room and went back into the corridor, going to very end where there was a greenhouse. He then doubled back to the middle of the corridor to reach another longer one that went down half of the structure. He attempted to open the door on his left, but it was jammed, so he went to the one on his right to see it was some sort of security room with monitors. He carried on to the next room where there was a washroom, and then the next room where there were sleeping quarters left and right along a short corridor. He examined each quarter, six small rooms with two beds each, but curiously with personal items laid about and even beds unmade. The next room was a lounge, and that led back into the main corridor. Derby checked the room across from this one to find an office space, and then a kitchen and mess hall next to that. Rather than continue to look into the rooms he could not get access to, he went to the end of the main corridor and checked the adjacent one. This corridor led to a manager office with more desks arranged in cubicles, a storage room on the right, and a pen on the left. Next to the pen was a corridor that led to the hangar garage where there were snowmobiles parked. The garage shutter was raised slightly, and a wind blew in through a bit of snow that had piled up in the crack. From this room, Derby went back and came around to a door next to the mess hall. He entered in to an infirmary with stretchers and counters, and a door that led into the room he could not get into.

The last room that Derby searched was a laboratory. The door he could not get into was jammed because it had a chair stuck on the doorknob on the other side. He looked at the chair and then at the steel table in the middle of the room. There was blood on the walls throughout the room, stained into the porcelain white ceiling tiles and tiled floor. He exited the room and proceeded to leave the compound, going out towards one of the satellite buildings. He attempted to open the door of one of them, kicking it down to look inside and see that it was a shed with some more crates around. He then went to the next and looked inside the frosted window. He came around to the door and then kicked it down, stepping into a larger shed where there was a twenty-foot long block of ice in the middle of the storage room. He looked carefully at the block of ice and could see something black on the inside, it was difficult to see, but it was long and slender, but with more than just four main appendages, but several like tentacles. Derby looked at the tall lanky creature carefully and then took a step back.

"What in God's name is this creature?" Derby questioned, taking out the journal from his jacket. He then stopped as he could hear the sound of motors on approach from afar. He put his journal down on a crate and then brought his weapon around, breaking the glass on the window and pointing it through with enough visibility to see ahead.

"Looks like company," Derby remarked, seeing the U.S. snowmobiles on approach. He readied his rifle and then left the shed, rushing towards the satellite structure on struts to climb up the stairs and walk around the balcony of the lookout tower. He climbed up to the rooftop and then laid down in the snow with his Gewehr 43 rifle, eyeing down the scope.

The multi-person snowmobile carried two fireteams each, and the individual snowmobiles two persons each to give twelve people scattering around the facility in teams to search for Derby. He stayed put where he was as he looked at them spread out, a team going towards the shed with the creature encased in case. He pulled the trigger at these two, taking one down and then the other in the reaction time. The rest of the servicemen immediately took cover behind the main building. He stayed put and raised the scope so he could look down the iron sights, picking off some soldiers as they took cover and then taking more shots while he was still hidden. The soldiers stayed in place, which prompted Derby to be the one on the move. He edged himself back towards the ladder slowly and then climbed down. He went towards the shed and took cover around the corner, going back around the other side to catch some soldiers by their flank. He removed his scope outright and kept the iron sights, laying down afterwards in the prone position and taking shots towards the Americans as they yelled out to each other. Derby could hear some yelling as though it was into a radio mic. He turned the corner and began to take shots at those near him before he moved in closer around the side of the other shed where he was some attempting to flank him.

When these soldiers were taken care of, Derby scavenged an M16 rifle, some ammunition, and then went back towards the lookout tower. He left the M16 at the base of the tower and climbed up around a snowy hill nearby to take position as some soldiers thought to come around that side. He opened fire at them from cover and then reloaded his rifle. He then stood up and came around to the other side of the building as it grew quiet. He ran towards the shed again, and then to the other one where he came towards another snow pile and spread out by it. He waited to see if more soldiers would come around. Rather than wait for them on the ground, Derby went back up to his perch on the lookout, using the mound of snow to climb onto the balcony and then the ladder. He then positioned himself from above on another pile of snow and waited.

Derby was able to pick off some soldiers as they made their appearance, but after a while longer, it grounded to a halt. From where Derby was perched, he could see something approaching from the horizon, and as it got closer the noise was recognizable as the Chinook helicopter. He aimed at the helicopter pilot as the cockpit faced him and the soldiers that came out from the rear hurried towards the opposite face of the compound. The helicopter then rose up and flew off back towards the U.S.S.

Justice. Derby was able to make eye contact with the pilot, which prompted forces on the ground to open fire at his position and for him to retreat.

The troops that arrived spread out around the compound and continued to lay down heat on Derby's position. He stayed put behind the mound of snow. They opened fire at him and he ditched the Gewehr 43 for the M16. He began to open fire at the soldiers as they attempted to reach the shed again, killing one and causing the others to retreat back to where they were hidden. An icy wind then blew over and Derby took the chance to reload. He then placed his rifle at the side and picked up the Gewehr 43, placing it with the scope facing the far side of the compound. He lay down some fire at the troops on the opposite-side near where the helicopter landed, and then he slowly took steps backwards to climb up a snowy hill behind him. From this perch, Derby had visual of all around again and stayed put as the troops moved in. He took the M16 again and watched with caution as the Americans began to expose themselves. He saw them approach the barn while another team came around the sides to flank Derby. As the troops were about to think they were flanking him, Derby opened fire at them, and then those further ahead near the barn shed with the ice. He caught around six soldiers by surprise, wounding another all from his position. The icy wind then picked up again and he disappeared behind the mound of snow to pull himself leftwards and fire at more of the troops near the barn shed and others that had taken up positions near the snowmobile. The troops that arrived spread out around the grounds and Derby withdrew and then reappeared from the sidelines as he caught them in their flank.

Eventually, the pressure was too much for them and a group of soldiers hopped aboard the snowmobiles and left. At the same time, the Chinook flew in and landed. Derby repositioned himself back at the lookout tower where he picked up his Gewehr and threw down the M16. When the helicopter finished sending out more troops, it shot its guns towards Derby as he took cover beneath the lookout tower, causing the windows to shatter and guns to rip through the walls above. He then looked ahead to where some troops were spreading out around the compound while another figure stayed back.

"Don't just stand there, kill him!" the figure shouted.

The helicopter began to make its pass around the compound again, which prompted Derby to stabilize himself on the mound of snow while the others got into position around and take a single shot at the helicopter pilot. The guns did not fire, and the helicopter began to spin out of control. Derby ducked down as it flew into the enemy line, hitting the smaller shed on the outskirts and causing a ball of fire to rise.

Derby continued to open fire towards the soldiers as they struggled to reach the larger shed. He took shots at them for another few moments until he reached his last bullet with the Gewehr and had to switch to the M16. He picked up the M16 and like before positioned the sights as though it was pointing towards the hostiles this time towards the compound. He then waited for an icy wind to pick up before he went towards the main compound and then the other side where some troops were. He picked up some ammunition, and then went all the way around to the other side of the compound while the American troops moved in to his dummy location. Derby continued forward as he approached the lone figure, Korah Kovner, with nothing but a handgun in his hand.

"Drop the gun," Derby remarked.

Korah froze in place and then turned around.

"I said drop it," Derby repeated.

"I should have known the rat in this wasteland was you."

"During the war, while in North Africa we earned the name Desert Rats because of our abilities to appear one place and then the other, scurrying around just like this…"

"You've got me. What are you going to do now?"

"I'm tempted to bury you with your ancestors here."

"Me? A descendant of the giants?" Korah questioned. "Don't fool yourself, Mr. Cabernet."

"Drop the gun."

Korah finally dropped it.

"Over there!" American troops shouted, opening fire at Derby. Korah kicked some snow towards Derby causing it to hit his face. He rushed over to some crates to take cover and then began to open fire back towards the Americans as they ignored the shed with the ice and instead focused their attention on Derby.

Derby took some shots towards the Americans and then moved himself to the right. He reloaded his gun and noticed the doors into the compound to be open. He followed Korah through them into the facility. He then walked slowly around the abandoned research station.

"Where'd you go, you slime," Derby shouted, looking around.

"Right here, Mr. Cabernet," Korah replied. "I'll tell you what, I really didn't expect you to make it this far. It did not take much to convince Secretary Clayton that we should approach you – he's quite the fan, although for the wrong reasons. He thinks you're misunderstood, but we all know you're the antisemite that you are."

Derby growled and began to go down the main hall. He then raised his gun up to fire towards Korah as he passed him at the end of the hall. He then stopped to face the other end as he heard American troops move in. They shot down the corner and Derby hid in the office spaces. He maneuvered himself through to come into the radio room, flanking the Americans and shooting at those that sought to come in. He then picked up some ammunition and stayed put.

"We met your friend, Dr. Jean-Baptiste Dumas, in Buenos Aires on his way out," Korah shouted. "A very neurotic man, I must tell you. Don't worry, he fled before we could kill him too, but we were able to search his belongings beforehand."

Derby grunted and began to go down the main corridor again.

"Tisk, tisk, tisk. I should have known that you had such an ironic background, all this time you spent speaking out against Nazi Germany and the Germans, seeking to distance yourself from them. You uphold yourself as an English gentleman who fought through the Second World War against the Nazi regime, but not only do your harbor antisemitic views like your enemies, but you're from the same background, *Herr Witzendorff.*"

Derby came to the end of the hallway and looked both ways. He then went towards the vehicle hangar.

"How does it feel? To know that your blood is the blood that you've hated so much since you were a young man? To know that all those people you killed while in service was not only for a vain cause, but your own common people too. It's no wonder you have so much... regret!"

Derby suddenly turned as Korah came out from around a corner with a knife. He stabbed Derby in the shoulder with the knife, piercing his flesh and causing him to drop the M16. He swung Korah off and put a hand around the knife in his shoulder, quickly taking his Walther pistol out and shooting at Korah as he ran away.

"You've got... nowhere to run," Derby remarked, holding the knife with his left as it stuck into his muscle. "Come out now..."

"Do you really think you can fight your way out of here? There's no where to run for you, Mr. Cabernet. It's over. Even if you were to escape, the hunt will not end. A greater bounty has already been set for you, greater than the one that was for Erich Liudolfings!"

"To believe I was fooled, not once, but twice, to fight another man's war..." Derby acknowledged. "I'll take what I have found here and make all the world know what shrewd imposters walk among us. That's all that you are, Korah, just another spawn of the devil. Even if I die here, the world will one day know the truth. Victory is always assured for the righteous, even if the war is over and it does not seem like you've won – God wins every time, and yourself and your kin, your father, Abaddon, will know eternal hellfire."

Korah appeared from around the corner, holding a chair. Derby deflected the chair and shot Korah in the shoulder. He then ran off. Derby pursued with caution, coming around the corner and then going down the right towards the exit. He looked outside and saw that it was quiet with no further reinforcements spread about. All that remained was a trail of blood that went into the frozen wasteland. Derby followed the trail, walking for a few minutes before he finally reached a figure in the distance. Korah appeared, on his knees, staring ahead towards the endless nothingness that was the Antarctic region.

Derby pointed his pistol at him, and without even need to shoot him, Korah fell over and onto his back.

"You've lost," Korah expressed with a wheeze. "The twenty-first century will be not the Jewish century, but the century of the Children of our rightful King who for years has been persecuted and oppressed by Christians like yourself, but will rightfully retake this world that prior to the start of the common era, was ours from the very beginning. All that awaits for us is a worthy leader, a true Messiah to lead us forward."

"Shut up, you lousy knob," Derby expressed, dropping his Walther pistol as he took a hand to the knife in his shoulder. "The Messiah already came two thousand years ago. Say it now, Korah, 'Lord Jesus Christ, Son of God, have mercy on me a sinner,' and be saved."

"You… you stupid goy… you've killed me, and now you want me to convert to your incessant religion? I hope you die a very slow and painful death…. I… I…" Korah began to wriggle and groan in pain. "J… Just kill me."

"I can't save you, Korah. Only Jesus Christ can."

Derby knelt down at Korah as he continued to hold a hand at the knife in his shoulder.

"Do you know what I'm going to do when I get out of here on that boat of yours, Korah? I'm going to finish my book, and travel to Germany and then Israel to let the whole world know what vile scum you and the rest of your cabal are. Your plan is foiled…"

Korah groaned in pain. The groans became more intense, as though they were a combination of anger and sorrow; malice and hatred, but after less than a couple minutes, he died. At that moment, Derby walked back to the compound where he was met with some American soldiers who pointed their rifles at him.

"Don't shoot, it's one of us!" an American soldier remarked.

"Identify yourself!" an officer yelled.

Derby looked at them, eyes wandering from each of them before he closed his eyes and fell over. The American troops quickly went towards him to tend to him.

Act 5, Scene 5

Derby woke up at an unknown amount of time later, opening his eyes to hear some medical equipment running in the ambience and people chatting quietly. He looked to his side to see some stretchers parked next to where he was lay, and then a mat sat next to him. He looked ahead to see some curtains drawn on the other side of the room and some rectangular windows next to them with views that looked out to the sea. Upon realizing that he was in the U.S.S. Justice, Derby lurched forward in a panic and pulled the covers off his bare torso.

"Easy there, Mr. Cabernet. Easy," a man with a Texas accent cautioned, standing up to keep him in bed. "You'll pull your stitches."

Derby looked at the man in the suit that was next to him. Secretary Clayton kept him in bed and then stepped back as Derby settled down. He smiled at him.

"You had me worried, Mr. Cabernet," Clayton expressed with a laugh, sitting down. "Kory told me that you and Erich didn't make it out of Iraq alive; that the Iraqis got you. Personally, I thought we lost you in Israel when we heard reports that the PLO had raided your location. All this time you were with him though…"

Derby looked at Secretary Clayton and then laid back.

"What has Mr. Kovner told you?" Derby questioned.

"Well, not much as I've had to return to the United States to get back to work. I left Kory in charge, really. He said he was attempting to gather information about what Mr. Liudolfings knew, but that was all… The men tell me they recovered you in Antarctica…"

"Where are we know?"

"Just off the coast of Brazil," Secretary Clayton replied. "I took the first flight I could when they told me that Kovner was MIA, possibly killed in action by a Nazi you guys were fighting out in the snow. The entire research station was destroyed as a result of the fight, and they found you wounded. I suppose the bastard got away; hard to survive in that climate."

Derby did not respond as he continued to stare at the ceiling.

"At any rate, one you're all better, we'll discharge you straight into Brazil if you'd like, and you can be on your merry way. Thank you for all your work with us, Mr. Cabernet. You've done Uncle Sam a solid. You should come down to the ranch sometime, it'd be a pleasure."

Derby did not respond as he felt the bandages around his shoulder.

"Yup, quite the wound you had, nearly bled out, so I understand."

"Can I ask you something, Mr. Clayton?" Derby questioned.

"Sure, bud," Clayton responded.

"I understand that you were involved in the investigation of the U.S.S. Liberty incident during the Six Day War," Derby expressed. "The incident in which Israeli fighter jets attacked an American ship. From your report, you cleared the incident as a mishap."

"Yes, a very unfortunate accident."

"I heard otherwise; that Israel intended to target that ship to bring the United States into the war with them. I suppose you know that to be the truth, and yet the Americans played it off to avoid tension between their partners in the Middle East. How does it feel, as a former navy captain, to have betrayed your fellow sailors that way? To have left all those victims down?"

"Now then, Mr. Cabernet, I don't think that's a fair analysis of the situation. I looked at it myself..."

"And yet you still cleared them..."

"Hold on now, partner."

Derby pulled the covers back and sat at the side of the bed.

"I don't want to sit idle here for another minute," Derby expressed, standing up. "I want to be taken to the coast so that I can contact my people... where are my things?"

"What things? You didn't come with things?"

"Dammit..." Derby muttered, "all my research... Nonetheless... I want to be let off. I have to write a book, Mr. Clayton, a sequel. You'll like this one... and when I'm done, I'm going to go to Israel to let the entire oppressed people of the Zionist regime know the truth of what a vile people exist in the depths of our society, and which have not only taken them prey, but seek to take prey the entire world."

"I'm confused, Mr. Cabernet. What sequel? You're not right in the head, partner."

"Oh, I'm quite alright," Derby responded. "This writing will be a sequel to by book on the Judean people, speaking about subversive activities from the last three-hundred years by people with Jewish names, of Jewish elites, all the way up to the Zionist occupation, and it will conclude with the revelation that these people were neither Jewish nor even human, but the descendants of a vile and demonic race of fallen angels who had subverted not just their people, but many more, and have caused the antisemitism of the last century, masterminded the occupation of Palestine, and seek to collapse Western Civilization and subjugate the entire free world."

Epilogue

"My dearest Derby, I hope this letter finds you well, if at all. I'm embarrassed, slightly relieved, but also a bit anxious as I write this letter. I just learned that all the letters that I had sent you since last spring have not reached you. They had never even left the post office as it turns out. Rather than send them all to you at once, I thought I would right this short letter to tell you that I have not forgotten about you, and I hope you have not forgotten about me. A few weeks after you left for France, I learned the most wonderful news that I was pregnant, and I kept that a secret from mother and father as much as I could before I had to tell them that this child was yours. They lambasted me, said that I would never see you again, but I held on to hope that I would because the gentleman I met at that party would not do the ungentlemanly thing to leave me behind. You did not respond to my letters though, and unaware that they never got to you, I thought the worst that you were either killed or did not wish to communicate with me. Nonetheless, I held on to our child, and just last February I gave birth to the most wonderful baby boy. I named him Everest, after that mountain you hope to conquer one day. I thought I should let you know, not only by surprise that I am here still, waiting for you when you return, if you are alive, but also that you have one more person waiting for you when you do. As much as I would love to have run away with you and have the wildest adventures in the New World, I hope that before you will take on this adventure of parenthood with me to raise our dearest child. Oh my Derb, please be alive… let me see your eyes again one last time. With love, Ophelia Mountbatten"

Derby looked at the letter with a stunned look. He looked around him as he stood in front of a fence to a prisoner of war concentration camp. Suddenly, the stunned glance in his face turned to a smile.

"Ophelia…" Derby muttered, "my Ophelia…"

"Good news?" a German-accented voice questioned.

Derby lowered his smile as he turned around and glanced at a prisoner behind the fence. The man was young, spoke in a coarse voice, and had buzzcut blonde hair and a sharp look in his blue eyes. He held on to the wires of the fence as he looked at Derby in a muddied dress, while Derby wore his battle dress with his tie and beret.

"As a matter of fact, very good news," Derby remarked to the prisoner, putting the letter into his pocket. "What business is it of you anyhow? Get from here…"

"The war is lost, all this suffering at its end," the young man replied, "and now here we are as defeated slaves barely kept fed well enough to survive. You've taken everything from us; from me, my wife, my son, our home. Now you won't even let me share in whatever joy you have waiting for you at home?"

"You listen here, you silly kraut," Derby rebuked, waving his finger at him. "Your government started this war when you invaded Poland, and you escalated it when you invaded Scandinavia and then France. You're behind these fences as we organize and process the lot of you, some of whom will be tried for your crimes committed against your own prisoners and enemies."

"And during these criminal trials, do I suppose your airmen will be tried for bombing our towns and killing our civilians too? Do I suppose your mishandling of some prisoners, the weaknesses of humankind and their wrath towards each other, will be treated the same way as with ours?"

Derby glared at the prisoner.

The prisoner straightened up and pushed himself off the fence. "Don't think yourself to be righteous because you won the war," he said. "This pitting of man against man, it is the greater crime that was made, and for what cause?"

"Against tyranny," Derby stated. "Against fascism."

"What about the tyranny of others towards German minorities in Poland? The tyranny of the Soviets? The fight against communism? When does the British Empire give up its tyranny towards the entire world? Towards India?"

Derby growled.

"I don't mean to vex you," the prisoner remarked, "but there is no justice in war. By all means, I should hate you, and the rest of the German people too for the suffering you have caused us because we had a vision for Europe that did not align with yours. Like me, many of us lost plenty, but I and most others do not hate you. A priest with us in the camp tells us to forgive and let forgiveness be greater than any justice that can come from any person. He says forgiveness is the greatest power against evil. You may not ask it from me, a lowly prisoner, but I forgive you, brother. I forgive you."

"What are you doing?" an officer questioned.

Derby immediately turned to his senior officer who approached. He was not talking to him though, but to the prisoner. He took out a whip from his belt and began to beat back at the prisoner through the fence.

"Off with you, German scum," the officer remarked.

Derby watched the prisoner off as a prison guard grabbed him from the other side and took him away. He then looked over to his senior officer and saluted.

"At ease, Cabernet," the major-general insisted. "I have orders for you…" he handed him a letter.

Derby looked through the letter and read it. He then looked back at the senior officer.

"We're being transferred to the Middle East?" Derby questioned.

"Correct," the major-general replied, "to Palestine. There, yourself and the rest of the regiment will relieve some garrison units there. Now that the war is over, it is time for His Majesty's army to disperse across the empire and bring it back under control. From what I understand, locals in some parts have grown unruly over the course of the war and it is now time that we show them an iron hand."

Derby looked at the paper again and then folded it. He looked back at his senior officer with a squint as the sun shone in his face.

"Apologies, with all due respect, Major-General, but I shan't be going with the unit to Palestine."

"And why the hell not?"

"Because I'm going to be getting married and taking care of my wife," Derby answered, "and I'm leaving the army at once, sir."

"We cannot give approval to [Zionism]. We cannot prevent the Jews from going to Jerusalem—but we could never sanction it. The soil of Jerusalem, if it was not always sacred, has been sanctified by the life of Jesus Christ. As the head of the Church, I cannot tell you anything different. The Jews have not recognized our Lord, therefore we cannot recognize the Jewish people."

– Pope Saint Pius X